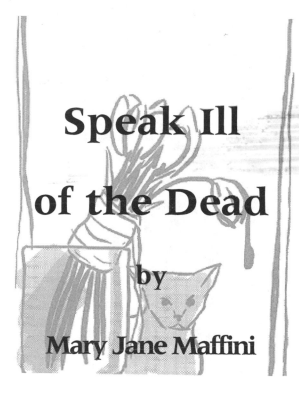

Speak Ill

of the Dead

by

Mary Jane Maffini

RENDEZVOUS
PRESS

Cover art: Christopher Chuckry

Le Conseil des Arts
du Canada
DEPUIS 1957

The Canada Council
for the Arts
since 1957

We gratefully acknowledge the support of the Canada Council for the Arts for our publishing program.

Napoleon Publishing/RendezVous Press
Toronto, Ontario, Canada

Printed in Canada

05 04 03 02 01 00 99   5 4 3 2 1

Canadian Cataloguing in Publication Data

Maffini, Mary Jane, date
    Speak ill of the dead

ISBN 0-929141-65-2

I. Title.

PS8576.A3385S63 1999   C813'.54   C99-931189-1
PR9199.3.M3433S63 1999

I am most grateful for the endless support and firm opinions of my writing group: Joan Boswell, Vicki Cameron, Audrey Jessop, Sue Pike and Linda Wiken. And also to Linda Berndt, Susanne Fletcher, Janet MacEachern and Dr. Lorne Parent for their advice, and to Georgia Ellis for the fictional use of her balcony. Many thanks to my publisher, Sylvia McConnell, for believing in me, and to Allister Thompson, the most courageous of editors.

Much of Ottawa is as it is portrayed, although it is only fair to mention that Justice for Victims and the Harmony Hotel are both figments of my fevered mind, as is St. Jim's Parish. Don't waste your time looking for them. Strangely enough, the one million tulips are real.

-MJM

One

That particular morning all I could think about was getting rid of Alvin.

It was the thirteenth of May. After the three feet of snow that came in November and stayed topped up all winter, I should have been paying attention to the signs of spring. I stomped along the bike path bordering the Ottawa River, not looking for groundhogs or robins and unaware of the fresh buds on the deciduous trees. Instead, black thoughts of Alvin clogged my mind.

All down Wellington Street and up on Parliament Hill thousands of tulips had popped out of the ground, on schedule for the annual tulip festival. I didn't notice them.

My mind was focused primarily on liberating my office from Alvin's presence, and secondarily on dealing with my large, meddlesome family, so Alvin or someone just like him never happened to me again.

By the time I picked up an extra large Colombian Supremo and honey oatmeal muffin across from my Elgin Street office, I was concentrating on the family part and my theory that I'd been switched at birth. That's how I account for being short, stocky and dark-haired in a family where everyone is tall, slender and fair. My sisters are long-boned and ash-blonde, beautiful still in their late forties. The pleats in their good wool slacks always lie flat; there's never a button missing on their silk shirts; their hair is just the way they want it to be.

I'm lucky if I can find my clothes on the chair in the morning, and my hair doesn't even bear talking about. And if I don't take the fifty-three minute walk to and from work every day, I go off the top end of the scale.

Even now, thirty-two years after my birth, my father still looks at me with surprise. It's a look I remember well from my childhood. Surprise—when he found me hanging upside down from a tree, or when he discovered six frogs in the bathtub, or when he read a note from The Nun of the Year saying I had played hookey from First Communion Class.

My beautiful sisters would just laugh. They were perfect. So they could afford to think it was amusing when I got fished out of ponds, ejected from Sunday School, stranded on the school roof. And one of them, Edwina or Alexa or Donalda, would rescue me, take me by the hand and make sure that even my father could see the humour in the situation. I would stand there, looking way up at a tall, fair man, hoping he would recognize me.

Donalda was named for my father, Donald MacPhee, and like him she was cool, detached, correct. Alexa and Edwina were named for my mother's brothers. Good Cape Breton names, although a bit out of place when we moved to Ottawa—a city of Barbaras and Beverlys and Susans. It's a tribute to my sisters' elegance as teenagers that they were never tormented about their names. Just floated through high school with their lovely long straight noses in the air, their blonde hair just so and lots of boys to carry their books. I suppose it didn't hurt that my father was the principal of St. Jim's.

All I got was the best name, Camilla, from my mother, who died when I was born.

My sisters returned to Nova Scotia to get good solid degrees in English at St. Francis Xavier or Mount St. Vincent or to train in nursing at St. Rita's. They returned with tall, respectable husbands—a dentist, an accountant and in Alexa's case, a doctor. Alexa's a widow now, but she still retains all the points she got for snagging the doctor.

As for me, I went charging through the University of Ottawa and wound up with a Law degree and no man in my life but Paul, whose dead face still smiles down at me from his picture on the wall in my office, three years after the accident that changed my life.

When I was growing up my sisters used to look at me with affectionate amusement—"Oh Camilla, how could you do that to Daddy's new car?" Now they pucker their perfect faces with worry and bite their Clinique-covered lower lips and try not to pester me about working seventy hours a week and forgetting to get my hair done.

My father still regards me with surprise.

But that's not the problem. The problem is he spends fifty percent of his time rescuing the children and grandchildren of old friends. People who, through no fault of their own, have fallen on hard times. Like Alvin.

"This particular boy," my father had said, meaning Alvin, "this particular boy never had a chance. Not like you, dear, with every opportunity."

I gave it my best defensive play.

"There's no space in my office for another person, Daddy. You know I just have the one room, and it's fifteen by fifteen, and it's full of files and equipment. Where would he sit?"

"That's just it, he could help with the files. Put them in the filing cabinets for you. He could answer your phone. Do the correspondence. Run the photocopier. You have a law degree, dear. Even if you insist on running this agency for victims, you don't need to do everything yourself. Give Alvin a chance. You won't even have to pay his salary. The government training program will pick up eighty per cent of it. At any rate this poor boy doesn't even want a salary, just a chance to get some experience. Having some help in the office will give you time to think."

Time to think? I definitely didn't want time to think—about Paul, about the kind of life we might have had if he had lived.

"Sorry, Daddy. No deal."

"Alcoholic father, God rest his soul, poor old Mike, and that brave little woman struggling to put all those children through university. Be a big weight off her mind. Mine, too. You don't seem to have any life at all, dear. Which reminds me, your sisters want to have a family dinner after Mass on Sunday. I don't suppose you'd consider going to…"

By the time I had tucked my styrofoam cup and my muffin under my arm, fiddled with my key and kicked open the door of the Justice for Victims office, Alvin had started his third week on the job. He'd already told me he was looking forward to a career in the World of Art, and that office work was not his first love.

He was in fine form that morning, and the sunlight glinted off his nine visible earrings as he brushed the remains of his breakfast from my Globe and Mail and into the wastepaper basket. "The Bear", a local rock station, blasted from the radio.

"Mitzi Brochu," he said.

"Gesundheit," I told him, as I moved a stack of research notes and put down my own breakfast. "I hope you're not coming down with a cold. But if you are, please feel free to stay home until you feel completely better. Better yet, have you considered going home to your mother in Sydney?"

But this subtlety was wasted on Alvin.

"Robin Findlay called. She wants you to go with her to meet Mitzi Brochu." The look on Alvin's face indicated this was some kind of big deal.

"Mitzi who?"

"You're kidding me, right?"

I wasn't. I scooped a stack of envelopes from the chair and sat down.

"Wow," he said. "You got to cut down on your working hours and get a life. Everyone in the country knows Mitzi Brochu. The Sultana of Style, the Queen of Cool, the High Priestess of…"

"Okay, I get the picture."

I remembered Mitzi Brochu, a scrawny fashion writer and broadcaster, with a poison pen and a tongue like a switchblade.

The phone rang.

"Justice for Victims," Alvin chirped. "No, I'm sorry, Mizzz MacPhee is in a staff meeting. No, no idea when. Sure, try later."

He hung up before I could snatch the receiver from his hands.

"What meeting? What meeting am I in?"

"This is important. This woman can make or break you. Any chance you could skip home and put on your teal suit? And ditch those running shoes?"

"No, there is no chance I will skip anywhere. And, furthermore, this woman cannot make or break me. I am not trying to make a fashion statement, I am running an advocacy agency for victims of violent crime. I don't give a shit about Mitchy Bitchy."

"Mitzi Brochu," said Alvin. "That's too bad, because Robin said it was really important. Incredibly important. Let's see, where did I put that message?"

He rummaged through the desk drawers one by one. Five minutes later, he located the message in the wastepaper basket and wiped a coffee spill from it.

"Harmony Hotel, this afternoon at 2:30. Suite…" he held the message up to the light, "it's a bit washed out…but I think it's Suite 815."

"Come on. I've got to get ready for Ralph Benning's parole hearing. And I'm way behind on the brief to the Department of Justice. Not to mention the membership drive…"

"Camilla, Camilla, Camilla. That's what I'm here for, membership drives and that stuff. It's called delegation, remember?"

"I do remember. I remember it was all here to do before you came and now you've been here for three weeks, it still is."

"I'll do it. I'll do it. But first, why don't I run over to the library and get you some background on Mitzi? You don't want to put your foot in it."

There was only one place where I wanted to put my foot. I thought about it. Sure would be easier to breathe in the minuscule office without Alvin. And easier to think without his radio. Really, that's the way I had set it up. To work alone, long and hard. The three visitors' chairs were just enough for the devastated crime victims and their relatives who found their shaky way to the office. The rest was all business. Phone, fax, photocopier and mile-high files. I loved my mingy little office—when Alvin wasn't in it.

He stuck his head through the door just as I was enjoying the foot thought.

"By the way, your sister called."

I forgot the foot. "Which one?"

Alvin shrugged before he closed the door. "I can't keep them all straight."

I knew it didn't matter which order I called them in, it would be the last one who left the message. The other two would have plenty to say. Sure enough, it was Edwina with an invitation.

"Why don't you come for lunch on Sunday? Frank will pick you up."

Lunch with my family comes off the time you have to log in purgatory, but no one wins arguments with Edwina, so I didn't bother. I was just finishing up with her when Alvin got back.

He tossed a pile of magazines on the desk. All back issues of *Femme Fatale*. All with the Ottawa Public Library stamp still on them.

"There you go, here's the sort of thing our girl Mitzi's written in the last two years."

"Alvin. The library doesn't lend these magazines. How'd you get them past the security system?"

"It's easy when you know how."

"Well, I can't survive without using the library for research. Don't get me into hot water with them."

I got up and stuck my nose out into the hall to see if any librarians had tracked Alvin back to the office.

He took advantage of my move to reclaim the chair at the desk. "Take a look at them. You'll get an idea about Mitzi, anyway, before this afternoon."

The Benning hearing was supposed to occupy my mind that morning and it did. I pored over the transcript of Ralph Benning's trial and the newspaper reports of the same. I reread notes from my interviews with Myra Anderson, the victim, and worked on a strategy for the hearing. I made a note to myself to talk to the prosecutor of the case. But it was hard to concentrate.

"Do you mind not whistling while you type?"

"What, I'm just a happy guy. It's better than you, grunting and snarling to yourself over those files." Alvin tossed a pile of envelopes into the wastepaper basket.

"What's wrong with those?"

"Mistakes on them."

Since Alvin's arrival our garbage rate had soared. We had become a fifteen foot by fifteen foot, four-basket-a-day office. I rescued the envelopes from the garbage.

"Put labels over them. If you can't think cheap, can you at least think green?"

"Sure."

Alvin flicked his coal-black ponytail over his shoulder and turned back to the typewriter. I pretended I didn't hear his next little remark about hormones.

The rest of the morning yielded little. By noon, I was hungry and faced with a pile of paper with Benning doodled on it over and over, surrounded by meaningless squiggles, crosses and puffs of smoke.

On a normal day, I like to eat a sandwich for lunch in the office. But Alvin was there, and I wanted to get away from him. He handed me the pile of *Femme Fatale* issues as I headed out.

"I can't take those," I said. "They are clearly marked Ottawa Public Library."

Rip. Slap. The covers landed in the overflowing wastepaper basket.

"Happy lunching," said Alvin.

As I walked away from the door, I heard him answer the phone.

"Sorry," he said, "I have absolutely no idea if or when she'll be back."

*　　*　　*

Elgin Street was showing the first signs of spring. Lily white, bare arms were sticking out of short sleeves everywhere as I shlepped along several crowded blocks to the Manx Pub. Time to get out the summer clothes. That shouldn't be hard, since I hadn't had time to pack them away over the winter.

I snagged the last table for two in the Manx and wiggled right in, spreading my coverless magazines out on the other side. I ordered the pasta special and began checking out the samples of Mitzi Brochu's style. Her prime targets were overweight celebrities and royalty ("Porky Princess Should Shun Public Participation"). The Princess was lucky enough to hightail it back to Europe after Mitzi skewered her. The media people were not so fortunate. Mitzi liked to take aim at the fashion foibles of television personalities too. "Dump the Frumps—Ship Media Fashion Losers Back to the Boonies" targeted female news anchors and talk show hosts across the country. One of our local news anchors, Jo Quinlan, got it right between the eyes with the headline "From the Barn to the Big Time". The caption under her photo shrilled "Beefy country look is out: time for a makeover, Jo-Jo."

Every now and then, Mitzi scored a double play: "Fat and Frumpy—Dual Deficit Punctures Polyester Politicians". The rear view shot of local political mover and shaker Deb Goodhouse bending over probably would have cost the photographer his life, if she'd caught him snapping on his wide angle lens.

Two minutes into the first article and I knew one thing: I had no desire to meet Mitzi Brochu.

Femme Fatale was reputed to be outselling *Chatelaine* and *Canadian Living*, the former leaders in the field of women's magazines. I was astonished that people paid to read it.

"Oh God, look at that," said my waiter as he deposited my plate on the table. "Mitzi Brochu, isn't she wicked? My favourite one was her TV piece on 'Ban the Bum'. A lot of people are still blushing over it."

"Hmmm," I said, only partly because I had a mouthful. And partly because I was asking myself what kind of person took such obvious pleasure in holding other people up to ridicule.

*   *   *

Even on the walk to the office, I kept asking myself why Robin Findlay, my oldest and closest friend, the most sensible person in the world, who dreamed about picket fences and children, slept in blue flannelette nighties and doted on her six cats, would want to see Mitzi Brochu.

When I opened the door, Alvin was pointing to his watch. "Robin called in a panic. You just missed her."

I made room on the desk for the pile of *Femme Fatale* and dug out my briefcase.

"Better hustle," he added. "It's a hike over to the Harmony. And she sounds like she's going over the edge. Oh, and don't give another thought to your threads, maybe Mitzi will keep her eyes closed."

*   *   *

Alvin was right. It was a hike to the Harmony. I clomped

along Elgin Street and snapped left at Laurier West, not giving a glance to the hundred thousand tulips in the park. People jumped out of my way as I plunged along the sidewalk. I'm told I get this look on my face when I'm concentrating. Sort of a short, square Terminator.

What was Robin upset about? Was Mitzi Brochu planning an article on creeping polyesterism in the legal profession? "Lumpy Lawyers on the Loose?" or "Barristers: the View from Behind?" That wouldn't have bothered Robin. From kindergarten through law school, she never worried about fashion or appearances at all, just went through life being her serene, reliable self. And it would take more than a mean-mouthed pseudo-celebrity to make her panic.

I was running through the fourth or fifth scenario (Robin had a client who wanted to sue the silk underwear off Mitzi the Mouth) when I passed the National Parole Board Office on Laurier West.

"Sorry," I said, without sincerity, to a man who had misjudged my velocity.

"Camilla MacPhee," he said, stepping back on to the sidewalk.

I looked at him, trying to remember who he was.

"Ted Beamish, remember me?" he said. "You were a year behind me in law school. I was a pretty good friend of Paul's."

"Right," I said.

"It's good to see you. I almost didn't recognize you."

"It's the running shoes."

He blinked. "No, something else."

I didn't want to dwell on this theme. Ever since Paul was killed, people keep telling me I look different. It bothers them.

"I can't quite put my finger on it. Maybe it's the way you…"

"So, Ted, what have you been doing with yourself since Law School?" Men always like questions like that.

"I'm at the Parole Board now. What are you doing?"

"While you try to make sure they get out, I try to make sure they stay in."

He flushed. A deep, mottled red clashing with his coppery hair. Then he plunged on. "Everyone deserves a chance."

"Tell that to the victims."

"Oh yes," he said, with the flush up to his cheekbones and rising, "I remember hearing you were heading up an advocacy group. I guess you have your reasons. Well, I have mine, too."

"Sure," I said, tapping my foot. Two-thirty was coming fast.

"Listen, you got time for a cup of coffee?"

"Late for a meeting."

"Some other time then." The flush flamed past his ears and kept going to the top of his head. And you could see it right through the thinner bits of red hair in front.

* * *

The Harmony had been designed back when people thought the nineties would be a time of tranquillity. Soft aqua shades on walls. Deeper turquoise in the carpets. Mountainous silk flower arrangements backing onto mirrors. The lighting was misty and indistinct, and generic music was oozing out of the walls. I tried to remember the Harmony Hotel slogan. What was it? Oh yes, "Harmony Hotels, where the client never has to worry."

There was no sign of Robin. I checked the slip with the phone message, but it was hard to read under the coffee stains.

At the registration desk, I asked for Mitzi Brochu's room.

"I'm sorry, I can't give you that information," the little

trainee with the big hair trilled. Her brass name tag said Stephanie.

"She's expecting me."

"Well, I can put you through by phone. She can give you the room number herself. Sorry, it's a policy." She handed me the house phone.

It rang and rang until I slammed it down. I gave Stephanie a dirty look and stalked over to a cluster of love seats.

I sank into the turquoise and silver striped upholstery to wait for Robin. I hoped she wasn't expecting me in whatever the suite was. But she wasn't. I spotted her capturing an elevator.

"Robin!" I bellowed, dashing for the elevator, but the door had already closed.

I got to the eighth floor without looking at myself in the mirrored walls but not without asking myself if the Mormon Tabernacle Choir could possibly have recorded their own version of "Satisfaction".

The eighth floor was done in shades of peach and gold. It would have been very relaxing if I hadn't been so revved up. I fished out the message again. Suite 8 something something wasn't going to get me to Mitzi, but I held the paper up to the light just in case.

One door stood open, with a maid's cart heaped with fresh towels and toilet paper and all those little bottles they put in bathrooms.

"Hello," I hollered into the room. "Halloooo."

A dark-haired woman in a uniform popped out of the bathroom and stared.

"Hello," I said. "Can you help me? I'm meeting my friend Mitzi Brochu here and I can't remember which room she's in."

"Sorree. Not speak mooch Engleesh." She smiled and shrugged her shoulders.

Fine.

The next step was to pound on the doors of every suite on the floor. Not so bad. The suites would be in the corners, four to a floor.

No answer at the first door. The door of the suite across the hall stood open. This must be it, I thought, starting towards it.

"May I help you?"

I spun around. A man had appeared out of nowhere behind me. He was tall, thin and very good-looking, with a slash of grey at each temple. And he scared the bejesus out of me. Until I saw the little brass tag that said Richard Sandes, General Manager.

I exhaled. In my line of work I deal with too many women who have come off second best in chance encounters with strange men.

"I'm looking for Mitzi Brochu. I have an appointment with her. Can you help me find her suite?"

He shook his head. "Sorry. We can't give out the room numbers of our guests. I'm sure you appreciate that when you're staying in a hotel. But we can connect you with her on the house phone."

"Tried that," I said. "Wait a minute. What's...."

I heard Robin cry out from the suite and I started to step through the open door into a little antechamber.

"You can't just go in there!" Richard Sandes yelped as I elbowed him out of the way.

We both recoiled as a long gagging shriek tore through the air and Robin stumbled out into the hallway, her eyes rolling back into her head. Her mouth opened and shut and opened again. All without a word. She clutched at my skirt with her bloody hands as she slid to the floor and passed out on the peach carpet.

Two

S omeone had hated Mitzi. Hated her enough to tie her arms to the curved ends of the brass bedpost, gag her, and stab her through the heart with a sharpened stake. Hated her enough to write a poem on the wall over her head. In blood.

> *Here she dies*
> *Full of lies*
> *Hell will be her*
> *Well-earned prize*

My stomach lurched as the still-red letters dripped on the wall. Mitzi's open, staring, dead eyes seemed to carry traces of the terror she must have felt as she died. Don't be stupid, I told myself, she's dead. She can't feel anything.

I concentrated on Robin, who was babbling and weeping. And throwing up.

The police should be able to help, I thought. In this case, I was off the mark. The troops were led by Detective Connor McCracken, sizeable, cool, and, under normal circumstances, probably quite good natured.

This time, he and his fellow detective kept asking all of us, but especially Robin, probing questions in that monotone they must learn in police college. If they'd had any training at all, they would have noticed Robin alternating between deep flush and dead white. Her hands shook during certain parts of her story. I knew what that meant, and I hoped the detectives didn't.

"You can't be here, you're also a witness," he said.

"Like hell," I said, "I'm her lawyer. Race you to the Supreme Court."

Detective Conn McCracken shrugged, sat Robin down in a chair and walked her through the events in Mitzi's suite. He was large, late forties, and looked like he might coach little league on the week-ends. He smiled at Robin and even patted her hand. The good cop. Soften up the suspect before you turn her over to the bad cop.

The bad cop was called Mombourquette. He had a rodent's face and mean little eyes to match. He was just waiting for a chance to take a bite out of Robin. I kept flicking my eyes from Robin to McCracken to Mombourquette to make sure everybody behaved.

When McCracken asked for the third time what Mitzi had wanted and Robin started to shake all over again, I put my foot down.

"Can't you see she's in shock?" I said. "She needs a doctor, maybe even a hospital. You guys push her around any more and I'll file a complaint with the Police Commission and you can read your names in the newspaper. Look at her. You can see her again when her doctor says it's all right."

"We need a bit more information," said Mombourquette, showing his sharp little teeth.

"I saw nothing," Robin said. She looked at me when she said it.

"What else do you need to know? She's already told you Mitzi Brochu, a well-known writer in women's magazines, invited her up to the suite. She didn't know why she was invited and when she got there the victim was dead. She didn't see it happen and she didn't see anyone leaving the room. She touched the body to see if there was still a pulse, and that's how she got blood all over her. And now, as you might expect, she's in a state of shock. Tell me, boys, would your mothers or sisters have behaved any differently?"

"Good enough," said McCracken, disappointing Ratface.

I decided that Robin would be better off with her parents than alone in her townhouse. I got up and called them, telling them to get the family doctor mondo quicko and suggest this would be a good time for a house call.

Of course, I knew Robin was lying to the police. I just didn't know why.

They say everybody is capable of murder under the right circumstances. But it would have taken a lot more than Mitzi with her trendy vindictiveness to turn Robin into a killer. And she never would have been able to tie those knots. She couldn't even manage that for her Brownie badges.

Conn McCracken took me aside, just before I bundled Robin into a blanket.

"You're Donald MacPhee's daughter, aren't you?"

"Yes."

"Jeez, I remember him from St. Jim's. And Alexa's your sister, right? I used to date her a bit. You were just a little kid when I saw you last. So, um, how is she?"

I found it hard to drop my antagonistic mood. "Alexa? So so. Her husband died last fall and she's still getting over it."

"Sorry to hear that," he said, not looking sorry in the least. "Well, tell her I said hi."

"Sure."

*   *   *

17

As we left the Harmony Hotel, escorted by a pair of police officers, the flash bulbs went off in the lobby and the TV cameras homed in. Jo Quinlan, strapping and capable news anchor, barred our way, holding her microphone, telling her viewers everything she knew about Mitzi's death.

The cameras got some nice footage of Robin looking like Bambi on speed.

Robin didn't say a word in the cab. She seemed to have crawled up inside herself and shut the rest of us out. Only the pressure of her hand clutching mine told me we were still connected. I was relieved when we got to her parents' home and found Dr. Beaver all ready for us. Her father and I slid her into her old bed and Dr. B.'s hypodermic did the trick. Even her mother ripped herself away from *The Young and the Restless* and stood there, wringing her hands.

"Robin's in shock," Dr. Beaver said. "Just shock. She'll be fine."

He hovered over her as she twitched and moaned in her sleep. He offered the same kind of down-to-earth advice we'd had from him as children, scared to get vaccinations. We'd always relaxed and giggled around him because he had huge buck teeth and looked like he'd be at home in a pond.

"You heard Dr. B.," I said to my unconscious friend. "You'll be fine."

She opened her eyes wide and squeaked, "The cats! What will happen to the cats?"

Oh no. Not that.

"She means her cats, the six she keeps," her father whispered. "They can't come here. Mrs. Findlay's allergic to cats. Oh my God, now Robin's going to fret about them."

I didn't need anyone to tell me what she meant. I am no fan of cats, and this particular six irritated me every time I dropped in to see Robin. But this wasn't the right moment to mention it.

"Don't worry about the cats," I said, feeling a sudden, regrettable largeness of spirit. "I'll make sure they're all right."

I gave Robin's hand a little squeeze and felt her squeeze back, just as her eyes closed.

Once Robin was out cold, Mrs. Findlay slipped back in front of the boob tube and lit up a cigarette. As long as I can remember, she's been addicted to soap operas. Once Robin told me her mother had been at the grocery store with a long lineup at the cash. When she realized she might miss *Another World*, she left her groceries and hightailed it home.

Robin's father and I just kept bumping into each other and not having anything to say. What could you say? I didn't want coffee. I didn't want a drink. I didn't want to try the lemon poppyseed muffins which were still cooling on the counter. Neither of us mentioned the police and their questions. We both knew Robin's troubles were just beginning.

"Don't worry, there's no need for you to hang around, chewing your nails. Thank you for helping. There's nothing you can do right now. You go home, and I'll let you know when she can talk," he said. "Camilla's leaving now, dear."

Mrs. Findlay butted out her latest cigarette and tore her eyes away from a blonde woman and a dark-haired man who were engaged in some kind of wrestling match under a sheet. And in the afternoon, too.

"God almighty, those two scamps, eh?" Mrs. Findlay lit another cigarette and pointed to the TV with it. But it was too late, an ad for detergent which would get your sheets sparkling clean replaced the wrestling scene. "That Nina. If they're not careful, her husband will catch them. Then there'll be hell to pay."

"I can imagine," I murmured.

"You just try and relax," said Mr. Findlay as he opened the door for me.

*   *   *

Just relax. Sure. You can picture just how relaxing it was at my place once my nearest and dearest got a gander at Robin and me on the six o'clock news. Hot and cold running relatives, everywhere you looked.

"Would you like a martini? Some warm milk? Toast? A nice boiled egg? Something else? Although there's not much in your fridge." That was Alexa. She believes in the efficacy of food and drink in the face of any disaster.

"Not really hungry."

"Would it help if I did a bit of this laundry?" Donalda. She's only comfortable in a well-administered household. Whenever she visits me, she perches on the edge of the sofa and stares into the kitchen at the dishes in the sink. "I could wash up those dishes for you, if you'd like."

"Sure, anything you want."

"I think your home would be much improved by the addition of some dining room furniture. Nothing too avant-garde, just a couple of nice chairs and a good table. I don't know how you can stand to have a desk in there. Why don't you spend a little of your money on fixing it up? You could even get a pretty desk and put it in the living room." Edwina. *House Beautiful* has always been her bible.

The burbling of decorating tips was drowned out by the squeal of the blender in the kitchen and the roar of the vacuum cleaner around our feet. Robin's cats took refuge in my bedroom. My father sat in the armchair in the corner and studied me with keen interest.

No one mentioned the murder. And I sure wasn't going to.

"Something else? What about a nice little rum and coke to settle you down?" Alexa never forgets our Nova Scotia roots.

To tell the truth, it felt rather good to have them bustling around, dispensing elbow grease and unsolicited advice, their voices blurring. Usually I protect my territory and independence and try to keep a handle on their surplus domesticity.

"A filing cabinet would help a lot. The light from your balcony would be perfect for a ficus benjamina. Can I top up your drink?"

The second rum and coke hit me like a piano from a second story window. As I crawled naked into my freshly made bed and curled into the fetal position, I could hear the gentle thudding of the washer-dryer and the hum of sisters chatting. I closed my eyes. Six cats settled themselves around my feet.

All that night and into the next day, Mitzi's dead face kept flashing through my mind, with Robin's wailing voice in the background. "No, no," she kept saying, "not dead. Not like this. Please not now."

*   *   *

"Crucified? Lord thundering Jesus," said Alvin, filled with admiration for my cleverness in finding myself in the right spot at the right time. "What did she look like?" He picked up the receiver he'd dropped on the desk as I sagged through the door. "She's here now, Mom, I'll call you back later." He hung up and looked at me with great expectation.

"I don't want to talk about it."

After a night of spinning in the sheets, fighting nightmares filled with dead eyes and silent screams, the last thing I wanted was to relive finding Mitzi Brochu. And the only way to avoid talking about it was to get Alvin out of the office. I decided the solution was a series of low-level yet time-consuming errands requiring stops all over town.

"Panty-hose?" he said, reading the list I handed him. "You want me to pick up your panty-hose? That's demeaning. It's bad enough I have to go to the print shop and the post office and the library and pick up cat food. But I draw the line at panty-hose. That's not part of my job."

"Sure it is. It's called Other Duties As Required. Take it or leave it. You can always go home to Mom."

I hoped Alvin would leave it, for good. But as a consolation prize, I hoped he'd at least be gone for a couple of tranquil hours.

In the meantime, I was counting on the Benning brief to take my mind off what we'd found in Mitzi Brochu's bedroom.

The Benning brief wasn't quite distracting enough. Mitzi, seen from different angles, superimposed herself on every page of notes. Even my endless doodles were gruesome.

And I kept thinking about Robin.

For my own peace of mind, I needed to know what Robin had been doing in Mitzi's room. And what she had meant by "not now."

The phone rang, jerking me back to the present. "Long distance, for Mr. Alvin Ferguson. Will you accept the charges?"

"No, Mr. Alvin Ferguson is not here and, no, I will not accept the charges."

The operator was pretty unemotional about the whole thing, but I slammed down the phone and made a mental note to check the next bill.

I couldn't concentrate on the Benning brief. And things administrative paled next to the enormity of being involved in a murder. What made her go there? Robin, sensible, flat-shoed real estate lawyer. Singer in the church choir. Disher out of food at the Food Bank. What was her connection with Mitzi Brochu, shredder of egos?

Mrs. Findlay answered the phone in a whisper.

"No, dear, she's still out like a light. Dr. B.'s been here again to give her something. She woke up at 6 in the morning and almost gave her father a heart attack, screeching."

"What was she, um, screeching?"

"Something like, 'you can't do that to her. I won't let you do that to her.'" A little quaver sneaked into Mrs. Findlay's voice. "Oh, dear, what do you think it all means?"

"I don't know."

I didn't either. But I had to ask myself, if Robin had seen the killer, had the killer seen Robin?

Why would she deny it? Especially to me?

Thanks to the vigilance of the local paparazzi, her face and name had blasted its way into every home in the region.

What had it felt like to preside over the media interpretation of the death of someone who had humiliated you on the pages of the magazine with the widest circulation in the country? Had there been a look of satisfaction on Jo Quinlan's face?

"Don't worry, Mrs. Findlay," I lied, "just make sure she's not alone. I think that will be much better for her."

"You're right, dear. Brooke's on her way home from Toronto now. She'll be a great help, I'm sure."

I murmured soothing remarks, casually omitting agreement that Robin's little sister would be a great help. I felt confident Brooke would be the self-centred and pampered vapour-brain she'd always been. It seemed inappropriate to mention this to her mother.

*   *   *

What the hell, I thought, I'm a taxpayer. And with Alvin out of the way, I was able to get to the phone.

"Oh, yeah," said McCracken, when I identified myself. "How are you today?"

I stopped myself from saying, "Oh, you know, the way I always feel the day after I've found my best friend *non compos mentis* in the presence of a warm corpse." Instead I said "Getting there."

"Great," he said.

"I'd like a bit of information."

"Not much I can say. Aren't you a defence lawyer?"

"Not usually. I'm an advocate for victims. My philosophy is toss the perpetrators in the hoosegow, slam the gates and turf the key."

"Oh," he said, "I guess that's good. I'm afraid I still can't give you any information. But how's your sister?"

"What's it worth to you?"

"Fingerprints."

"Shoot."

"Nothing but the deceased, your little friend and the housekeeping staff."

"My sister's fine."

"Do you think she'd mind if I gave her a call sometime?" he asked.

I cleared my throat in a meaningful way.

"We've interviewed all the staff and the other guests and no one saw anyone except your friend Robin enter the scene of

24

the crime. Ms. Brochu had no apparent enemies."

"My fanny, she didn't. Did you ever read anything she wrote?"

"I'm telling you what the witnesses tell me."

"Maybe you should talk to them again."

"Maybe. But the way I hear it, your friend was upset before she ever got near the victim."

This was true and I knew it, but I just kept silent on my end of the line. Until it was McCracken's turn to clear his throat.

"Hard to say with Alexa," I told him. "You better just give her a call and find out."

"Thanks a lot."

"No problem," I said.

Alexa wasn't home when I dialled.

I nibbled my nails for a long time after talking to McCracken. It sounded to me like Robin could turn out to be an easy solution for the police. I would have to make sure that didn't happen.

I knew Robin hadn't had enough time to kill Mitzi. But I didn't even need to know that—I knew her.

Alvin, considerate as always, had laid out a few more issues of *Femme Fatale* with Mitzi articles for me. He'd added a note, suggesting I might find them amusing.

Mitzi, it turned out, had an annual feature, "Mitzi Picks the Glitz and Mitzi Picks the Zitz." These issues, Alvin mentioned in his note, were hard to come by, as someone had already stolen them from the library. Lucky for me (he said) he had friends.

"Mitzi's Glitz" turned out to be a mix of svelte men and women with impeccable style sense and verve and hectares of spare cash for clothes. A dozen glitzers in all, but no real surprises. The wife of a department store magnate, a bakery magnate and a magazine magnate. And, of course, the magnates themselves, indistinguishable in white tie. A CBC cultural guru. A model whose furry eyebrows, pointy cheekbones, and pouty lips were on every second cover of *Femme Fatale*. A real estate developer. A classical guitarist. An actress. A former Prime Minister. Mitzi had burbled on in praise of their superb taste and élan.

Who gives a shit, I thought. But the real fun stuff was reserved for the "Zitz". Poor old Zitz. Just minding their own business and then one day, one too many cream puffs and, poof, they've made the list.

Jo Quinlan and Deb Goodhouse were way down on the Zitz list at numbers 11 and 12. Still, they were on it. No wonder there weren't any copies left on the local stands.

I'm not a person who cares about appearances, my own or others, but still I was surprised Jo Quinlan would have let herself be photographed wearing those particular spandex shorts and that halter top. Particularly in profile. Although from the gas barbecue in the background, the tongs in her hands and the look on her face, it appeared the scene was her own backyard and the photographer had just stuck his nasty little camera over the fence.

"Massive Media Menace" was the caption over Jo's photo. Underneath it read: "Try mud-wrestling, dear, you already have the wardrobe, and leave the screen to those who don't fill every inch of it."

Still, Jo Quinlan got off better than Deb Goodhouse. Or "The Goodhouse Blimp", as Mitzi dubbed her. The rear view shot of Deb Goodhouse walking up the stairs of the Centre Block of the Parliament Buildings had a cartoon string drawn around her ankle. The angle of the camera had enhanced the rear expanse. "Is our Princess of Polyester full of hot air or worse? Will she rise in the House and float through the ceiling? If looks could kill, she'd be six feet under," the commentary read.

The articles featured pictures of Mitzi too. Looking much better than the last time I had seen her. Emaciated, with blood-red lips and a crow's nest of black hair. All in black with bare shoulders, black gloves past the elbow, black hose and pointed black spike heels. The photo of Mitzi floated without background, a judge, ruling without mercy on fashion crimes.

Somebody had taken revenge on Mitzi. Just a glance at these articles told me there would be a long list of candidates. Not to mention the hundreds of others who must have suffered at Mitzi's hands. I hoped the police would do a good job of checking out Robin's competition. If not, I decided I'd have to do it myself.

Alexa was home this time when I called to warn her.

"Oh good, Camilla," she said. "I was just about to call you. Edwina wants us all to have dinner at her place. Six o'clock…"

I interrupted. "I had no choice but to suggest you might be willing to get a call from this cop you used to know in high school. Sorry. But you can always take your phone off the hook."

"A policeman? Oh, not Conn McCracken, was it?"

"Yes, look, I'm sorry…."

"What did he say?"

"Nothing much, just how were you."

"What did you say?"

"I said you were so so."

"Oh, Camilla."

"And I told him that Greg died."

"That's all?"

27

"What did you want me to say?"

"I don't know. Did he ask how I looked?"

"No, he didn't."

"Oh."

"Anyway, he might call you and you can tell him how you look yourself."

"Oh, Camilla."

"Gotta go, I hear the dreaded Alvin approaching."

"Wait a minute. Wait a minute," Alexa breathed. "Does he still have all his hair?"

"I didn't notice."

"For God's sake, Camilla," she said and hung up.

The only good thing about being the boss is making up rules and then changing them without reason or warning as you go along. So when Alvin crashed back into the office, dropped his bags, and snarled something about how can you stand all those fucking tulips all over the place, I beamed as I picked up my jacket and opened the door.

"So long, Alvin. There's plenty to keep you busy. I see about fifty linear feet of filing on the floor. By tomorrow, I expect to be able to see the pattern of the carpet."

His wail followed me down the stairs. "Don't you want these panty-hose?"

Three

After twenty years or more, the tall respectable husbands collected by my sisters had begun to settle into middle age and to develop creeping hairlines, baby paunches, and minor peculiarities, some easier to adjust to than others. Take, for example, Donalda's husband, Joe, each year withdrawing more and more into a world of his own, of golf and fishing and imaginary trophies. Or Edwina's Stan with his collection of dribble glasses, plastic dog turds and fake vomit. I wish I had some kind of coin for every time I encountered a whoopee cushion in the passenger seat of Stan's Buick LeSabre.

"Better take it easy on the baked beans," he always said.

I suggested to Edwina that perhaps Stan was developing Alzheimer's and should be locked away for his own protection, but I noticed she still kept sending him to pick me up for family get-togethers. This dinner was no exception.

A hand mirror lay on the passenger seat as I opened the door.

"Would you mind moving that?" Stan said.

As I picked up the mirror, it screamed with laughter and kept on laughing after I threw it on the floor.

"Perhaps you should get your hair done more often," Stan said, between his own screams of laughter.

"Perhaps you should get a life, Stan," I suggested, not laughing but giving some thought to screaming myself.

HAHAHAHAHAHA, howled the mirror from the floor,

just before I picked it up and chucked it out the window.

Stan was still sulking when we reached Nepean and pulled into the driveway, which I think Edwina vacuums twice weekly.

"Aw, Camilla, the girls would have gotten a big kick out of that at dinner," he said.

"Like hell," I told him.

If "the girls" had sent Stan to get me into some kind of a mellow mood after a distressing day spent mulling over Mitzi's death and Robin's continuing state of withdrawal, "the girls" were going to be let down.

They were hanging around the entrance, three vultures with dish cloths, when we arrived. I could tell they'd been bustling around the kitchen, discussing my mental state, when they'd heard the car. Now they were trying to look like they'd all accidentally ended up near the front door just as we got there.

They scanned my face and turned to Stan. He shrugged, before perking up a bit.

"Wait a minute," he said, flinging open the door to the basement and thundering down the stairs. "I think I have something else that might do just as well."

"Are you all right?" Edwina asked.

"Well, I'll never look in another mirror again."

"He's just trying to cheer you up, dear."

"Let's chat in the living room," said Donalda, steering me, as if I hadn't been there a thousand times.

Edwina's entire house is picture-perfect polished mahogany, pastel brocade, flowers in silver or crystal vases. In the living room, my father glanced up from the newspaper, peering over the top of his little half-moon reading glasses. He matched the decor. Eighty-year old gentleman, distinguished, white-haired and slim, seated in wingback with matching ottoman.

"Hello, um, Camilla," he said.

"Can I get you a little drink?" Alexa asked me. Her colour was high and she had a sparkle I hadn't seen about her for months.

Donalda looked at my father after Alexa left the room. "Do you think she has a fever, Daddy?"

"No idea, dear," said my father, with a flicker of worry.

"Maybe she's in love," I said.

"Oh, Camilla."

Dinner was wonderful. Edwina knows her way around a kitchen and I have to confess it's very pleasant to sit on well-padded dining room chairs, surrounded by the warm glow of mahogany, eating good food off Minton china. She presided over the distribution of the roast lamb stuffed with spinach and chèvre with the air of an artist at a show of her work.

And, in my family, we always find things taste even better when we're discussing people who are not present.

"She did?" said Donalda, as we heaped the lemon rice onto our plates "Well, I'm not surprised. Did you see what she had on?"

"No wonder he practically dived down the front of her blouse," said Edwina, passing the squash soufflé.

"Exactly," said Alexa, and reached for the broccoli, "and I know we're all human, but I don't think church is the place for it."

My father just concentrated on the food. He doesn't approve of gossip. I concentrated on my food too, since I didn't know any of the people whose blouses were under discussion.

When the neighbours and other parish members had been dealt with, they turned their attention to the murder. I was waiting for it. Mitzi Brochu's murder had captured the imagination of the magazine-reading public in a big way.

"A crucifixion," said Alexa, shivering. "It's too gruesome."

"Well," I said, "it wasn't really a…"

"Somebody absolutely had it in for her," said Donalda.

"No kidding," I said.

"Not surprising when you think about the sorts of things she wrote about people," Edwina pronounced. "She literally ruined careers and brought terrible embarrassment to people, right here even in our community. People who were just minding their own business and had nothing to do with her. She just selected them and burned them." I wasn't sure how the words were getting out with Edwina's lips pursed like that.

"I know," sighed Alexa, twisting her napkin. "Poor Deb Goodhouse."

"She is a little bit broad in the beam, but even so…" Donalda didn't get to finish her sentence.

"Her beam is not the issue. The woman is a well-respected politician and a wonderful contributor to the community. She's given a lot of herself to environmental projects and to helping the third world and what does she get in Canada's best-selling women's magazine? Not a word about her achievements, just her backside. After I read that article, I cancelled my subscription."

Well, I bet that showed them, Edwina, I thought.

"Poor, poor Deb." Alexa was still milking the poor Deb theme.

I'd never given a moment's thought to the Hon. Ms. Goodhouse before I read the article in *Femme Fatale*. Somehow she seemed to be important to my sisters.

"She some kind of a friend?" I asked.

The three of them turned and looked at me.

"Oh, Camilla," said Alexa.

"Of course, she's a friend," said Donalda. "Don't you remember? We all went to St. Jim's together. She used to be at the house all the time."

"So what was I then? Seven years old?"

"All the same. You must remember Deb."

"Right," I said, referring to woolly memories of a beefy brunette scattered among the long blondes, all of them giggling and smoking cigarettes and listening to Pat Boone in the upstairs bedrooms.

"You must remember how excited we all were when she won her first federal election." Edwina gestured around the table to indicate that I was not only unaware, but also alone, in my lack of excitement.

The other girls nodded, as did my father and Stan. Joe smiled to himself, managing a hole-in-one on his internal golf course.

"I guess I missed it."

"It was around the time of…" Edwina started to say Paul's death but was silenced by the tensing of muscles around the table, signalling the topic was about to change. Every one in my family is always worried that any talk of Paul will plunge me into some internal chaos, from which I will never recover. I'm not so sure they're wrong. We don't get nearly as agitated over Alexa's much more recent widowhood. The topic veered to the highlights of Deb Goodhouse's career.

"So was she upset by these articles in *Femme Fatale*?" I asked.

A rustle of relief around the table confirmed the tricky topic of Paul had not caused me to plummet into instant depression. I guess I was as relieved as anyone else.

"Oh, yes," said Alexa. "She was very hurt. They were terribly personal and insulting."

"And even worse," Edwina broke in, "she thought they trivialized everything she'd been working on. You know, these women politicians, it's a pretty tough life for them, and then, to have the only article ever written about you in a national magazine focus on your backside, well...." Edwina became speechless at this point.

"Quite an effect," I agreed.

"Not only that, but her blood pressure went practically through the roof," said Alexa.

"Indeed?" I said. "She must have hated Mitzi."

"God, yes," said Alexa, avoiding my father's flicker at her minor profanity, "Deb felt like killing her."

Everyone made a point of letting me know this was just a figure of speech, only an emotion and not a reality, and Deb Goodhouse could never have crucified Mitzi Brochu, in case I had drawn that conclusion from Alexa's remarks. Even Joe came back to earth during the brouhaha.

"Don't worry about it, girls, I wasn't about to call the police."

"Well, of course not," they said in unison, and changed the subject yet again.

"So, how's Robin doing?" Donalda asked.

"She's still in bed."

"Still in bed!" said Edwina.

"Dr. Beaver's been giving her sedatives. He says she's too emotionally fragile to be up yet or to be on her own."

"What does he know about emotional shock, you tell me that?" said Donalda, "If she were my daughter, I'd send her to the vet before I'd let old Bucky Beaver look after her."

"Tell me about it," said Alexa. "I'm surprised he didn't recommend mustard poultices to draw out the poisons in her system. Or maybe he did. Camilla?"

34

"Sorry to disappoint, but I think it's just good old fashioned tranquilizers."

"Well, none of my business, of course, but Robin hasn't really led such a sheltered life. I mean, she is a working lawyer and she did do a lot of legal aid work before she went into real estate law and, sure, it's traumatic finding a dead body, but don't you think she's over-reacting?" asked Edwina.

"I'd like to see how any of you would hold up if you stumbled across a crucified, bleeding corpse, still warm."

"Pass the lamb, dear," said Stan.

"On the other hand," said Edwina, "you stumbled across the very same bleeding corpse, still warm, too, I believe. And yet, here you are bouncing off to work and indulging in a full and active social life."

Fighting off the memory of dead Mitzi while I slumped around the office and getting dragged off to family dinners with shades of the Spanish Inquisition was more like it. Still, Edwina had a point. Robin was overdoing it.

"Unless," Edwina continued, "Robin killed this woman. Then she'd have a reason to feel so upset."

"Edwina," said my father.

And I'd thought he was dozing at the other end of the table.

"I know, Daddy, but she was there, all covered in blood and she won't tell anybody why she was in that room and now she's verging on a catatonic state. Something's very strange about all that."

"Oh, Edwina, you can't think Robin would kill anybody. We've known her since she and Camilla were kids. It's not possible," said Donalda.

Donalda was right. It was far, far more likely I would kill somebody. And even that was out of the question most of the time.

Edwina was not one to give up when she was onto a good angle.

"Maybe Mitzi Brochu had something on her and was going to do an article on it."

"Oh, right, Edwina," I said, "and what would Mitzi have on Robin? Putting too much milk in the cats' dishes? All of Canada would rush to the newsstands to buy that issue."

"You may be her best friend, but you don't know everything about her."

"Yes, I do know everything about her. And I know she didn't, and she couldn't kill anybody."

I felt unshakable certainty about this. I'd thought for hours about Robin and what she could have done. I'd examined every memory I had of her since the day in kindergarten, when we'd first shared the red crayon and become friends for life. Robin was always the one who helped the smaller kids with their overshoes and zippers. Robin always helped the old ladies cross the street. Robin would give anyone her last dime. Robin didn't kill Mitzi.

But Robin, Robin, Robin, I thought, why are you lying?

"Maybe," said Alexa, "she was in love and…"

This startling suggestion was followed by a strangled gasp from Donalda. We all turned to gawk at a set of teeth complete with full gums, sitting in the middle of the table next to the silver vase with the six baby roses. The teeth grinned in a mad parody of every denture advertisement ever made.

For a minute there was total, and uncharacteristic, silence at the table. Until Edwina reached forward to wipe that smile off her Irish linen tablecloth.

"HAHAHAHAHAHAHAHAHA," roared the teeth. "HAHAHAHAHAHAHAHHAAHA…" Startled, Edwina dropped them into her Minton vegetable platter.

So that was what Stan had been prowling around in the basement for. A suitable replacement for the laughing mirror.

"HAHAHAHHAAHAHAHAHAHAHAHAHAHAHAHA HAHAHAHAHA," howled the teeth from on top of the broccoli.

With the exception of me and Joe, who didn't return to earth this time, everyone collapsed with laughter. Donalda's shoulders shook and her head bobbed. Alexa wheezed out heeheehees until twin streams of tears ran down her cheeks. Edwina had a full-bodied boom, not unlike the teeth in the broccoli. Even my father had to smile. Stan was a happy man.

"Get that damn thing out of here before I toss it," I said.

Stan stretched toward the broccoli where our new friend was starting to wind down to a "hahaha".

"She'll do it!" he squeaked. "She threw the mirror out of the car."

"Oh, Camilla" said Edwina. "He's only trying to cheer you up."

"He'll have to try a lot harder," I said.

Donalda reached over and patted my hand. "We all know how worried you are. But Robin will be okay. Her mother told me Brooke's on her way back from Toronto. That should make a big difference for Robin to have her sister here."

Sure, I thought. It will mean there's that much less attention for her when she needs it the most. Brooke will siphon off every extra bit of tender loving care the Findlays were lavishing on Robin. They won't even know it's happening. If I knew Brooke, it would be just little things, but soon her mother would be busy altering clothing and making special little meals for Brooke's friends, and making her bed and picking up after her. And what was this "on her way back" business? Toronto was a fifty minute flight or a four-and-a-half-hour drive. Why wasn't Brooke at home already?

Somehow I couldn't see Brooke soothing Robin after her nightmare. On the other hand, Robin, like her parents, would do anything for Brooke. Maybe even get out of bed to help out with the added workload Brooke always presented. Brooke might be good for Robin, but for all the wrong reasons.

As we started to clear the table, I got instructions to relax in the living room with the boys. Does all this special treatment make me the same kind of person as Brooke? I wondered as I lounged on the sofa. A user, a burner-up of the good will of others?

Alexa brought me a fresh cup of coffee. She leaned over and whispered, "He hasn't called yet."

My thoughts of Conn McCracken were not fond. I'd already had a couple of chats with him and all the information had been flowing one way. I had a feeling I would keep on hearing from him until he found out why Robin had gone to see Mitzi Brochu and why I'd gone with her. Whenever I'd ask him something, he'd indicate in that big, comfy way of his, that he couldn't answer me.

"Count your blessings if he didn't call, Alexa," I said, thinking that the fewer complications any of us had in our lives, the better.

"Oh, Camilla." She bit her lip as she flounced back to the kitchen.

I couldn't help noticing she was wearing red lipstick for the first time since her husband had died.

My father eyed me warily from the armchair at the end of the living room. Finally, he spoke.

"Tell me," he said, "how's Alvin getting along?"

Four

Back in my apartment, I was so well-stuffed with lamb and rice and broccoli that I was ready to settle down for the rest of the evening. I shifted from novel to novel, from task to task. The phone at the Findlays' was busy. And there were too many cats, everywhere you looked. I was getting used to them and even recognized the damn things. The black one, the white one with black markings, the ginger Tom, the tabby and the grey Persian. And the plump little three-coloured number, which Robin said was a calico cat. I didn't know their names and didn't plan to find out.

It was just before nine and I decided to try a few chores to bore me to sleep. Reading the week's papers, locating the week's laundry, washing up the week's dishes. Not that I cherish these chores, just that I find it better in the long run if I attend to them. And they are soporific.

But the visit from my sisters earlier in the week had thrown the schedule off. The laundry was done, and there were only the breakfast dishes in the sink. Most of the papers had disappeared. Figuring I could limp on for another week without indulging in drudgery, I shook the Persian off the remaining papers and retired to the balcony with a lamp, an extension cord and a clear conscience.

My apartment building is perched on the edge of the parkland which borders the Ottawa River Parkway. The balcony looks down on the Ottawa River from sixteen stories. To the North lie the Gatineau hills, green and rippling even in mid-May. I can see the bike and pedestrian pathways like ribbons along the river. And to the East, the green-roofed Parliament and Supreme Court buildings. A turn of the head shows downtown Ottawa, highrise clusters with more blotches of green, some with green rooftops and others consisting of mundane blocks of concrete and glass, creating wind tunnels. I could make out the mellow pink of the Harmony Hotel, the top stories glowing between two office towers.

The Harmony Hotel, where Mitzi Brochu had checked into a spacious peach suite, expecting luxury and finding death.

The Harmony Hotel, where Robin had kept an appointment and discarded her mental health.

The Harmony Hotel, I thought, is the key to understanding everything.

I chucked the papers back into the corner of the living room and lifted a cat from my favourite pair of running shoes.

It was time to start sticking my nose in. And I knew the place to start.

Forty minutes later, I walked into the lobby of the Harmony Hotel.

Another girl with big hair was working the Reception Desk. This one's tag said Naomi and she didn't trill, she chirped.

I flashed my driver's license in front of her, and said, "We found a few gaps in the Mitzi Brochu investigation. Can you confirm a few facts, ma'am?"

It wasn't my fault if she mistook me for the police. Her eyes widened.

"What kind of facts? I wasn't on duty that day. But I'm sure one of the others…or even Mr. Sandes could…"

"Don't worry about it. You'll be fine. I just need you to check the files to see if anyone was sharing Suite 815 with the victim on this trip. Or on any of her previous trips."

"One minute, please," she breathed and vanished through a door behind the counter.

I was drumming my fingers on the marble surface, when a voice behind me said, "Good evening, Ms. MacPhee, will you join me in my office?"

The day had not been good to Richard Sandes, perhaps because he was still at work at night. His hair was a little greyer than I remembered it and there seemed to be extra space in his suit. I remembered him being very sick in the powder room after we'd found Mitzi's body. Very sick and for a very long time.

"Smoke?" he said, passing me the package.

"No, thanks."

But his smile was still in working order. His eyes were rich and dark, like Belgian chocolates.

"Naomi seems to be under the impression you are a police detective, Ms. MacPhee. I wonder why?"

I shrugged my shoulders. "What can I say? Young people, they're very impressionable."

The crow's feet around his eyes crinkled up, but his mouth was busy with the cigarette. I couldn't tell whether or not he actually smiled.

"What can I do for you?" he asked.

"I'd like to know a few things about Mitzi Brochu. How often she came here. And if there was anyone who usually stayed with her."

"Why?"

"I'm trying to find out why my friend went to see her and asked me to come along."

"Didn't she tell you?"

"Well, I didn't actually talk to her before the murder, it was all accomplished with messages. And after, she hasn't been well enough to badger about it."

"I'm sorry?"

"She's tranked to the ears because she was so traumatized by finding the body. Well, you remember the state she was in when we got there?"

"How could I forget? I was pretty traumatized myself. You mean the poor girl's still out of it?"

"Right. Can't or won't eat. Can't get out of bed. Starts to shake if there's the slightest reference to Mitzi Brochu. Dead or alive."

"That's too bad."

"So, you can see why I would like to get a handle on why Mitzi wanted to see her."

"Weren't the police any help?"

He raised an eyebrow when I snorted.

"Okay," he said, "I think I understand how traumatic it must have been to find the body. The whole tragedy is still haunting me."

"You're going to help me?"

He shrugged his shoulders and smiled. "I remember the state your friend was in."

"Thank you." I slumped back in the chair.

"Do you want a cup of coffee or something?"

"Something," I said, not knowing what. My stomach was clenched.

"All right, shall we chat in the bar? It's pretty quiet on Sunday night."

"Good."

"I'll just check a few details and be back in a couple of minutes."

42

While I was waiting, I looked around. The office reflected the aqua theme of the Harmony foyer and hallways. Very restful with the oak furniture and the silk flowers. But all business, except for two photos on the bookcase. A plump blonde girl, about ten years old, grinned from one. An older version of the same girl, svelte and elegant, even in sports clothes, stood with Sandes and a woman in front of a boat. Richard Sandes looked different in the photo. Heavier, happier, casual in beige boating gear.

I was still standing by the photo when he came back.

"Your family?"

He nodded.

"Your daughter?"

"Yes."

"She's beautiful."

He smiled and I realized I was disappointed. I'd been hoping for his sister and his niece or something. It had been a long time since I'd felt the pull towards a man, a long time since Paul.

The bar was peach rather than aqua. We settled into peach-patterned tub chairs. The waiter materialized immediately. There are advantages to sitting with the manager. It occurred to me the tension in the tummy was nothing more than nerves, but even so I chose a double order of suicide wings and a light beer to wash them down.

Richard Sandes had a Perrier and a cigarette.

"So," I said when the order had been taken, "what can you tell me?"

I guess someday I'll have to work on smoothing out my conversational skills. But he didn't seem to mind.

"Miss Brochu stayed here whenever she stayed in town. She liked the Harmony and the brass always insisted on making a big deal out of her. There was talk about using her in an ad campaign for the Harmony Hotel chain. She got preferential treatment, so I guess that's why she chose us over the Hilton or the Westin or the Chateau."

"Hmm," I said, "she didn't strike me as too harmonious."

"True," said Richard Sandes, "but she was very well known and popular, well, maybe not popular, but she got good media coverage and people liked to read about her and liked her broadcasts, so it must have seemed like a good idea to the decision-makers."

"Did she get free rooms?"

"No, but she got the suite for the price of a standard room, provided we weren't booked solid for a convention or something."

"How long has that been going on?"

He stopped for a second and looked at me.

Maybe I was getting goopy from those suicide wings. I dabbed at my mouth and fingers with a napkin. I'd lost the habit of worrying about how I looked to a man.

"I don't know," he said, "I've only been here for six months. I'd have to check the files."

"Oh," I said, distracted from my Mitzi probe, "where were you before?"

"Toronto."

"Quite a change to Ottawa. How does your family like it here?"

Richard sipped his Perrier for a second before answering.

"I'm here on my own."

I didn't know quite what to say. There are many reasons for being in a new city on your own. Most of them you shouldn't pry into.

"Do you like it here?"

He shrugged. "I don't get out much. I've been putting in pretty long hours. But I like that and I like the Harmony."

"It's a beautiful hotel. I can see why you like it."

"Yes. I hope I can stay on."

"Would they move you without…"

He smiled at me. A crooked smile with a lot of sadness in it.

"I'm the manager at a showcase hotel where a star client was murdered. In a very showy way. The Official Philosophy of Harmony Hotels is to provide a place where clients don't have to worry. There's a lot of heat right now. Somebody's got to carry the can, and I'm the ideal candidate."

"That's not fair."

"Life isn't always fair, Ms. MacPhee."

"Right. Tell me about it."

He waved the waiter over to refill our drinks. I was surprised to see mine was empty. There's something about suicide wings.

"So," he said, "what did you want to know about Mitzi Brochu?"

"Everything. How often she came here. Who stayed with her. Who came to see her. What she was like."

"Oh, is that all?"

I noticed he was laughing.

"Well, whatever you can tell me," I said, laughing too.

"Let's see, she came down about once every two months. I have no idea who came to see her. Hotels are not in the business of keeping tabs on clients."

"What was she doing here?"

"In the hotel?" His eyes twinkled.

"In Ottawa."

"The scuttlebutt is she was writing a book on federal politicians. On their personal style or something."

45

"A book on Members of Parliament?"

"I heard on M.P.'s, Senators, the Prime Minister, the back room boys, everyone and everything."

"Have you ever read her stuff?" I asked.

"Yes."

"Then you know what she was like. A lot of people would want to avoid being in her book."

"Perhaps not enough to kill her."

"Humph," I said, getting back to the suicide wings.

"Even though you might like it to be a conspiracy of parliamentarians."

I thought he had a point, so I tried another approach.

"Did you know her well?"

"Not really. She only stayed here three times since I've been here."

"Did you like her?"

"Not in the least."

I raised my eyebrows and sipped my beer.

"She wasn't very likeable."

I had to agree.

"And she upset a lot of people before she died," he added.

I knew what he meant. She'd been able to upset me a lot even after she died. Case in point, here I was on a Sunday night in a bar with a man I'd just met. Something I'd never done before in my life.

"I know. Robin was one of them."

"And you say she's still in shock."

"That's right. And the police want to talk to her as soon as she's well enough."

"Too bad," he said. With sympathy.

"Right."

Our conversation slid into personal matters, likes and

dislikes, what chance the Jays might have this season, what it was like to live alone in Ottawa.

Much later I looked at my watch and shook it. The time couldn't be right. I had to get home to bed like a good little girl or I wouldn't be able to catch up on the Benning case tomorrow.

"Gotta go," I said, whipping out some cash and looking around for the waiter.

"It's on the house," Richard said.

"Thanks." I was on my feet, still marvelling at the fact I'd had two beer on a work night.

"Something I said?" he asked, rising.

"No, just pressures of work. Time for me to hit the hay. Do you mind if I call you if I have other questions?"

"No problem."

As we walked back to the foyer, where the big-haired receptionist was chirping at new arrivals, I decided to grab a cab. It was very late by my standards, and the walk by the river was just a little too isolated at night. I'd had enough big, strapping clients who were victims of vicious predators to be under any illusions.

"Thanks, again." The front doors opened, and I walked towards the cab stand.

Richard took me by surprise as he caught up to me. He took the Blueline driver by surprise too.

"Can I give you a lift?"

The last surprise was when I realized how much I wanted that lift.

I found myself smiling as I waited for the parking valet to arrive with Richard's car, and I was still smiling as we pulled on to Wellington Street and turned left.

"Usually I walk," I told him.

"It must be nice. Especially with all the tulips."

"What tulips?"

"The million or so tulips that are about to bloom," he said, flashing a look at me.

"I guess I haven't really noticed them. You sort of take them for granted when you've lived here most of your life."

As we slipped along the Parkway, the river glittered in the May night. In five short minutes, we drew up in front of my building, and I felt a jab of regret.

"Good night," I said, regretting the regret.

"We seem to have gotten off topic. Aren't you going to ask me about her boyfriend?"

"Whose boyfriend?" The words slipped out before I could stop them. Mitzi's boyfriend, of course. "What about the boyfriend?"

"I think he lives here in Ottawa, but he was always in her room. Every time she was in town."

"But not this time."

"Oh yeah, this time, too."

"Well, where was he when…"

"According to the hotel staff, they had a knock-down drag-out dust-up, the night before. Bad enough for the other guests on the floor to phone and complain about the noise."

"Do the police know?"

"They do."

"This is good news. They might leave Robin alone."

The little question still nagged me inside. If the boyfriend was the bad guy, why would Robin be lying?

"What's his name? Mitzi's boyfriend."

"Wendtz. Rudy Wendtz."

We said good-bye for the second time and I smiled at the memory of Richard Sandes, all the way from the car to the elevator and from the elevator to the sixteenth floor and all along the hallway to my apartment. I kept smiling up to the point where I spotted my neighbour, Mrs. Parnell, moving her walker back to her apartment after her outing to the garbage chute. It's hard to keep smiling once you've spotted Mrs. Parnell.

I nodded to her and made a futile attempt to pass without engaging in conversation about anything I might have done to provoke her. She might be in her seventies, but she is a woman who embodies the word "formidable". I've heard other neighbours speculate about her links to power in former governments, even insinuations about intelligence work in World War Two. Whatever the scuttlebutt about her past, at this point in her life Mrs. Parnell was content to occupy her time being a pain in the butt.

"Excuse me, Ms. MacPhee," she said, staring down at me over her remarkably long nose, reminding me of every nun who ever caught me making a paper airplane in Religion class. Her ability to terrorize was not diminished a whit by the fact that she leaned on the walker. Somehow she managed to hang on to a cigarette in a long holder everywhere she went.

Mrs. Parnell is the sixteenth floor's keeper of the public morality. She has two passions, music, opera in particular, and making sure no one, but no one, gets away with anything, but anything.

"Oh, hello, Mrs. Parnell," I said, once I was sure there was no escape. "Lovely evening."

She was five-eleven if she was an inch and I could feel myself shrinking as she continued to stare down at me. Why I, a thirtysomething lawyer, nasty as the next guy, should be intimidated by a tall, awkward old lady in a mud-coloured sweater with holes in the elbows was beyond me.

"Ms. MacPhee, is it possible cat noises have been heard coming from your apartment?"

"Cat noises," I said, shocked. "Certainly not, Mrs. Parnell. What would ever give you that idea?"

"I have ears, Ms. MacPhee."

Yes, and the less said about them the better, I thought. What the hell, the best defense is a good offense, somebody once said. It seemed to me to fit the occasion. I gave it a try.

"I also have ears, Mrs. Parnell, and may I suggest you have confused the howling of vowels from one of your gruesome operas with feline sounds in the vicinity. And who can blame you?"

"Well!" she said, moving herself and her walker back into her apartment with remarkable speed and slamming the door.

I whipped open my own door, slid through and closed it. A great chorus of meows greeted my arrival.

Five

Yes, this is Alvin Ferguson. Yes, I will accept the charges."
Alvin held his hand over the receiver and shot me a
meaningful look. "It's my mother, it's quite personal. Would
you mind waiting outside for a couple of minutes?"

It was Monday morning at ten, and I was still standing in
the doorway of Justice for Victims, clutching my muffin and
coffee. I opened my mouth just as Alvin reached over and
closed the door.

I sat on the stair sipping my coffee, nibbling my muffin
and listing all of the things I would like to do to Alvin. I'd
finished the coffee, the muffin and the list, and was getting up
to go back in to insert the telephone somewhere painful, when
I heard the "excuse me." It was What's-his-name.

"Oh, hello, um…" I said.

"Ted. Ted Beamish. You remember, I ran into you the other
day outside the Parole Board Office."

"Right."

"We talked about having a coffee together sometime when
we ran into each other."

Well, he had talked about it.

"I saw on the news that you and Robin Findlay were there
right at the scene of the Mitzi Brochu murder. That must have
been right after we bumped into each other. I'm sure you must
have been very disturbed by it."

"You bet."

"So I didn't like to call you right after the...um, incident, but I thought I might try today. It's a new week and..." A band of sweat formed on his upper lip.

I might as well have coffee with the guy, I thought, since there was no point at all in strangling Alvin with a witness present.

"Sure, why not?"

"How about the Mayflower?"

As we settled into our booth, I wondered what we would find to talk about. It doesn't bother me to sit there and not say anything, but it seems to make other people a bit edgy.

I ordered coffee and sat there.

Ted Beamish ordered carrot cake with his coffee and started talking.

"I had a lot of leave accumulated so I thought I'd take today off and get a few errands done," he said.

"I'm an errand?"

The flush raced up his face.

"Of course not. It's just I had some free time and I was on Elgin Street and I thought I'd drop in and see if you weren't too busy to have coffee. To tell you the truth, you didn't look too busy."

"You mean because I was sitting on the stairs? They're my favourite place to sit and contemplate when I have a tough problem."

This seemed more reasonable than the truth, that I had been turfed out by the office help who needed to discuss an urgent and private problem with its mother.

"Do you have a tough problem now?"

I thought of Robin and Benning and Alvin.

"Yes," I said, "several."

"That's interesting. The stairs, I mean."

"Works for me," I said, although I never intended to sit on them again.

"Tell me about Justice for Victims," he said. "I heard you set it up yourself."

"Right."

He wasn't one to give up, and he was nudging about my favourite subject. It was possible I was going to be lured into conversation after all.

"What do you do?"

"Well," I said, feeling my motor turn on, "victims are the forgotten players in our legal processes. I'm running an advocacy agency for them. Justice for Victims represents the interests of victims in dealing with various parts of the government and the judicial system. We lobby for or against proposed legislation which we think will affect victims. For instance, changes to the Young Offenders Act. We offer support for the victim in dealing with the system. Often a victim is victimized all over again by the time a trial or a procedure is over. Or they're terrified when a criminal is about to get paroled back into their community. They don't know what to do, they don't know what their rights are."

"Sounds great to me." He gestured to the waitress for a refill. "How do you get funded?"

He'd hit the sore spot.

"We're a membership organization. Anyone with an interest in justice and victims can join for a small fee. I'll get you an application form," I grinned. "You'll get a newsletter out of it, and sense of doing something good. And I get a constituency to mount letter writing campaigns to the feds when necessary. I ask for donations, too."

"And you can make a living this way?"

"More or less. We get grants from various levels of government and personal and corporate donations. I supplement with a bit of legal work on the side, and I get asked to participate in task forces looking at the victim perspective."

I didn't tell him my expenses were minimal to run Justice for Victims. The office was sub-let from the association next door. Alvin came subsidized, although not quite subsidized enough. I also didn't mention I had to top up my own living expenses, not that they were high, out of Paul's estate. Still it was worth it as far as I was concerned.

"I can see why you would be so committed to victims' rights, after what happened to Paul. And that guy getting away with it."

I didn't let myself think about this too often. The wounds were still there. Paul, brilliant and funny, would have been thirty-four in three weeks if a drunken lout hadn't polished off a two-four of beer, then lurched onto the road with his RX-7 and mangled Paul's little Toyota. It had taken three hours to cut his body from the wreckage. Longer than his killer served.

"One year suspended sentence. Gotta give the guy a chance. After all, he never killed anyone before." My hands were choking my coffee mug as I talked. Choking the drunk driver, choking the judge.

"Tough on you."

I wanted to change the subject. I wasn't in the habit of discussing just how tough it was.

"Right," I said, "so what else are you going to do on your day off?"

"I'm treating this like a Saturday, so I'm doing Saturday stuff," he said. "Drop over to the market and get a few things, go to the library and stock up, see how the tulips are coming up…"

Those damn tulips again.

"…maybe go to a movie tonight."

He'd been looking into his empty coffee cup, but now he flicked a glance at me.

"I don't suppose you'd feel like a movie tonight."

"I'm not ready to see other people yet. Sorry."

This time the flush surged up past his hairline and down through his shirt collar. I could have sworn his hands got pink.

"Oh, of course not," he said, "I realize that. Just talking about a couple of people watching a movie."

"Don't mind me, I'm being a jerk," I said. "I've got a lot on my mind and it's making me surly."

I noticed he didn't leap to deny this.

"This thing with Mitzi Brochu has thrown me. You remember Robin, I guess."

"Of course," he said. "I remember seeing the two of you together a lot at law school.

"Well, she's just devastated by the whole thing and doesn't seem to be getting over it, so that's a strain. The police have been complete creeps about it."

"Hmm."

"So the point is, once life gets back to normal and I'm not such a jerk, sure, let's get together and go to a movie. Maybe Robin could come too."

That might be just what she needed, I thought to myself. And this little guy might be the perfect match for her. Pleasant enough. Appreciates tulips. Probably likes cats too. Maybe a movie with a single man would be enough to get Robin to climb out of bed and comb her hair.

"I'll get your number," I said, "and let you know when would be a good time."

He wasn't the type to insist on paying the bill. He got a point from me for that.

"I'll be off to the library," he said as we stepped out of the Mayflower and into the very bright sun.

"I've got some stuff to check out. Let's walk over to together," I said. Death Row reprieve for Alvin.

"Sure."

He was the kind of person you could be comfortable with, without talking. I liked that.

As we reached the corner of Elgin and Laurier West, across the street in Confederation park, 15,000 tulips exploded into view. He stopped to look. Robin would have too. This could be a perfect match.

We jostled by the camera-toting tourists enjoying the Festival of Spring. By my calculations, there was a tourist for every tulip.

"So," I said, while we raced the light across Elgin, "did I ever tell how I feel about the parole system?"

"Let's not ruin a perfect morning."

We said good-bye inside the library. I galloped up the stairs to reference and he headed for fiction. He was planning to do the W's. Wodehouse. Westlake. Wright. Wolfe.

I was planning to do the W's too. Wendtz.

There was only one Rudy Wendtz in the city directory. He had an address on the Queen Elizabeth Driveway and his employment was listed as prmtr. After a while, I figured out this must mean promoter. But what did promoter mean?

I let my fingers do the walking and sure enough, in the yellow pages under Promotional Services, I found "Events by Wendtz".

What kind of events, I wondered, give you the kind of income you need to live at that address on the Queen Elizabeth Driveway?

* * *

Back in the office, there was no sign of Alvin. With luck, he'd caught the first flight back to Sydney to resolve the family crisis.

Wherever he was, I had free access to the phone. I checked in with the Findlays. Robin was in bed.

"Perhaps when Brooke gets here..." Mrs. Findlay let her sad, flat voice trail off. "It'll be good to see her."

"Well, yes," I said, "especially after her long walk."

Mrs. Findlay always pretends she doesn't hear my Brooke comments.

"And you too, will you be here tonight?"

"Count on it," I said.

"Oh, that's good. Robin has been finding the visits from the police very upsetting. Wait a minute, here she is. She says she wants to talk to you. Are you sure you should be out of bed, dear? Dr. Beaver says..."

"What police? What visits?" I shouted into the receiver. But no response.

"Camilla?" Robin sounded like an exhausted mouse. "I think they're going to arrest me."

*   *   *

She looked like hell when I shot through her front door twenty minutes later. In sharp contrast to the perky, bright, blue flowers marching across every free inch of the Findlays' kitchen, Robin had definite grey undertones. She was wearing an old United Way campaign tee-shirt with tea stains down the front, grey jogging pants with a hole in the knee and pink pig slippers. Deep half-circles were gouged under her eyes. Her blonde curls hung in greasy strands. She clutched a china cup of camomile tea, and her knuckles were white.

Why? I asked myself. I'd seen the same body, minutes afterward. Why was she so psyched out? Not that it wasn't distressing. Not that you wouldn't have nightmares. I still jerked awake in the night with Mitzi's dead eyes winking at me. But I wasn't reduced to a psychiatric case. Logic told me that stable, sensible, unimaginative, dependable old Robin should have been in the same state I was. After all, it wasn't someone she loved or even someone she knew as far as I could tell. I knew it could be explained, and I knew Robin was keeping something from the people who loved her. I wanted to grab Robin and shake the truth out of her.

So instead I said, "You look like roadkill."

It was intended to make her laugh. But all it got was a little nod of agreement.

"I know," she said.

"More coffee, Camilla?"

"No thanks, Mr. Findlay," I said, watching him wipe his hairy hands on his blue and white checked apron. I tried to remember if I'd ever seen Mr. Findlay without an apron.

"A little lemon coffee cake?"

He slid the lemon coffee cake towards us on small blue-rimmed plates. Forks and blue napkins arrived on the table seconds later.

Mr. Findlay's coffee cake is not the sort of thing I'm ever going to turn down. I was through mine in a flash. Mr. Findlay had replaced the first piece while both of us watched Robin fiddle with her little plate, never even touching the fork. Her nails were bitten to the quick.

I took a deep breath.

"Tell me what the police asked you."

Mr. Findlay scuttled from the room.

She looked at me with unfocused eyes.

"A lot of things."

"Like what?"

"What was I doing there, did I know her, was I angry with her, did I kill her."

I nodded. I understood why the police would ask that sort of thing. Of course, they didn't know Robin like I did. You couldn't blame them for seeing guilt in Robin's refusal to say why she went to see Mitzi Brochu that afternoon.

"It was awful," said Robin. Whether she meant finding Mitzi or being grilled by the police was unclear.

"Who questioned you?"

"I don't remember his name. But he came here to my parents' house and he badgered and badgered. He thinks I killed her. I know it." She bit her lip.

"Was it the retriever or the rodent?"

A tiny flicker of Robin's old smile twitched.

"It was the ratty-looking one. He kept trying to trick me."

Mombourquette. I shivered. I hated the thought of his rodential mind. And even more the idea of him invading the Findlays' blue-flowered territory, trying to trap Robin for a murder she could never have committed.

"They'll be under pressure from the media to get an arrest. I was there with the body. Covered with blood."

She caught me by surprise. The old Robin spoke for just a minute before disappearing back into the sedative-induced mental mire.

"You'd better get a good defense lawyer. You don't even need to talk to them without a lawyer present. You know that."

She half-smiled.

"You're a good lawyer."

"I mean a defense lawyer. One of the big ones."

"I want you."

Robin had always been stubborn, even from the first day when we met in kindergarten and she wanted the red crayon. Some people might have interpreted her collapse as wimpiness, but I knew it was just another way of being obstinate.

"I don't get people off," I said, "I try to keep them in jail. This is not the right attitude for your case."

"I don't care."

"Well, if you don't care about yourself and your chances, do you care about your parents? And your sister? They'll want you to have the best."

I had felt the parental presence of the Findlays throughout the conversation. I hoped they would rush in to offer reinforcement, but it was just Robin and me, locked in a struggle of wills.

"You or nobody," she said, with that little smile.

"Shit." But I knew I was hooked. She had gotten the red crayon, too, way back in kindergarten. I'd backed right off because I was so happy to have a new friend with blonde curly hair and eyes like cornflowers. Only then did she share it with me.

I knew why she wanted me. In practical terms, I was just as good as the next guy. My five years in criminal law before starting up Justice for Victims gave me the tools I'd need to mount a competent and spirited defense. But more than that, I was the only lawyer around who loved Robin and would do damned near anything to make sure she was all right.

Having won her point, Robin closed her cornflower eyes. Her smile faded. So did her colour. I didn't think she could get any paler, but I was wrong.

"I have to go back to bed now."

As I helped her up the stairs to her bedroom, I tried again.

"You'll have to tell me why you were there, if you expect me to help."

"Not now," she said, as she slipped between the pink sheets with the white ruffles, looking like a sallow stranger in this familiar room. "Not yet."

Mr. Findlay was waiting for me, with what looked like tears in his eyes, when I got down stairs.

"She's asleep already," I told him.

"Thank you for taking her case. We hoped you would."

I didn't have the heart to tell him it wasn't the best thing at all. That you get what you pay for. In this case, the fee would be nothing, and the defense lawyer would be blinded by affection, and someone who usually played for the other side.

Mrs. Findlay was staring at the television as someone's previously unknown illegitimate child inserted herself as a new character on *Another World*. She didn't hear me say good-bye.

"It will all work out," Mr. Findlay called out to me, as I climbed into my car.

*   *   *

"That's right. Wendtz," I said to Conn McCracken when I reached him by phone that afternoon. "Rudy Wendtz."

"What about him?"

"Do you realize he was Mitzi Brochu's boyfriend?"

"Your sister has an unlisted telephone number. Do you realize that?"

"Yes, I do."

"She's a bit hard to locate."

"I suppose she is."

"I was trying to get in touch with her soon."

"So, this Rudy Wendtz, you talked to him?" I asked.

"I can't seem to remember. I got a lot on my mind."

"I think I have that number somewhere."

"Oh yeah, right," he said. "Wendtz. It's all coming back to me now."

"My sources tell me he and La Belle Mitzi had a major battle the night before she died."

McCracken coughed.

"Right," I said, spitting out Alexa's number.

"The guy's a vampire," said McCracken, "just like the victim. Even looked a bit like her."

"What about the fight?"

"What about it?"

"Check the statistics, Detective. Eighty percent of women who are murdered are murdered by their significant others."

"Coincidentally, a substantial portion of killers turn out to be the person who reported the murder."

"That would be me, in this case. Bring on the cuffs."

"Course, we don't know, maybe you ducked in, did the deed, ducked out again, disappeared and dashed back in time to discover the deceased with Robin." A long, wheezy chuckle followed this.

"You have the mind of a poet, too bad you're developing asthma. Should see a doctor."

He kept on chuckling.

"Back to the subject of Wendtz," I said. "I hope Mombourquette put him through the wringer and then hung him out to dry."

"I interviewed him myself. I hate to be the one to break it to you, but Wendtz had a business meeting with three associates between the time Mitzi was last seen alive and the time you called in."

"Oh, sure," I said. "Like some so-called promoter's associates would never tell a fib to the big scary policeman. And what do you mean sicking Mombourquette on defenceless women while you get the vampires?"

"Sorry you don't like it, but your little friend is still our prime suspect."

"Fair enough, but you're the one who's going to look like a putz in the local media when the killer turns out to be someone else."

"Would you mind repeating that number?" he said, just as I hung up.

I was alone in the office and that was good, since I could swear in private.

I nibbled at my nails and tried to work on what they call a three-pronged strategy. One, try to keep Robin from getting arrested. Two, work out a foolproof defense in case she did get arrested and, even worse, had to stand trial. Three, try to find out what her real involvement with Mitzi Brochu had been.

My mood was not enhanced by the five person-to-person collect phone calls for Alvin.

I picked up the sixth and snarled, "I told you he's not here."

"Camilla?" Alexa's voice came through after a pause.

"Sorry."

"I just wanted to tell you I'm going to the lake for a few days to open up the cottage. I wanted to check you'd be all right."

"Why wouldn't I be all right?"

"Well, you know, finding that body…"

"That was last week."

"Even so, it must have had an effect on you."

"Have a good time."

"I don't suppose…"

"You don't suppose what?"

"Never mind, I'll call you when I get back. If you need anything, Edwina and Donalda are there. And Daddy."

"Good-bye."

Great, I smiled to myself, Edwina and Donalda and Daddy. I could put them to work. Shadowing Rudy Wendtz maybe.

This was such an amusing thought, I was still smiling when Alvin's shadow darkened the door.

Anyone else but Alvin and I would have felt sorry for him, his face was so grey, his eyes so clouded, his pony tail so wilted.

"Oh, it's you," he said. "Some people called for you this morning,"

"Who?" I said. "I didn't see any messages."

"They said they'd call back."

Any single-cell scrap of sympathy I might have felt evaporated.

Alvin reached over and picked up his backpack from the floor. "Gotta go," he said. "Family emergency."

"What a shame. Well, take your time. We all have to have our priorities. And if you can't get back from Cape Breton, I'll understand."

My facial muscles ached from suppressed joy.

"What are you talking about? It should all be settled by tonight. By the way, I did a little research on your friend Mitzi Brochu. That pile there's got every article she ever wrote and that pile next to it is newspaper articles about her and reviews of her TV specials. Everything's in date order with the most recent items on top. See you tomorrow."

When Alvin's good, he's very, very good. He's particularly good *in absentia*. I spent the rest of the afternoon combing through the articles by and about Mitzi Brochu. It proved to be a potent dose of a poisonous pen. Mitzi had been a lot of things. Nice was not one of them.

Alvin had been very thorough. There was even a picture of Wendtz. Rock promoter Rudy Wendtz, according to the caption. He was shown sampling sushi with Mitzi, she glittering and malevolent in black velvet and metal, he with a two-day growth of beard and slicked back dark-blond hair ending at his shoulders. He looked like a man who worked out. And weren't those tattoos an adorable touch?

Articles on Mitzi were plentiful and while one or two bleated about the effect her call to "diet or die" had on the already precarious eating habits of teenage girls, most gushed about Mitzi's wicked wit and unflagging sense of style.

When I had finished wading through the world of the late La Brochu, I slapped the magazines on the table and considered taking a Gravol.

She had her favourite targets: actors, politicians, TV personalities and a Toronto model she compared to a grouper.

Deb Goodhouse had been the butt of insults for years. I thought Mitzi's jabs had been a one-time random effort to skewer women M.P.'s in general. But Mitzi articles dating way back had rearview shots of Deb and curare-tipped remarks about her sense of style. Running a close second was Jo Quinlan, who averaged two major slams a year by Mitzi. I wasn't sure who suffered the most slings and arrows: Deb or Jo.

I flipped through the magazines and checked the little credits area in the front. The photographer was the same for all the Deb and Jo pictures and many of the others. He smiled out from a photograph that made him look very, very good. I fished the scissors from the desk and snipped out the picture of the photographer.

Sammy Dash was his name, a man who obviously loved his work.

Six

Alvin was settled in at the desk, humming, so I found myself huddled in the back of the office, surrounded by work I should have been doing. It was just after nine in the morning, but already I did not feel like working. All I could think about was rat-faced Mombourquette waiting for his chance to scurry through the Findlays' front door and drag Robin off to the station, still in her pink pig slippers.

No, the best thing, I told myself, was not to sit in the office listening to Alvin sing his favourite Fred Eaglesmith song for the eighty-second time. The best thing would be to get out and stir up a little dust to distract Ottawa's finest from my very, very vulnerable client. I had a few strong options based on reading about Mitzi's favourite victims. A phone call was all it took, and I was on my way.

"You're spooking the horses," Alvin sang, "and you're scaring me."

"Good," I said, just before I slammed the door.

*   *   *

Deb Goodhouse was one of those rare women who look good in red. Very good. Her hair was still dark brown, almost black, cut in a dutch-boy style. Her dark eyes and ivory skin showed to advantage with her red blazer and matching slash of lipstick. She looked like Snow White, grown middle-aged and professional. She smiled and shook my hand till my bones ached. But I could tell she was not at all glad to see me.

"Well," she said, "imagine. Alex and Donnie's little sister. What can I do for you?"

I wondered if she could have been one of the handful of Ottawans who had missed the sight of Robin and me being hustled away from Mitzi's murder site by the cops. Somehow I doubted it.

Still, she'd been willing to see me, which was the only way I could have gotten past the long-faced security guards and into the labyrinth of offices in the West Block of the Parliament Buildings.

Deb Goodhouse's assistant, tall, beautiful and black, had ushered me in through the antechamber to the M.P.'s office.

"Thanks for seeing me. This is great," I said, gawking like the rest of the tourists on the Hill. I had got past the area designated for the public.

The soft leather padding on the door made me wonder, but Deb Goodhouse's office was less opulent than I expected, even taking the leather sofa, the brass floor lamp, and the very good rug under the mahogany coffee table into consideration. A television set stood within easy view from the desk or the sofa. Citations from dozens of civic organizations hung around with portraits of former Prime Ministers. A small Canadian flag sat on the desk.

"I always wondered what it was like inside a Member of Parliament's office."

Deb sat behind her massive desk, her fingers pressed together in a tent. She wore red nail polish and a chunky square-cut silver bracelet with matching earrings. Her body language said "shut up and get out of here", but her red lips stayed curved in a tight little smile.

Mitzi had done a real number on her. I thought back to phrases such as "Polyester Goes to Parliament", "Pound for Pound the Voter's Choice" and "The Hulk on the Hill". It seemed absurd to think of Deb Goodhouse in those terms. She was a large woman, but polished and attractive, looking younger than her fortysomething years. Her overall image was one of competence and calm. Of course, she was a little tense, but that was because I was there.

"Mitzi Brochu." I met her eyes as I said it.

"What about her?"

"I'm sure you know she's been killed, and in a most gruesome manner. A client of mine is being investigated for the murder and, as part of the background work for the defense, I'm looking into what kind of woman the victim was."

A little snort escaped from Deb Goodhouse's red lips.

I stopped.

"Go on," she said.

"Well, there were some Ottawa people she liked to skewer in her columns and on her broadcasts. You were one of them. That makes me think you couldn't be a fan. I wanted to get a sense of how the non-fan would describe her."

I sat back in my chair. Alex and Donnie's little sister from hell.

"Well," she said, "how would you like to pick up your mail some day and see your flowered butt in full-colour spread across the pages of one of your magazine subscriptions? Of course I wasn't a fan. She didn't *want* me to be a fan. She wanted me to be one of her victims." She paused and watched my face. "I don't make a good victim, Ms. MacPhee."

"Doesn't surprise me. But what did you think of her? What emotions did she arouse in you?"

She laughed.

"You don't get elected, you know, by giving in to your emotions on every little thing. You've got to save your energy for what counts."

"So she didn't bother you?"

"Of course, she bothered me. Wouldn't she bother you?"

"She did bother me. And I wasn't even one of her victims."

"Neither was I, Ms. MacPhee. She wanted me to be, but I wasn't."

"I'm sorry?"

"My mother always told me three things, 'Doing well is the best revenge, look at yourself and see the truth and make sure you find the opportunity in every situation.'"

I raised an eyebrow at her.

"When Mitzi first started to skewer me, as you call it, I was pretty steamed. I talked to my lawyer and I slammed every cupboard door in the house."

I liked this approach. It was the first feeling of warmth I'd felt for her.

"Then I tried my mother's advice and took a good look at myself. In the mirror. I saw a woman who was large and dumpy and wearing plenty of flowered polyester, but no make-up. At the same time, I saw a woman who'd spent a career fighting to help other people—street kids, refugees, the working poor—but the only time she splashes across the pages of a national magazine is when some shark-woman in Toronto decides she's not fashionable."

For someone who saved her emotion for what counted, Deb Goodhouse's neck was very red. Her lips were now clamped in a steely line.

"Not fair, really," I encouraged.

"Of course, it wasn't fair. But that's not the point."

"What is the point?"

"The point," she said, pointing a red fingernail at me, "is I decided to take a few lessons. It doesn't pay to be a laughingstock in this business. I didn't sue the witch, that would just draw attention to her. But I changed my appearance, dropped the polyester, got professional advice, modified my hair a bit. Just gradually, over a year or so. And I didn't say boo about Mitzi and her campaign of mockery. I got a lot of sympathy calls and visits from other people who thought I might be upset and a few smirks from so-called friends. But I've weathered it."

"What about the photographer?"

"What about him?"

"Did you have any reaction to him?"

She shrugged. "Why should I? He was just doing his job. Mitzi was the driving force behind the articles."

"Tell me, why did Mitzi pick you?"

"Who knows? Because I was there, I guess. I asked myself that often enough. I think she just liked to single out women who were doing something real and important and hold them up to ridicule."

"Did you ever meet her?"

She shook her head. "Never wanted to. I might have had trouble holding my tongue, and I wouldn't have wanted to read my comments in the media."

"So," I said, "you must have hated her, though."

"I didn't hate her. I have better uses for my energy."

I thought her snarl took away from the sincerity of the statement. Deep down, Deb Goodhouse had harboured a red-hot hatred for Mitzi Brochu. Too hot to hide behind a cool exterior. Too hot to cool down even after Mitzi's death.

"I'm sure you have."

"Anything else you need to know, Ms. MacPhee?" She

pointed at her in-basket. "As you can see, I have plenty to do."

"You've given me lots to think about," I said.

I stood up and shook her hand before she could take the initiative. It was sweaty, not at all like a politician's should be. Stress can do that to you.

I said good-bye to the beautiful assistant, leaning over her desk to shake her hand.

"Sorry," I said, "I didn't catch your name."

"Manon. Manon Bruyère," she said, with some reluctance. She seemed to think I was up to something.

I was.

Deb Goodhouse bellowed for her and I left, smiling.

I was still smiling as I strolled out of the Centre Block, through the tourists, and down the Hill to Wellington Street. Eighteen thousand blood-red tulips nodded at me, pleased with my results.

I thought about the woman I had just visited. The shoulder pads on Deb Goodhouse's very good red jacket had been designed to draw the eye away from the size of her arms, but in my mind, there was no doubt about it: Deb Goodhouse would have been strong enough to hoist skinny little Mitzi by those ropes. Things were looking up. Another day like this and I hoped to be able to present a package of possibilities to the police.

*   *   *

"What kind of knots were used to tie those ropes?" I asked McCracken. I thought coming straight out with it would be the best approach. I thought wrong.

"That number doesn't answer," he said.

"It doesn't?"

"That's right."

"Well, I'm sure it's her number. I ought to know. I've been returning her calls for enough years."

"Well, she doesn't appear to be there."

"She could just be out shopping."

"I don't think so. I tried all last night. And this morning from nine o'clock on."

"Hmmm, well, I'm kind of busy now trying to find out what kind of knots were used on Mitzi. Once I find out, I could look into why Alexa isn't answering her phone. In the meantime, I guess you could say I'm tied up."

"Reef knots. Some people call them square knots."

"What kind of people use square knots?"

"Sailors and boy scouts among others," he chuckled.

"Thanks. Oh, and Conn, I just remembered. Alexa's spending a couple of days opening up her cottage. Too bad she doesn't have an answering machine."

"Oh, thanks a lot."

I could feel the chill on the line.

"Think nothing of it," I said.

For my next phone call, I had to pinch my nose to change the sound of my voice. First, I found Manon Bruyère's telephone number in the government telephone book.

"This is Mabel Hubley calling from the Headquarters of the Girl Guides of Canada. We're double-checking our list of famous former guides. Can you tell me if Ms. Goodhouse is one?"

"Well, of course, she is. You must know that. She's been on your Board of Directors."

Oops.

Manon's voice changed. "Wait a minute. Who did you say you were?"

But it was too late. I had what I needed.

72

* * *

I was alone in the office, planning my next coup, when Ted Beamish knocked. It was time to close up for the day and I'd sent Alvin off to the public library to get some books on knots. I'd made him promise to borrow them officially.

"Hi," Ted said.

"Hi," I answered, wondering why he was there.

"Can I come in?"

"Sure, why not?"

He settled into the chair, placing his briefcase on the floor and loosening his tie with the little palm trees.

"Just on my way home from the office and I thought I might check to see if you wanted to try that movie tonight. And bring your friend."

"Robin's not in shape for a movie."

"Oh." Disappointment flashed across his face. I swear all the little palm trees on his tie drooped a bit.

"She's a bit slow getting over finding Mitzi's body. And the police are hassling her."

He looked like a little red-headed kid whose popsicle had melted too fast.

"I'll tell you what, I'll talk to her about the movie. Maybe that'll cheer her up a bit and speed the recovery." I beamed at him, hoping he'd leave me alone.

"Sure," he said.

"I'm sure she'll want to go the minute she gets the old pep back."

"Right."

"No, I mean it." I had no idea of how she'd react to the

73

three of us going out to a movie. But I had an overwhelming urge to protect him.

"Okay. Do you think I could drop in with you and maybe help to cheer her up?"

I could just imagine what would happen if Robin discovered I'd brought one of Ottawa's rare available bachelors to see her with her hair in strings and her feet in pigs.

"I'm afraid she's sedated. Not allowed any visitors except family. They make me sit in the living room, and they relay my messages to her whenever she regains consciousness."

I could tell he didn't believe me.

"But I could go to the movie with you later. We could even grab a hamburger or something."

I couldn't believe this was happening. Hadn't he been the one who jumped the gun about asking me to a movie? And here I was pleading with him to make it happen. And all because I didn't want the little jerk to look sad.

"I guess so," he said.

"Good. Good. Good. Good. Well, I'll give you a call as soon as I get home." I stood up and slipped into my jacket, hoping he'd get the hint. "You'd better give me your phone number."

*   *   *

Brooke arrived from Toronto just after I settled in at the Findlays'.

"Surprise," she said as she swept into the room, trailing garment bags.

I was surprised all right. Surprised it had taken her six days to manage the five hour drive from her Toronto penthouse.

74

We all looked up from the chocolate chip cheesecake muffins Mr. F. had just served.

With the exception of me, everyone switched into "Brooke's here" mode, rustling about, fussing. Fetching her a chair, then a cushion for the chair, then a glass of wine and cup of coffee. Fretting because the coffee couldn't be cappuccino. Trying to tempt her with the muffins.

Brooke leaned back, stretched out her mile-long legs and lit a cigarette.

"So many things are happening. I've been so frantic. I can't wait to tell you all the news."

They leaned forward in anticipation. Mrs. Findlay with the same expression she uses to watch the soaps. Mr. Findlay with a tray of mixed baked goods he'd assembled for Brooke. Robin still in the pink pig slippers. In fact, Robin hadn't taken her eyes off her sister since Brooke blew through the door.

"Big new assignment," said Brooke, smiling and taking a sip from the wine.

She was wearing long, long, tight, tight jeans and a washed out blue tee-shirt. No make-up, no jewellery. Of course, she was getting a little long in the tooth for a model, close to twenty-five. But she was still breathtaking. Her parents and sister were, in fact, almost holding their collective respiration waiting for the news of the big assignment. I picked another muffin from the plate and asked myself how Elmvale Acres could have produced an amazing specimen like Brooke.

"Okay, just a little bit, Daddy," the amazing specimen said, accepting the plate of goodies.

She picked up a brownie, took a tiny bite, put it back on the plate and licked her fingers. Everyone smiled in approval. Except me.

Perhaps you're just jealous, I suggested to myself, because

you're not five-eleven, a hundred and eighteen pounds, and ash blonde with azure eyes and full pouty lips. Perhaps.

"It's official. I'm going to be the face they use for the new 'Walk in the Woods' campaign. I'm the 'Walk in the Woods' woman! It's all signed. Nothing can stop it now."

Everyone gasped. Well, not everyone. But even I did a few mental calculations. "Walk in the Woods" make-up, toiletries and bath products were the biggest phenomenon in the Canadian beauty business. All natural products, no animal testing, great colours, politically correct and reasonably priced. "Walk in the Woods" was rolling over all the old stand-bys and even the new players in the cosmetics industry.

Even I had to admit it was some kind of big deal.

Mrs. Findlay turned to me. "Isn't that wonderful? Our beautiful daughter. She's just like Nina on my show, isn't she? We're so proud."

I thought it would be inappropriate to gag, but it was tough resisting.

There was lots of other news from Toronto. Who Brooke had seen, lunched with, where she'd eaten dinner, what parties, what contacts.

What tripe, I thought, but everyone was spellbound, even Robin, who should have known better.

Brooke had lots of new clothes too, in the garment bags. Things needing a little nip here or a tuck there. Mrs. Findlay scuttled for her sewing basket. Mr. Findlay trotted out to the car to pick up the rest of Brooke's luggage. Robin sat there, transfixed by her sister. And chewing her nails.

They didn't pay too much attention to me as I left.

*　　*　　*

After the Findlays, Ted Beamish seemed normal. Once I had called him, he insisted on picking me up to go to the movie. I'd slipped into my favourite old jeans and yanked on a pullover. The warm May day had been replaced by a nippy night with a frost warning, but you could still smell the fresh green leaves in the air.

He ordered bagels and lox at Nate's, while I went for the traditional smoked meat sandwich. The Bytowne was right across the street and *Hear My Song* was playing.

"So," he said, once we were settled in and our food had arrived, "how's Robin doing?"

I crunched my pickle and thought about how Robin was doing. Better perhaps with her sister there, taking her mind off the murder. But not good. I thought back to her waxy skin and glazed eyes. Eyes following her sister's every move, eyes filled with questions. Not once had Brooke referred to Robin's experience. Except for an airy little cheek kiss, she hadn't acknowledged her at all. Brooke liked to be concerned with Brooke. For this she was rewarded, in life and by her family.

To Ted I said, "Not great. She's a long way from being better."

To myself I said, what are you holding back?

"That's too bad. Well, keep me posted. We'll get out together soon enough, I guess."

Later as we sat in the theatre, I considered this. I'd thought he wanted to go out with me. But maybe he'd been angling for Robin all along and I was just too arrogant to see it. But if he did want to go out with Robin all along, why wouldn't he just call her up and ask her out? She would have been tickled. Not bitchy like me.

It did not compute, and in the dark of the theatre I turned

away from the screen to look at Ted Beamish, enigma.

He blinked and offered me some more popcorn. What the hell, I told myself, you think too much.

*   *   *

The next morning, the sun was splashing deep-pink stripes across the sky as I rose. I got up early and ready for action.

I had a lot to do if I wanted to keep my buddy out of the hoosegow. Of course, six cats had to be fed before I did anything.

The temperature was about 13 degrees Celsius as I sat out on the balcony in my fuzzy-green winter housecoat, sipping from a large mug of extra-strong Colombian and making lists. Stuff to pick up at the grocery store. Things to do at the office. People to talk to. Suspects to badger.

The pink sun accentuated the bit of the Harmony Hotel visible from the balcony. I added Richard Sandes to my list of people to talk to.

The temperature was inching up as I stalked down the path by the river. It was the first time in days I'd had the mental space to enjoy the blue and silver ripples on the water, to listen to the birds, to grin at the nosy groundhog. The grass along the sweeping lawns separating the Parkway and the shore was deep-green and dewy, and the deciduous trees sported clouds of tiny, fresh leaves. It was going to be a great day.

I clomped into the Harmony about 40 minutes after I had left home.

Two young women, wearing the house uniform of deep turquoise jackets and navy mini-skirts, were at the reception desk. One was Stephanie, the trainee I remembered from my first visit. The other one was Naomi. She'd been on duty the night I had visited Richard in his office, and later at the bar.

They both had very big hair and fresh faces. One wore little flats and the other one had on spiky pumps. I looked down at my Nikes and wondered if it was time to change my look. At least when visiting the Harmony.

Mr. Sandes was in a meeting and would not be available for another hour, they explained. My disappointment must have showed because they offered to take a message, in stereo. I wanted to move a little faster in my investigations, not that I was dying to see him.

I left my work number, telling myself it was just business.

As I turned to walk away, I remembered something and decided to try my luck.

I dug the magazine picture of Sammy Dash out of my purse and asked them if they had ever seen the photographer around the Harmony when Mitzi was staying there.

A little spark of tension flickered among the three of us. They exchanged glances.

"No," said Stephanie.

"I don't think we can discuss anything like that with you before we talk to Mr. Sandes," said Naomi.

"There must be some things you do without checking with Mr. Sandes," I pointed out.

"Right," said Naomi, "but this isn't one of them."

I decided I liked her.

I'd been hoping they would have identified Sammy Dash as one of Mitzi's frequent visitors and maybe offered me a little poop on him. Their reluctance just made me more interested in Sammy, the long shot.

* * *

"Alvin," I said, "you're looking lovely today."

He flashed an inky look at me from behind the cat's eye sunglasses he was, for some reason, wearing in the office. His hair was glossy and caught in a smooth ponytail and there was a scrubbed look about him and his black clothing which I was sure he would try to eradicate, if only he realized it. I sniffed the air. Sure enough, fabric softener.

I had made up my mind if I couldn't beat Alvin, I would join him. Although I felt like beating him.

"Some guy named Sandes called you."

I'd have been damned before I would have let Alvin know about the little frisson I felt at this news.

"A date?" asked Alvin.

"No, not a date. And not your business."

Stuff like that just rolls off Alvin.

This was where the joining not beating came in.

"You hang around with an artsy crowd. Did you ever hear of a photographer named Sammy Dash?"

He scrunched up his face in an effort of recalling. Very uncool, I thought.

"Nah," he said, "don't think so."

"Oh," I said, simulating grave disappointment with some success.

"I suppose I could find out. I've got a lot of connections in that line."

"Would you?"

"Sure, I'd do it right now, but I have all this typing to do." He pointed to the one letter and three envelopes I'd left for him in the box I'd labelled TO DO ALVIN AND MAKE IT SNAPPY.

I figured I could do the letter and envelopes myself before Alvin hit the end of Elgin Street on his way to the cafés in the

Byward market. Where everyone wore black. Where you'd go to find out about a photographer named Sammy Dash.

"Sayonara," I said, trying to resist pushing him out the door.

As his feet thudded down the stairs, it began to dawn on me that Alvin might turn out to be useful. An Archie Goodwin of sorts.

Once I was sure he was gone, I picked up the message from Richard Sandes. Archie Goodwin had neglected to write down the number. I pulled out the telephone book and found the Harmony. As I lifted the receiver, I could feel my heart pick up the pace a bit.

For God's sake, I told myself, it's not time yet. Paul's only been dead three years. You're not ready. You're not interested in other men. And even if you were, would you pick a man who must be past fifty, with a grown family, wherever they are? Too ridiculous.

I dialled the number.

"Richard?" I breathed, when the switchboard connected us.

Seven

Jo Quinlan was naked, drying her hair in the ladies changing room of the health club of the Chateau Cartier Sheraton. She turned off the hair dryer when I spoke to her.

"Nice place," I said, after introducing myself. "Isn't it a bit out of the way for you?"

"I like it. It's pretty much on my way home from work. I don't have a lot of spare time, so if you can tell me what..."

"I know what you mean." It wasn't like I had all the time in the world. "Finish up. I'll wait."

She flicked the dryer back on, waving it around and fluffing her hair with her fingers, squinting with dissatisfaction. I thought her hair looked great. Deep auburn, little soft kinky waves, cut a bit asymmetrical. I figured her haircut cost more than my month's groceries.

I waited.

When she finished, she flicked off the dryer and tucked it into a blue and violet gym bag. She stared at herself with narrowed eyes in the mirror. I didn't think she liked what she saw. It was hard to figure why.

I saw a woman, close to six feet tall, with broad shoulders and tan skin dusted with light freckles. She must have been a star basketball or volleyball player back in high school, and she was still in shape.

I felt easier asking her questions once she'd put her

underwear on. Ladies changing rooms rattle me. It's a legacy from the nuns.

"Mitzi Brochu," I said, as she pulled on a cream-coloured silk man-style shirt.

I didn't miss the quick look she shot me.

"What about her?"

"She mentioned you in several articles."

She'd turned away from me and slid herself into a pair of faded black jeans. But even from behind I could see those strong shoulders tense.

She turned back to me. "I noticed."

"I'm not surprised. They were extraordinarily vitriolic. And deliberately cruel."

"Tell me about it," she said, snaking a tan woven leather belt into the belt loops of the jeans.

"Any idea why she picked you as a subject?"

"None. I came home one night and there was my subscription to *Femme Fatale* and there was I, paraded for all the world to see. Photographed in front of my dad's barn down in Buckingham. The caption read 'Which one is the barn?' How would you like that?"

"I wouldn't. No one would."

"Right." She tugged on a tweed blazer with tan, black, cream and hunter green in it and pulled the shoulders straight. "Mind telling me why you're asking me these things?"

"Not at all. I'm a lawyer and my client is suspected by the police of putting Mitzi out of her misery. I'm trying to find out more about Mitzi and her relationships."

"Can't say I blame you. Did your client get the *Femme Fatale* treatment too?"

"No. I don't think she ever had anything to do with Mitzi."

"Hmm," she said, and I could tell she was thinking back.

"Okay, she's the little blonde lady who left the Harmony. You were with her, if I remember correctly. Robin Findlay."

"Right." I remembered that Jo Quinlan was a reporter first and had a good grasp of the background.

"Did it give you any satisfaction to know that the woman who'd made you miserable had one of her victims turn on her?"

Of course, this was quite out of line, but I asked it anyway. Jo picked up her black leather purse and her gym bag before she answered.

"Mitzi Brochu didn't make me miserable. Sure, she tried and I'm certain that she would have tried again. But it didn't work. I wasn't miserable and I never would have been. Irritated, yes. Pissed off, yes. But not miserable."

She met my eyes with her steady green ones. And I believed her.

"And since you asked me straight out instead of beating around the bush, yes, her death did give me a certain satisfaction. She was playing with fire. And maybe someone snapped. Possibly someone who was afraid to be the next victim. Whoever it was did the world a favour. But it wasn't me. So I guess that doesn't help your client much. Good luck elsewhere."

I was thinking about her comments as she strode out of the changing room, leaving me surrounded by bodies I had no wish to see. I caught up to her as she was climbing into her Toyota Supra in the parking lot.

"Why did she single you out from among the media?"

"God damned if I know," she said, settling herself in and fastening her seat belt. "I never figured that out. She did, and she sicked her photographer on me, and that's all I know."

"What about the photographer?"

"What about him?"

84

"What's he like?"

If Jo had managed to keep a cool head during the chat about Mitzi, she had a bit more trouble talking about Sammy Dash. Her hands clenched around the wheel and the muscles on her neck stood out in ropes.

"He's a shitty little weasel who stalks his victims with great enjoyment. You can see it in his beady eyes when he catches you. Maybe he's just mad at the world because he can't get it up."

"Can't he?"

"How the hell would I know?" She pressed the power button for the window and I yanked my hand out just in time.

I looked after her for a long time after she peeled out of the parking lot on two wheels. Maybe she hadn't killed Mitzi Brochu, although she was strong enough and she had motivation enough. But Sammy Dash would have the fight of his life if he ever ran into her in a dark, lonely place.

And she'd given me a very interesting comment to chew on.

*　　*　　*

When I arrived at the Findlays' around six, everyone had already eaten. The fragrance of roast chicken hung over the kitchen and the living room, where Mrs. F., surrounded by sewing gear, was concentrating on the television screen. A man and a woman (Clarissa and Jake) lay naked and alone (except for the camera crew) and not only that, they were about to say something of great importance.

"Hello, Mrs. Findlay," I said.

"Shh. Not now, dear," she said without taking her eyes off the screen.

Mr. F. grabbed my arm and hustled me into the kitchen,

closing the door so we couldn't break the spell with any idle chatter.

"Lemon meringue pie?" he whispered.

I almost explained that I was going out and shouldn't eat dessert first, when I recognized the small-minded beliefs that lay behind such a statement.

"Love some."

"Good girl. New recipe."

"How's Robin?"

"So-so. Here, we'll take this upstairs and you can try to cheer her up."

Together, we crept past Mrs. F. and up the stairs with a plate of pie and a pot of tea.

Robin was propped up in her bed talking to Brooke when we opened the door. Brooke broke off in mid-sentence. Both of them stared at us as if we were some new species of spider. Pushing her father aside, Brooke left the room without a word, but with a backward look at Robin that said lots. Mr. Findlay crept out after her. The scent of Brooke's expensive fragrance hung around after she left, irritating me.

"You're dressed up," Robin said, leaning back on her pillow and closing her eyes.

"No, I'm not," I said, pouring the tea.

"You are so."

"Not. And anyway, how would you know? Your eyes are closed."

"Look at your shoes."

"People wear high heels all the time."

"People, yes. You, no."

"It's no big deal."

Robin sat up, and for the first time since the murder, looked a bit like her perceptive self.

"Don't recall seeing you in a skirt after work hours. Ever. With your cashmere sweater yet."

"I felt like a change."

She leaned forward and squinted at me.

"I do believe you're wearing make-up."

Maybe I'd overdone it. My black pumps with the challis skirt and the good sweater. The lipstick was a bit much, I thought. I wasn't that used to applying it.

"Tell me you're in love."

"I am not in love," I snapped. "I am just making incredible personal sacrifices for you."

"You must be. Lipstick. My God." She fell back against her blue and white flowered pillowcase, laughing. Just like the old days.

After two minutes, I told her to shut up.

"I'd hate to think of what you'd do if you saw someone in an evening dress, for God's sake. You'd have to be put down."

"An evening dress," she howled. "Camilla in an evening dress."

Robin's old self was reappearing, and what did it matter if my ego had to be sacrificed to make it happen?

"I'm doing it for you," I said, with a small martyred smile.

All I got in response were snuffling, choking sounds.

"I'm busting my butt investigating other suspects in Mitzi's murder in order to get the police off your back, and what do I get for it? Mockery and derision."

The mockery and derision stopped as the words came out. The blood drained from Robin's face, and she sank into the coverlet.

"Oh, don't do that," she whispered.

"Why not, for God's sake?"

"You might...get hurt."

"Don't be silly. What could happen to me?"

"Look what happened to Mitzi."

"That happened because Mitzi was Mitzi. Nothing like that is going to happen to me on the streets of Ottawa."

"Please, don't do it. Leave it to the police."

"The police, may I remind you, are sniffing around you. They think all this collapsing in bed looking like a stale pudding is exactly the type of thing a remorseful crucifixionist would do. What the hell is wrong with you? What do you know about the murder? Who did you see? Stop lying to me, Robin."

"I told you. I didn't see anything. Nothing."

When Mr. Findlay tiptoed through the bedroom door with Robin's latest dose of medication, he found her lying with her eyes closed.

I, on the other hand, was sitting there steaming. Robin was making herself sick about this. And refusing the very type of activity that could help her. Bullshit, I said to myself, I just can't stand this kind of bullshit. What really bugged me was that underneath the signs of weakness I could sense a steely stubbornness. Maybe she hadn't seen anything, but she was damn well deflecting attention from someone. Who and why were the questions.

"It's been very hard on us," Mr. Findlay whispered in the hallway, "having her like that. Thank heaven Brooke's here, or I think her mother's heart would break. Thanks for coming. It usually cheers Robin."

Right.

As I passed by the living room on my way out, Mrs. Findlay was on the phone to her friend.

"Honest to God, Marge," she said, lighting a cigarette. "Clarissa told him about the baby. I couldn't believe it."

She gave me a little wave without breaking stride in her conversation as I left.

They told me later that Robin just lay upstairs, not speaking, until the next day, when the police came back.

*   *   *

Driving back downtown, I thought about Robin and whatever she was hiding. I've known her for twenty-seven years. She was holding back something, and knowing Robin, it couldn't be for her own benefit. Therefore, it was for someone else. Since Mitzi's murder had been brutal and vicious, even taking into consideration Mitzi's nasty side, under normal circumstances Robin would not have tried to protect someone who would do such a thing. Not unless it was someone very special. Someone close.

I thought back to an episode when we were in seventh grade. Someone had broken Mrs. Findlay's prize possession, a Royal Doulton figurine. Tensions had run high in the Findlay household, and Robin had taken the rap for it. Even though I'd been sitting next to her on her blue chenille bedspread when we heard the crash. Even though I'd told her parents that. Even though she'd been grounded for a month, and God only knows what emotional havoc was heaped on her by her loony mother. Even though.

Robin had kept a pale-faced silence throughout, never once protesting her innocence. Never once pointing her finger at the real culprit, a seven-year-old vision of blonde hair and blue eyes and sweet smiles.

And Brooke, of course, had never confessed.

By rights Robin should have been jealous of the much younger little brat who got all the attention, but she never was.

Always supported, always defended. Since I was the little brat in my own family, there wasn't a lot I could say about it to Robin. Brooke was another story.

"You've had your First Communion, Brooke," I'd made a point of saying at the time. "So I guess you realize that you'll burn in hell for this. This is a double mortal sin and your soul doesn't have even one little tiny patch of white left on it."

Deep down I'd suspected that Brooke wasn't worried one bit about God and his helpers. She knew she could wrap them around her little finger.

"Leave her alone," Robin had told me, her eyes still red-rimmed from her mother's last verbal blast. "She's just a little kid."

"Old enough to fry."

Brooke had started to cry at that point. She had an amazing trick of crying while still looking beautiful. No blotches, no red eyes. Just little rivulets of tears and a trembling pink lower lip.

"Better go home now," Robin had told me, as she reached down to comfort her poor, trembling little sister. "See you tomorrow at school."

"Sizzle, sizzle," I mouthed at Brooke as I left, making sure that Robin didn't see me.

The memory of that encounter was crisp and vivid, even though it was nearly twenty years old. And two things I knew: Brooke hadn't changed a bit. And neither had Robin.

*　　*　　*

Even the soothing tones of the Harmony couldn't quite dispel my miserable mood. The ambience in The Tranquillity Room should have been enough, given the string quartet and all. The poached Atlantic salmon helped a lot, and so did the chocolate pâté and raspberry coulis. Still, I was on edge. As we sipped our cappuccino, Richard Sandes leaned across the white linen tablecloth and gave my hand a squeeze. Warm and protective. Like a father.

"Maybe she's right," he said.

I gazed into his deep-brown eyes and said, "Don't be silly." Ruining the mood.

He gave me one of his sad smiles, but I thought I saw a flicker of concern cross his face as he beckoned for the waiter.

The waiter practically vaulted over the serving table to get to us. He managed to maintain his dignity, although I couldn't help noticing his toupee was a bit askew.

"Armagnac?" Richard asked.

"Better not. I've got my car."

Naturally. I'm the only person I know who would take her own car on what was turning out to be a very romantic evening of investigation.

"Don't worry about that. I'll get you home. Your car will be fine in our parking lot overnight. Armagnac for two, Gilles," he told the waiter.

"Yes, Mr. Sandes."

Richard and I exchanged grins as the waiter hurried off to get our drinks. He paused before one of the tall mirrors to straighten his hair. It couldn't be easy, I thought, serving dinner to the General Manager.

I returned to the subject du soir.

"You don't know her, Richard. She's always been level-headed and calm. She's had plenty of time to recover her emotional balance since finding the body."

I couldn't figure out what there was about this man, but here I was blabbering on about Robin and my fears. Maybe there's something about seeing a corpse together that helps to break down conversational barriers in later encounters.

He shook his head. "I don't know about that. It was so gruesome. I'm still waking up in the middle of the night, dreaming about it. And I'm a tough old goat, not a young woman who stumbled onto a murder scene alone."

The Armagnac arrived before I could say something cranky. In the interests of keeping the very pleasant evening very pleasant, I decided not to talk about Robin anymore.

Instead we talked about me growing up in Ottawa, my family, my weird job, even a bit about Alvin. The Alvin parts caused Richard to laugh, lightening his face, warming it.

I didn't ask him much about his personal life, and he didn't volunteer much. But the questions were bouncing around in my head, questions I wouldn't hesitate to ask a man who didn't interest me. Things like: are you planning to stay here permanently, does your wife have some kind of job commitment in Toronto that prevents her from joining you, are you separated, divorced, growing apart? Things like: do you feel lonely, how did you vote in the last election, what do you like for breakfast? I stopped myself at that last thought. Careful, careful. Don't be an idiot.

"So," I said out loud, all business, "thanks for your information about Rudy Wendtz."

Richard had been nursing his Armagnac with a semi-smile on his face. His head snapped up at this.

"I've been thinking. I shouldn't have told you about him at all. This is a very dangerous situation, and he's a pretty sleazy guy. The police know about him. I think you should let them handle it."

"Too late," I said, "I've already tracked him down. And are you sure the police know about him?"

I didn't mention that I hadn't been able to talk to Wendtz yet. Some things are better left unsaid.

"Oh yes," said Richard, "I made a point of letting them know. Just on the off chance he didn't turn up in their investigation. Although it's unlikely they would have missed out on someone so close to...the deceased."

I nodded. We both knew that.

"Who knows what they'll turn up about him."

"What do you mean?"

He hesitated, "Well, I've got reason to believe he's involved in some pretty bad stuff."

"Like what?"

Richard shrugged, "Dealing drugs, I'm pretty sure."

"What makes you think so?" I asked, having drawn the same conclusion myself on the very slim grounds that this guy had a lot of money and not much job to show for it.

"Information from the staff. They talked about everything Mitzi did and anyone who spent time with her. They tell me that Wendtz is involved in big league stuff. No facts, mind you, just gossip. But I believe it."

"Hmmm." Alvin could be put to work on this one too.

He smiled at me, "I hope we're not going to be talking about this all night."

"No," I said, meeting his eyes. "Just one more thing."

A sigh and then, "What is it?"

"The photographer, Sammy Dash, what do you know about him?"

Richard thought for a minute. "Not a lot. He was in and out. Acting like a big shot. Aggressive little creep. Making a play for good-looking women all the time, especially the tall, slim ones, and always looking for a shot that would sell. You know, paparazzi type."

"Wow," I said, with mock amazement, "here in Ottawa. Imagine."

"Exactly. Here in Ottawa, they don't like that sort of thing."

He glanced away, and I spotted a well-known politician dining with a less well-known, but most influential, pillar of the consulting community.

"That must have given you a bit of grief."

"It did. I had to speak to Ms. Brochu and tell her to keep him on a leash, or our special arrangement might have to end. I couldn't risk a complaint whispered in the ear of the CEO or the Chairman of the Board by some outraged politico," he twinkled. "And I enjoyed telling her, too."

The Ottawa river glittered as we drove along the Parkway. The usual blackness was lifted by the vigorous full moon beaming down on us. Aretha was belting out "Chain of Fools" on the car stereo, and I was thinking about Richard's wife.

As we pulled into my quiet crescent and rolled to a stop in front of my building, I found it difficult to breathe.

Ask him, my internal voices screamed, ask him about his goddam wife. But all I managed was a goofy grin. It reminded me of all those nights after the Saturday dance at St. Jim's, grinning at a new boy who'd walked me home.

Richard was much more mature.

"Please promise me that you won't go barging after Sammy Dash or try seeing Rudy Wendtz."

"I'm a big girl, Richard. I won't step into the basement with either one of them. I promise that."

"Funny," he said, "I'm not sure that you realize how dangerous big players in the drug game can be, although in your line of work you should. And keep in mind that something very bad happened to Mitzi."

"Mmm."

"Mmm nothing," he said in the tone he must have used with his daughter over the years. "You call me, or the police, or someone very large and mean if you decide to have any dealings with either one of them."

"Thanks, Mom."

He gave me a look that defied interpretation, but I was used to living on the edge.

"Good night, Camilla."

He brushed a light kiss over my forehead. It could have been the kind of kiss you exchange in those first tentative moments when you think you may be falling in love with someone, and you are quivering with suppressed emotion. Or it could have been the kind of kiss you bestow on your favourite aunt as she recovers from a bit of bladder repair in the hospital.

As I jabbed my key into the lock of the interior door to the foyer, I wanted to scream "Just where the hell *is* your wife, anyway?"

Eight

Sammy Dash lit his Gitane with care and respect, sucked in the results, and looked right through me.

I was perched at the next table in a black-walled café, watching Sammy watch the ladies. I'd followed Alvin's list of likely sites for spotting Sammy, and sure enough, by the end of my round in the Byward Market area restaurants, bingo. I decided to let Alvin put his feet up on the desk for ten minutes on Monday morning.

Two women in jeans, sweaters and Birkenstocks sipped their second refill of coffee and wrinkled their sensible noses as the first whiff of the Gitane passed their way. I watched with amusement as they pointed out to the waitress the incongruity of Sammy exhaling right underneath the sign that said Non-Smoking Section.

The waitress was a curvy teenager in a black knit top and mini-skirt, which went well with her fishbelly skin, scarlet lips and fuck-me shoes. Her black hair was pulled up and off to one side in a Pebbles Gone Wrong look. The chewing gum was a nice touch, too.

She goggled at the two women. Then shot a glance at Sammy. He leaned back in his seat, exhaling a jet stream of Gitane exhaust in the direction of the complainants.

The waitress rolled her eyes and chewed her gum.

"Well," she said, "there's nothing I can do about it. Would

you mind moving over by the window? No one's smoking over there."

"What do you mean, there's nothing you can do about it? Tell that asshole to butt out. Tell *him* to move over by the window," said one of the women.

"Well, I can't. He owns this place."

"To hell with this," said the woman. "We're out of here. Permanently." She scraped back her chair, scooped up the tip that had been resting on the table and shoved the bills into her jeans pocket.

The waitress watched them stomp through the front door.

She shrugged.

Sammy smirked.

The café lost some business, Pebbles lost her tip, the two women lost their warm after-lunch glow. Everyone lost except Sammy Dash.

I could tell he'd enjoyed himself.

Sammy Dash made for good watching. He was lean and sinewy, not too tall, a great build for a sleaze photographer. He was wearing a black tee-shirt and chinos, tight around the crotch. Brown hair, cut short, and blue eyes, sharp and foxy. A black leather jacket, European style, hung over the back of his chair. His legs sprawled in the aisle, feet bare inside his sandals.

The café was crowded and noisy, but no one messed around with Sammy.

I had a gut feeling he was a key factor in Mitzi's misfortune, and I wanted to get a better sense of what made him tick before I talked to him.

I watched him all the way through an open-faced smoked salmon on brown sandwich and then through my cappuccino.

Eye contact was his specialty. He singled out women who were already escorted. Tall women. More than one had to put a hand on her partner's arm to head off a confrontation with Sammy. Sammy grinned whenever that happened.

When he sauntered out the café doors, I was right behind him. Still behind him when he climbed into a dark green Porsche and slid into the traffic. Naturally, he had a vanity plate.

How much money do photographers make, I asked myself as I eased my way into the traffic behind him. The middle-aged man in the grey Honda Accord behind me seemed to feel he'd been cut off. I waved back at him and blew a little kiss.

*　　*　　*

Robin's trip to the police station capped the day.

"They did what?" I asked Mrs. Findlay. The phone shook in my hand.

"They took her in for questioning. To the police station."

"When?"

"Hmmm. Just as *Another World* was coming on."

"When is that?"

"Two o'clock," Mrs. Findlay huffed. "And there's no reason to snap at me, Camilla MacPhee."

Snap, I thought, I'd like to do more than snap, you vapour-brained old bat. But I injected a note of respect into my voice and asked, "Who took her in? The big guy, McCracken?"

"No, the small one with the pointed nose."

"Who went with her?"

"With her? Nobody."

"NOBODY?"

"I'm not going to mention your tone again."

"She went alone with the officer?"

"That's right. Her father was out when they came."

"And Brooke?"

"Brooke had an important appointment this afternoon. She couldn't break it."

"Right. And you couldn't leave because *Another World* was on."

I hung up, resisting the urge to go over there, kick in the door and insert her, head-first, into the television set.

* * *

The police station is new and concrete and designed to create the impression of efficiency. Not even the murals can soften its sterile, forbidding atmosphere.

McCracken met me at the Criminal Investigation desk.

"Where is she?" I said. "I've got the right to see her."

He had the good sense to turn red.

"She's at the General."

"At the General Hospital?"

McCracken's voice was gruff. "She collapsed during questioning. Hit her head on the desk, I guess. Anyway, they took her by ambulance, and when I went by earlier, they said she was going to be all right.

"Let me get this straight. You took a sick woman from her bed, allowed her to be brought in by a sadistic little weasel, and then let her injure herself?"

He grunted.

"I'm her lawyer. Nobody called me. You think you can get away with running things like it's a police state?"

"She tried to call you. You weren't in your office. Nobody knew where you were."

Alvin. I'd kill him. But I didn't lose time plotting Alvin's death. McCracken was my target.

"When this case gets cleared up, you guys are gonna get roasted for badgering innocent citizens."

"Look, I understand how you feel. Mombourquette got a bit too…zealous. She's okay. Her father's with her now."

"Her father!" I exploded, even though I felt a wave of relief. "This woman is not only innocent, but she might have seen the real killer. Do you think the sixty-five year old muffin-meister will be able to protect her if the killer decides to eliminate a witness?"

"This isn't New York," McCracken fought back. "We think your friend is the real killer."

As I turned and stormed out, McCracken called to me, "When can I get in touch with your sister?"

When you can go ice skating in hell, McCracken, I thought.

Turning, I said, "My sister's a busy woman and a very attractive one. She seems to have developed a strong interest in a man who's just entered her life."

"Who?" McCracken blurted.

I shrugged. "The woman's got to have some privacy. But I can tell you, she's all keyed up waiting for his phone calls."

McCracken slumped a bit at that. What can I say, he deserved it.

* * *

Robin had been sent home by the time I reached the hospital. When I finally got to the Findlays', she looked as bad as I'd expected. Her father didn't look much better, his face grey as he sat next to her, holding her pale hand.

"Oh good," I said, "I see the family finally rallied around."

"They couldn't go with her," he said.

His eyes watered, and I knew he realized what that said about his family. And he knew I did, too.

I gave him a little hug.

"Sorry," I said, "I know you're one of the guys in the white hats."

But Mr. F. wasn't thinking about himself.

"Look at her. What's wrong with her? What's happening to Robin? I can't understand it."

"I don't know. But I'm sure going to find out, no matter what."

I meant it. I had a lot to find out and I still wasn't sure where to go next. But I didn't care who got dirt on them, if it meant getting Robin out of this mess.

* * *

Back in the office, I was still steaming. And there was no sign of Alvin to take it out on. I'd had a twelve-ounce Colombian to calm me down, and for some reason it wasn't working. I was too jangled to even consider tackling any of my cases, so I settled for making notes on Mitzi's murder in a little book.

I started a few lists. Like who had a reason to kill Mitzi.

I thumbed through the issues of *Femme Fatale* which were still stacked on the desk, looking for other local people who'd been skewered. Deb Goodhouse and Jo Quinlan were the only two who showed up. I put them on the list.

I left a note to Alvin instructing him to get to work finding out who else in the Ottawa area had been roughed up by Mitzi, either in print or on the air.

Of course, Mitzi's killer could have come from anywhere, and I knew it. Still, I told myself I'd deal with possible non-

Ottawa candidates later on. If I had to.

I added a bit to Alvin's note, instructing him to get a list of everyone Mitzi had ever targeted in any medium and their address. And to do this quickly. I underlined "quickly" twice, adding "P.S. Alvin, if at anytime in the future I receive a call from, about or in any way pertaining to Robin and you do not give a clear message and stand on your head to locate me, I will truss you up with the telephone extension wire and ship you back to Sydney in an urn."

I felt a certain satisfaction when I turned my attention to my own list.

I added Rudy Wendtz's name, in light of their big argument the night before Mitzi's death. And I put Sammy Dash's name, too, just because I hated the little jerk.

Then I remembered Richard's comment about Mitzi's next project. A book on Members of Parliament, senators, backroom boys. That could make for a pretty long list. I translated it to political connections and added it to the other names.

On my To Do list, I made a note to find out who had complained about Mitzi's fight with Rudy and what the other guests had heard.

Would Richard help me get their names, I wondered.

Five minutes later, I knew the answer.

"You must be kidding. How long do you think I'd hold onto my job if I gave out that kind of information and you badgered my clients?" Amusement wafted over the phone lines. "I hope you're a good sport about it, because I'd really like to see you again."

"Me?" I said, "Richard, Goodsport is my middle name. Why don't I drop in for a drink in your very nice bar when I finish up here at the office?"

"Great, I'll wait for you."

I had a smile on my face as I hung up and departed the office for the ATM down the street. I hoped that Richard would forgive me my trespasses.

*   *   *

"I can't give you that information," Stephanie gasped, her big hair quivering with outrage.

"That's too bad," I said. "I would be grateful." I pushed the symbol of my potential gratitude towards her on the polished top of the reception desk at the Harmony.

She took a quick look at the warm red-orange tones of the fifty and quivered a little bit more.

"No," she said, "Mr. Sandes would be very upset. I could even lose my job." Her eyes strayed to the bill.

I added a second one to the first. She licked her lips.

"All right. It would take a little while, but I could mail you the information."

"Sure," I said, tearing the fifties in two and handing her one half of each. "And when I get the information, I'll send you the balance on my account."

She wrote out her home address on a piece of Harmony stationary, and I handed her one of my cards. We'd just completed our little transaction, when Stephanie gulped.

I turned and saw Richard heading towards us.

"Here he is, dear," I said, "no need to call him for me at all. But thanks for your help."

Stephanie nodded, whitely, and tried to smile.

I didn't have to try. My smile bloomed by itself as Richard got closer.

*   *   *

103

As I unlocked the door to my office the next day, the phone was ringing.

Alvin had left a note. Gone out, it said.

I answered the phone myself.

"Where have you been?"

"Alexa, it's not like you to be peevish."

"Just answer the question, dear. Don't be evasive."

I decided to answer the question before Alexa and I tossed any more adjectives at each other. "I've been all over the place. There was a murder, in case you forgot, and Robin was brought in for questioning. I've been busy."

"Robin was brought in for questioning!"

"Don't you listen to the news?"

"I just got back from the cottage. Where is she? Don't tell me she's in…."

I reached for my cup of coffee to steady myself and interrupted her. "They haven't arrested her. They'd have to show probable cause. And since she didn't do it, that's unlikely."

"God, I hope she's got a good lawyer."

"Me."

"Camilla!"

"I know, I think it's crazy too. But she insists."

"Do you have to deal with the police and everything?"

"That's a really silly question from a sophisticated woman." She sighed. "I know."

We both knew why she'd asked it.

"He hasn't called me, you know," she said.

"You've been at the cottage."

"Well, he could have left a message."

"Didn't he?"

"There were a lot of clicks."

"I don't know what to tell you."

"Why do you think he wouldn't leave a message?"

"Jeez, I don't know. Maybe he was afraid his wife would overhear him."

After Alexa hung up on me, I spotted the envelope from Stephanie. The girl certainly was quick on her feet. I smiled at the contents. Sure enough. Three names, three addresses. Check-in times, check-out times. Room numbers at the Harmony. Home and work phone numbers. Stephanie was a girl who'd go far. I tucked the two half-fifties into a envelope and scribbled her home address on it. Alvin could get a little exercise delivering it. And I made a note to say nice things about her to Richard.

Now I had a little ammo in my war against Wendtz.

I picked up the phone.

Of the two people I reached, neither had clear memories of Mitzi and Rudy's dust-up. Both were a bit confused about why I was calling.

Connie Dietz was my biggest hope. She'd had the room next to Mitzi's.

"Sorry, Ms. Dietz will not be back in the office until May 25." The voice was prim and officious. I couldn't resist shaking it up a bit.

"This is regarding a police investigation." True enough. "Ms. Dietz was staying in the hotel where Mitzi Brochu was murdered. We're double-checking to see whether she heard anything of importance the night before the murder."

"My heavens, I didn't know anything about that. Ms. Dietz is travelling in the United States. You mean she was near that murder?" All signs of primness had disappeared from the voice.

"Can I reach her? Do you have her itinerary?"

"Sorry. She's on holiday."

"I imagine you gave that information to my colleagues when they called earlier anyway."

"Well, no. I take all the phone calls here, and this is the first I've heard of it. Perhaps they just left a message. Here, let me check Connie's voice-mails for you."

I sat on the line listening to rustling sounds until she came back.

"There's a few here from Ottawa. A Sgt. Mombourquette. Would that be it?"

"Right on."

"Well, I'll certainly get Connie to contact you the minute she shows up. And, Officer, good luck with the case."

"Thanks, but don't tell her to call me. I'm on the road quite a bit. I'll contact her. Thank you."

There was a breathless good-bye from Ms. Prim as she rushed to get off the phone and spread the news.

Not much information, but it told me Mombourquette had quit after leaving one piddling message. But then, his money had always been on Robin.

I picked up the phone. At least the defense had Connie Dietz in its back pocket.

"Merv," I said, when the call connected me to my favourite tame Mountie, "you've gotta help me. Robin's in real hot water."

"Who is this?" Merv asked, "Not Camilla, is it?"

"Of course it's Camilla."

"High time you called me back."

"What do you mean, it's high time I called you back?"

"What the hell do you think I mean?"

"Sorry, Merv. Are you saying you left messages for me?"

"Yes, I'm saying I left messages for you."

It wasn't necessary for him to mimic my expression with such enthusiasm.

"Oh," I said, deciding to overlook the mimicking, "well, I didn't get any messages." I made a little note on the desk pad —Kick Alvin's Butt.

"Yeah, well, who's the guy who answers your phone? He needs some kind of lessons in something."

"Yes, Merv, he does."

"Right." Still sulking.

"Anyway, Merv, I'm calling you because Robin's in big trouble and…"

"Well, I know Robin's in big trouble. Anyone in the country who's read the headlines or listened to the news knows. Being found in the room with Mitzi Brochu's body is big, big news. Why the hell did you think that I was calling and leaving all those messages?"

"Okay, so you know. Of course, I guess I just have been too busy tearing around to pay attention to the media. The police are focusing on her, and I've been scrounging for alternatives."

"Jesus. Those guys are such peckerheads. You met this Mombourquette?"

"Yup. He's got it in for Robin." So far so good. Merv was getting steamed. He'd always had a soft spot in his heart for Robin, ever since we were teenagers and he was the young Mountie living across the street.

"I don't know how anyone could even think for one minute she could hurt anybody. Does he look like a wharf rat or what?"

"Probably has a tail under his cheap suit," I said.

"Jeez, somebody's got to do something. Have you been over to that loony bin lately?"

"You mean the Findlay place?"

"I went over. Her mother's stuck in front of the television having orgasms over the soaps and her father's baking all the time, except when they're both fussing over that useless bitch of a sister. And here's Robin practically in a coma. Have you seen her?"

"I have, Merv. And I am doing something. And this is how you can help."

"Shoot."

"One of the guys I want to know about is Sammy Dash. Can you check out the computer for his license plate and get me the guy's address? And listen, you can tell if someone's got a record from that file, right? I need that too, and if he's got a history, I want to know for what."

"You know I'm not supposed to give you stuff like that. I can't even get into the files without giving a reason. I'm a year from retirement, and you want me to be breaking security."

"Right. I'm sure you'll think of a good official reason to check him out."

"You just make sure you keep an eye on Robin. She needs you."

"Sure will. Oh and Merv, that's S-A-M-M-Y D-A-S-H."

*   *   *

Alexa was sitting in my living room when I got home that night, much too tall, blonde and elegant for the surroundings. She tapped her long, patent leather toes on the leg of my table. After five minutes, I finally had to ask her what was wrong.

"Why are you doing that?"

She fixed me with a long, dirty look. "He doesn't have a wife."

"Who?"

"I think you know."

"Oh, well, how was I to know he didn't have a wife?"

"Well, now you know."

"So he called, did he?"

"No, he didn't, but I asked around. I have sources."

"And no wife."

"That's right."

"You don't think he's gay, do you?"

Her voice went up just a smidgen. "No, I don't think he's gay."

"Just wondering, a man of that age. Not married..."

"He's divorced." She snapped it, sounding like a rifle report.

"Divorced! Does Dad know?"

"What does Dad have to do with it?"

"Well, I mean, here's you, nice Catholic lady, widowed, entitled to see other nice Catholic widowed people and here's him, D-I-V-O-R-C-E-D. You'll be the talk of your Parish."

Alexa sat up very straight.

"I'll cross that bridge when I come to it."

Nine

I drove over to Elmvale Acres Saturday morning. Robin looked even worse. She must have lost twenty pounds since finding Mitzi.

"She was just pretending to eat a bit before, and now she's not even pretending. We're so worried." Mr. Findlay stood by the door with a pan of lemon loaf held in his oven mitts.

Mrs. F. nodded her head from the sofa, which was something, I guess, acknowledging that the situation was serious. Even though her mind was on a taped episode of *The Young and the Restless*.

Mr. F. was glum. Rejection of his food struck at his self-image, I'm sure.

I still wasn't prepared for the sight of her, shrunken and grey. It was hard to believe that anyone whose colour was that bad had blood in their veins. The skin on her face was loose.

"Robin," I whispered when we were alone, "you better start eating or old Dr. Beaver's going to stick a tube through your nose, down your throat and force feed you. Nibbling on your Dad's fresh lemon loaf is a more pleasant alternative. Trust me."

She tried to smile. "I do trust you. I just can't eat. I just can't. And I don't want to."

The rest of our conversation went nowhere. Just like every time I'd spoken to her since the murder. One thing I knew. I couldn't count on Robin for help with the investigation.

"What did Dr. Beaver say?" I asked Mr. Findlay on the way out.

"He's going to put her back in the hospital if she doesn't start to eat. Maybe get her some psychiatric help. She doesn't want it."

"Shhh," said Mrs. Findlay from the sofa.

Must have been an important part.

*   *   *

I spent the rest of Saturday in the office trying to catch up. I worked halfway through one mountain of paper, but two more had sprung up. Tomorrow, I said, and went back to thinking about Robin.

Since the murder, everyone's reactions to Robin had been emotional. Poor Traumatized Robin. Or, in the case of the police, Guilty as Sin Robin. It was time for me to take a more reasoned approach to my friend and her very big problem.

I worked through a little flowchart of possibilities. For instance, Robin either killed Mitzi or she didn't. I couldn't bring myself to believe she had, so I pursued the no side. Robin either saw the killer or she didn't. If she had seen the killer, she either knew the killer's identity or she didn't. If she saw someone she didn't know, she would have no apparent reason for not describing him or her. If she knew the killer, she was refusing to talk for some reason that made sense to her. Fear? Protectiveness? If it were fear, who could scare Robin so much that she would not describe a murder to the police?

Robin and I knew many of the same people. Of course, she's met quite a few more people through St. Jim's Parish and the Humane Society and dishing out food at the Food Bank and even her office. But somehow, I didn't think these organizations would be the sources for Mitzi's murderer. Just to be on the safe side, I made a note to nose around in all four. But my heart wasn't in it, these were not people to inspire fear. And Robin, for all her fragile blonde looks and current attacks of the vapours, was no chicken.

Fine, then. The last variant was that Robin saw the killer and chose to protect him or her for some reason. I chewed on my pencil and tried to figure out what reason Robin could have to protect a killer.

When I slunk out of the office, full of questions, I bumped into Ted Beamish.

"Think nothing of it," he said, dusting off his knees.

"Sorry, Ted, I wasn't expecting anyone. It's Saturday."

"Sure, I know."

"What can I do for you?"

"Well, I was heading for the Mayflower and I…I saw your light on and I thought I'd see if you had time for a beer, catch up a bit."

A good enough story, except that my office was past the Mayflower, and you can't see the window from the street.

"Why not," I said, before realizing that I was ticked off at Mr. Ted Beamish, but good.

"How's Robin?" he asked as we sat down and ordered.

"If you're so concerned, why didn't you ask me about her when she was taken in for questioning?" I snapped.

"Taken in?" Ted turned white. "If she's being questioned, why are we sitting here?"

"You're telling me you didn't know about this?"

"I've been away at a hearing," he said. "God, poor Robin. Why would they suspect her?"

"Because she was the last person to see Mitzi before she was found dead, because only her fingerprints and Mitzi's were found in the room, because…"

"Sounds pretty fluffy to me."

I nodded. "And because I think Robin is protecting someone."

"Who?" he inhaled.

"Well, I'm not sure, but she either knows or suspects someone of killing Mitzi, and she's making herself sick over it."

"Who?"

"I don't know who, or I would have my elbow in his throat right now. But maybe someone from work, or church or her volunteer stuff. I think I'll nose around a little bit."

"I'll help you." Ted's face lit up at the prospect.

"No, that's all right…"

It fell again as I started to turn him down. Wait a minute, I said to myself.

"…that'd be great, Ted. Why don't you schmooze the girls in her office and the Humane Society. We can both do a bit of the Food Bank."

He was nodding. "I can do that."

"Sure," I said, "I'll just confine myself to stalking the criminal elements. I feel more comfortable having my own niche than spreading myself all over the map."

"I'd like to see her, too," he said.

"Sure," I lied, knowing Robin wouldn't want to see any new man in her current state, "I'll set that up for you."

"What do you mean set it up?"

I could tell by the look in his eyes that I had gone too far.

"I'll just drop in myself sometime tomorrow and give her some encouragement." He said it in a way that didn't allow for argument.

* * *

By eight o'clock on Sunday morning, I was at Robin's, surprising her father in the middle of making cinnamon rolls.

"These'll be ready in half an hour," he said, as I skipped up the stairs.

"I can't," Robin whined, as I manoeuvred her into the bathroom.

"You'd better," I told her, as she sat on the little blue chair, and I rummaged through the dozens of shampoo bottles, "Otherwise an attractive male colleague is going to drop in to see you and find you looking like a bleached sardine."

"What do you mean, a bleached sardine?" she asked, leaning her head against the wall and closing her eyes.

"Pale and greasy."

I looked up from under the sink to see she was laughing, just a little silent shake, but it gave me hope.

While Robin was in the shower with a lemon fragrance shampoo, I kept up a running conversation, talking about Ted Beamish, talking about Alvin, talking about anything but the murder. I was on the alert, ready to grab her if she collapsed.

Mr. Findlay whipped into her bedroom and changed the sheets when we were out of the room. He left a pot of steaming coffee, two blue and white china mugs and fragrant, warm cinnamon buns with icing glaze on top.

Back in bed with her yellow hair blow-dried and smelling lemon-fresh, she leaned against the blue roses on the pillowcase.

"Ted Beamish," she said, "I can't quite place him."

"I don't know how you could forget him. He's..." I searched for the right word... "dashing. And persistent." True enough, and more appealing than pudgy, red-headed, receding-hairlined and forgettable-faced.

114

"Persistent?"

"You have no idea. But listen, you'd better get on a little warpaint. I don't know if he's persistent enough for a bleached sardine."

Robin managed a little pink lipstick, a smudge of blue eyeliner and a few sweeps of mascara before she fell back on the pillow.

I had no mercy. "Cheek stuff," I hissed, "what do you call it?"

"Blusher," she whispered.

"Where is it?"

"In my purse."

I rummaged through gum, keys, at least seven pens, chequebook, a banana that had to be removed at once, two notebooks, sunglasses, dozens of little notes about things to do, perfume, an address book, wallet, a tennis ball, two packets of tissues, lottery tickets, a Mars bar and her blusher.

I dropped the banana into the wastepaper basket and the room took on the scent.

Dabbing on the bit of blush gave Robin an illusion of health, if you didn't look too closely. If you didn't notice the loose skin and glazed eyes.

"There," I said, waving a hand mirror in front of her face, "you look great. And we can see your breath on the mirror, so we know you're alive. This is good. When he comes through that door, he's going to fall right off his horse."

I don't know why she thought that was so funny. I found myself laughing, too. We howled until tears ran down our cheeks. Even though two minutes earlier I'd been acting with all the humour of a women's prison warden. At least Robin, the real Robin, was still kicking underneath her shrunken exterior.

The door to her bedroom burst open and our laughing choked off.

"For Crissakes," Brooke shrieked, sticking her head in, "don't you know people are trying to sleep?"

"My apologies, Brooke. We shouldn't let the psychological recovery of your sister interfere with something as crucial as your rest."

I would have continued on, but she was gone before I got revved up. She slammed the door, too, but only after she called me a bitch.

"Oh dear, poor Brooke," said Robin, all signs of laughter disappearing.

"Poor Brooke, nothing," I said, filling the mugs with coffee and handing one to Robin. "You have the right to laugh."

"I heard her come in at three last night. She must be exhausted."

"Maybe it's time poor Brooke thought about you a bit. Maybe you're the one who needs special attention and care. Maybe there are more important things in this world than Brooke and her stupid career as a vacuous face on the cover of a vapid magazine."

From the look on Robin's face, I'd gone too far again.

It took two cups of coffee, a bit of cinnamon loaf and a lot of soothing talk before she smiled again. We patched up the makeup and she gave my hand a little squeeze.

"I know it's hard for you to be so nice and patient, Cam. Thanks."

"Well, anyway, at least you look okay in case what's-his-name shows up."

Before heading back to the office, I straightened up the room. In the process I knocked over Robin's purse. I did my best to replace everything in some kind of order, but after a while I gave up and piled in the chewing gum packages, notes, stamps, eye shadows, pens and other stuff. At least the banana was gone.

The writing on the last note caught my eye. Rudy Wendtz, it said. Nothing else.

I looked over at Robin.

"He might not come," she said.

"He'll come."

"Maybe not."

"Even supposing he doesn't come, which he will, you still got yourself fixed up and you look very nice and fresh and I'm sure you feel a lot more comfortable."

I didn't mention finding Rudy Wendtz's name in her purse. I would ask Robin about Rudy Wendtz when the time was right. She smiled a little bit when I left.

All the way home, I thought about that note. What was it doing there? How did Robin know about Rudy? Had she known him before she got summoned to Mitzi's suite?

*   *   *

The next day, there was no Alvin in the office. While getting rid of him had been my major preoccupation not too long ago, now I was bothered by his continuing, unexplained absence.

A plain brown envelope with my name typed on it lay on the floor next to the door. I picked it up and tossed it onto the desk.

Alvin hadn't been in to pick it up. Another strike against him. Still, his absence meant I could get to the phone without pushing him out of the way.

I called Ted Beamish.

"Now?" he said. "It's not even ten o'clock. I can't just disappear on the taxpayers' nickel."

"Make up the time," I said, trying to sound like I must be obeyed, "we're talking someone's mental health here."

"I was planning on dropping in to see Robin on my lunch or after work. I was going to call first."

"Don't wait. Don't call. Go now."

After a pause, he said, "All right. I guess I can do that."

"But first," I said, "tell me what you found out schmoozing the girls at Robin's office and the Food Bank and the Humane Society."

"Well, not that much. No one at the Humane Society knew anything. They were just worried about who was looking after her cats."

And well they should be, I thought.

"At the office, I schmoozed the girls as you suggested. They seemed to feel Robin had been under some kind of strain for about a week or so. No one knew what, she just seemed very worried and distracted."

"For a week?"

"Thereabouts. No one's sure. And they can't link it to anything. But they'd been talking about it themselves even before the murder."

"Hmm. You got a contact there now you could just call for a bit of information?"

"Sure."

"See if you can find out if she received any calls from her sister."

"The model?"

"The one and only."

"She's kind of self-focused, isn't she? I hear it's all me, myself and I."

"You got it."

"Let me think, what else," he added. "Right, the Food

118

Bank. I tracked down two of the other volunteers who were on with Robin last week. One of them remembers her being very distressed, very distracted. It turns out this was the night before the murder. Something happened to her that day. This person didn't know. But she might have told someone else. A close friend."

I shook my head. I was her closest friend, and she hadn't confided in me. Probably because she couldn't reach me. If only I'd been at the office when she called. If only I'd intercepted her at the Harmony before she went into Mitzi's suite. If only…"

Ted's voice interrupted me.

"Well? What do you think?"

"Good stuff. Well, you should head off now. Robin needs you."

I noted a trace of resentment in his good-bye.

Job number two was to find that little twerp, Alvin, and drag him back to indentured labour where he belonged. Or set him loose and find someone who could do the job. Yes. I could fire him for deserting his post.

I ripped Alvin's file from the drawer and found his address. While I was searching for a pen and a piece of paper on the desk, I spotted the plain brown envelope again

Probably his notice, and he was too chicken to give it in person, I thought as I ripped it open. Inside was a single sheet of white bond. Sammy Dash, it said, DOB 29/03/58, no outstanding warrants. Previously convicted of possession of cannabis. Did not serve time. Several charges of assault on former girlfriend, later dropped. Suspected of involvement in cocaine traffic. Never charged.

Sammy's address was included too. Well, well. Thanks, Merv.

When I found the pencil and paper, I copied Sammy's address along with Alvin's. I also cast a guilty glance at the pile of work. It seemed to me it had taken on an eerie, green glow and was beginning to pulsate a bit.

I'll get to you, I said. The phone was ringing as I skipped out of the office.

*　*　*

Alvin was surprised to see me. Perhaps because I was leaning against his doorbell and had been doing so for five minutes. There was some interesting graffiti on the walls, and the corridor had a faint scent of illegal substances.

"Camilla," he said, "What are you doing here?"

"Looking for you. What the hell do you think?"

"Gee. That is a surprise. Come on in."

A surprise.

"I thought maybe you were dead. But, of course, that may have just been wishful thinking."

"I wasn't expecting you. The place is a bit of a mess."

The place was less of a mess than I would have expected.

"I'll get you some tea," he said and disappeared from the room before I could tell him he was fired.

I headed for the sofa with the leopard-skin covering, passing the ancient refrigerator, painted silver, which was the focal point of the living area. There was no other furniture in the room, unless you counted the CD player and the chrome coat rack holding Alvin's best studded black leather jacket. Or the toilet with the exuberant ivy growing out of it. No sign of the mess Alvin had alluded to, although it was hard to tell if the walls were clean or not, since they were painted black. The same applied to the floor, which was a giant abstract painting

120

of household appliances and cleaning products, with a high-gloss finish. On a wall it would have been a mural. Was it a flooral? I wondered.

I had to sit down, since standing on the flooral gave me the feeling of hurtling through space.

The Hammerheads blasted from the sound system at about 100 decibels, so I decided to fire Alvin in the kitchen and avoid the tea thing altogether. On the way, I discovered the mess.

The large table in the dining "ell" was covered with magazines, newspapers, print-outs and cassettes. More were stacked on the ground. Sheets from flip charts had been ripped off and taped to the walls. Each contained long lists of names under different headings, like *Femme Fatale*, the local satirical magazine *Peeping Tom* and its relatives in other cities, and Mitzi's broadcasts. There were also lists by type. Alvin had cross-referenced many of the names from one list to another.

So that's what he'd been doing. It was going to be tough to fire the miserable little creature now.

"How are things at the office?" Alvin emerged with a silver tray carrying an old pink and gold china tea pot, creamer and sugar bowl and two cups and saucers, with tiny silver spoons. He passed me in the ell and plunked himself down cross-legged on the floor, leaving me to decide whether I would join him or perch on the sofa like a fool.

I picked the sofa. The floor made me dizzy.

"Well," he said, looking up, "you got here just in time. I'm at the last list. Some interesting stuff is showing up there. We'll have our tea and then see if you can find the most important patterns."

"Sure," I said, adding, "beautiful tea set."

"Thanks, it was my grandmother's Anniversary Rose. Mom

gave it to me when I left. She figured it'd just get broken by the other kids at home. I think it adds a nicely jarring note of discontinuity with the floor, don't you?"

"Indeed," I said, as Alvin poured my tea.

"So, where did you get this very interesting floor design?"

He looked at me with surprise. "I painted it, of course. What did you think that I did with my spare time?"

I hesitated to mention I'd thought he spent his spare time frying his tiny brain with chemicals. Instead I said, "Beautifully done, Alvin. Tremendous precision, especially with the electric can openers."

Was it my imagination, or did the faintest trace of a blush cross Alvin's chalky cheeks?

When the tea was finished, we moved to the dining room to inspect the project.

Sure enough, there were patterns all right. Alvin's list entitled Key Targets identified them by type.

Women Politicians, Royalty, Television Personalities, Singers, Actors and Models, and Anyone Fat were the headings Alvin had picked.

"Everyone she ever targeted in print or broadcast fits into one or more of these categories," he explained.

"I guess people like to see the powerful and popular get skewered. It gives them a sense of superiority if the winners have warts."

"Right," said Alvin. "Look at the tabloids the next time you're in the supermarket. They'll give you tremendous insights into human nature."

I considered the spectre of Alvin in the grocery store.

There were few surprises when we reviewed the lists. Each name had a check mark for every time Alvin had found a reference to that person in print or on air, he explained.

"It wasn't easy getting video copies of her broadcasts," he said. "You'll have to reimburse me for some expenses encountered by a certain individual in getting them."

I opened my mouth to speak.

"In cash," he added.

I let that pass and noted that Deb Goodhouse had thirteen checkmarks, compared to one or two for most of the others. Alvin had circled her name in red marker.

On the media list Jo Quinlan was also circled in red, no doubt because of the nineteen checkmarks.

"Almost every show and every 'Zits' article had a little dig about Jo Q.," Alvin said.

Nothing much of interest in the Singers and Actors list. A country-style singer had three checks by her name, as did an east coast pop fiddler. A great lady of Canadian theatre merited two. The initials B.F. were the last on the list with a question mark and a cross reference to the lists labelled Models, General Gossip and Coming Soon.

Brooke Findlay's name appeared on all three.

I walked back into the black living room and poured myself another cup of Earl Grey.

Ten

I spent the evening examining the many complex lists compiled by Alvin, trying to find a few other leads. By midnight, I gave up. Jo Quinlan and Deb Goodhouse were still on my own, and they'd been joined by Brooke Findlay.

Brooke, according to Alvin's mysterious sources, had been lined up in Mitzi's sights, scheduled for a special treatment in the coming months.

"Why?" I'd asked.

He'd shrugged. "Unclear about that. Lot of shifty looks and sly remarks."

"Like what?"

"Like 'Ask Rudy, if you have the guts.'"

"What's that supposed to mean? Is this guy supposed to scare me?"

"I don't know. He scares everyone else."

"Give me a break. Do I have to drag every little bit of information out of you?"

"Okay, okay. He's supposed to be like some kind of major supplier, you know."

"You sure?"

Rays from the only light in the room glinted off Alvin's black cat's eye glasses. Coupled with the pointer in his hand, he looked like a deranged fairy godmother.

"Don't be dense. That's the word on the street. Big time.

And too hot to handle. Nobody tangles with Rudy Wendtz."

"Hmmm."

* * *

All night I dreamed about killing Brooke Findlay in a variety of satisfying ways. In my dreams, justice prevailed and I found myself serving a ten-year sentence of Family Dinners. I jerked awake at eight o'clock when the phone rang.

"Dinner tonight," Edwina said. "My place. Don't try to weasel out of it."

My God, it was starting.

"I won't resist, Edwina. Will it be a long one?"

Silence drifted back to me over the phone.

"What time," I asked, assuming she was still on the line, "and are you sending a guard for me?"

"Very funny. Stan will pick you up at six thirty."

"All right."

"And, Camilla."

"Yes?"

"Do not, and I mean this, do not provoke Alexa."

"Moi?" I asked.

But she'd already hung up.

* * *

It was after nine when I stepped out of the shower and dried my hair. I decided not to wait until I got to the office to make my first call.

"Oh sure," said Merv. "I'll just drop everything and find out about this guy for you. I was just sitting here waiting for your call anyway."

"Very funny, Merv. But I'll understand if you abandon

Robin to her fate. Pressures of work. Nothing to be done about it."

Merv made some sort of animal noise before he hung up. It sounded promising to me.

I was wearing my pumps and my best court suit. I took my camera, just in case I needed it, and my Nikes, just in case I had a chance to walk somewhere.

One last call before leaving.

"She's asleep," Mr. Findlay whispered.

"How's she doing?"

"A bit better. She had a visit from a very nice young man yesterday. Seemed to cheer her up. Maybe you could call a bit later in the mornings. Brooke needs to rest until eleven."

I let the Brooke remark slide. At least Ted had done his Boy Scout bit and visited Robin.

As I stepped into the hallway, it occurred to me a photo of the cats might cheer Robin. I opened the door, said the magic words "Meow Mix", and snapped the six of them as they whipped into sight.

"So long, guys," I said, closing the door and almost tripping over Mrs. Parnell's walker.

She opened her pursed-up mouth to say something.

"Smile for the birdie," I squawked, as I clicked the shutter. Darned if she didn't blush.

I left for work with a good plan for the day. Beaver through the Benning file then move on to see Rudy Wendtz, as soon as he might be awake. I decided on eleven as the trend.

When I pulled into Rudy Wendtz's driveway, I had to admit to myself that not one word of the Benning brief had made it past my eyes and into my brain, where it could have done some good. Tomorrow, I promised myself.

It was the perfect spring morning, bright yellow sun, bright blue sky, bright tulips in many colours. The temperature was a bright twenty degrees and climbing. The teal wool suit, although bright, was beginning to feel hot and scratchy, and it crossed my mind that I should get some new warm-weather clothes. But first things first.

Rudy Wendtz was polishing off breakfast in his conservatory which overlooked the canal. Very pleasant. His cotton terry robe had set him back a couple of hundred bucks. His bare feet were resting on a leather ottoman as he lounged in a leather chair, enjoying his breakfast cigarette.

Wendtz was large. Under the terrycloth robe lay long, powerful muscles. The presence of exercise machines and weights in the room may have contributed to the impression. There were no plants in this conservatory, but then you can't have everything.

He didn't get up when I was shown in by the large, lumpy individual who answered the door. Just studied me from behind semi-closed lids, while he blew out smoke. From the look on his face, I would rate about a 2 on a good day.

I didn't care. Rudy didn't rate too high with me, either.

I could see why Mitzi had kept him, though. He had a certain something, in that he was well over six feet and he radiated power. He looked as though he hadn't shaved for several days, and he had a serious case of bedhead. His eyes were the eyes of a snake, and perhaps that's why he looked dangerous.

"Yeah?" he said.

"Good morning," I trilled. "How are you today?"

"I'm doing okay," he said.

I didn't doubt it. The three-story brick house, with its location on the Queen Elizabeth Driveway and its view of the sparkling canal, its long, green lawn, its conservatory and its

God knows what else, must have set him back a few bucks. The black Mercedes in the driveway was a good indicator, too.

"Terrific," I chirped. "I wonder if you can help me?"

"Maybe."

"Great. You see my friend, Robin Findlay, was unfortunate enough to find the body of Mitzi Brochu, who I understand was a friend of yours. The police are being quite difficult about this, and I thought that I would chat with people involved and try to find out something that could help a bit." I beamed at him.

The large, lumpy individual poured out a mug of coffee for Wendtz. They both looked at me.

"Oh lovely," I said. "I take mine with just a bit of cream."

Glances heavy with meaning were exchanged before Large-and-Lumpy lumbered off. He returned with a black mug for me, filled it and added some cream. He looked like he was measuring my neck for a garotte.

"Mmm," I said, taking a sip. "I hear you were great friends."

"Who do you hear that from?"

"Oh, here and there, everyone seems to know."

"Do they?"

"Mmmm. Yes, they do. Wonderful coffee."

"My special blend," said Large-and-Lumpy, with a shy pride.

"Just great," I said.

"And a bit of French roast."

"Good enough to market," I said, thinking I had made a friend.

"I don't think I can do much for you, Miss Um…?"

"Oh, I'm sure you can, Mr. Wendtz."

He turned the full force of his snake eyes on me. I sipped a bit more coffee and smiled.

"You see, I think that whatever Mitzi was working on might be the key to her murder. I know she was a very good friend of yours, but she seemed to alienate a good many people with her work."

Wendtz lit another cigarette, and Large-and-Lumpy looked at me with understanding. I felt certain that Mitzi had alienated him, all right.

"I don't know what she was working on."

"You don't?" I said, gazing with disappointment into my empty mug.

"No."

"That's too bad."

Large-and-Lumpy moved around my chair and refilled my mug. I beamed at him like a soul mate.

"We didn't mix business and pleasure," Wendtz said, shooting a bit of smoke in my direction.

"A shame."

He shrugged. This was a man born to shrug.

"There are some local people who were singled out by Mitzi for persistent treatment. I wondered if you might know whether they were targets for coming articles. It's possible that one of them might have snapped. You see, I'm sure my friend couldn't have done it. She's too gentle and soft. She spends her time in the soup kitchens and feeding stray cats and rescuing other people."

"Sorry, I can't help you," Wendtz said. His sneer might have been intended as a smile, but he lacked the practice.

"What about Deb Goodhouse?"

"What about her?"

"Mitzi slammed her often enough. Was she in the works?"

"I don't know."

"Jo Quinlan then. She was a favourite target."

Was that a flicker that passed between Wendtz and my new friend?

Wendtz looked at his watch, which was large and Swiss and cost more than my car. He looked back at me. I smiled.

A pregnant cloud of silence hung in the air.

I think Wendtz was getting ready to splatter me all over the wall when I stood up.

"Sorry, gentlemen," I said, "you are excellent company and I am tempted to spend the morning here with you in idle chatter, but I have important work to do, and I cannot allow you to entice me away from it."

Large-and-Lumpy nodded. Wendtz looked at both of us in disbelief.

At the door I turned. "Oh, and Brooke Findlay, was there any connection between her and Mitzi?"

Bingo. Large-and-Lumpy gawked at me, more in sorrow than anger. Just as well, because enough rage flashed across Wendtz's face for both of them. Most people get hot when they're angry. Wendtz radiated coldness. I felt my body temperature drop, even in the thrill of finding a connection between Rudy Wendtz and Brooke Findlay.

Now we're cooking, I thought, as I reached for the door to let myself out.

Large-and-Lumpy beat me to it.

"You shouldn't of said that," he whispered as I left.

*　　*　　*

I wasn't one block away from the house when a car pulled up beside me. A portable flashing light was perched on its roof. McCracken was inside.

I pulled over, surprised at how my heart was thumping. Large-and-Lumpy, for all our instant rapport, had made me very, very edgy. To say nothing of his keeper.

McCracken's laid-back good humour was eclipsed by a somber stiffness. It didn't look right on him. Big men like that should be good-natured and outgoing.

"What the hell are you doing at Wendtz's place?" he asked, leaning over my window.

"What you should be doing, McCracken. Investigating."

"You'd better leave that to us."

"Glad to, if you'd do your job and arrest a certain well-known member of the underworld who we both know probably offed the victim with a smile on his face. Instead of badgering gentle cat lovers to their grave."

"He didn't do it."

"Of course, he did it. And we both know it. And I'm going to prove it while you sit on your duff."

McCracken's eyes bulged. "Interfere with this case any more…"

"What any more?"

"…and I'll arrest you, for all kinds of interesting things."

"I'd enjoy that, McCracken. We'd both make a splash in the media."

McCracken stood up. "Hang around Wendtz and you'll make the papers all right. Some sad little missing persons announcement. Use your brains on this one, for God's sake."

He started back to his car. I knew he hated to ask me about Alexa, and I wondered how long he could hold out.

Not long. He turned and walked back.

"You know, you may have stirred something up here. Who knows what you're going to have to deal with as a result. These guys are pretty dangerous. Here's my home number in case you ever have to get in touch with me. It's unlisted. Any time you need help or advice." It must have hurt him to say that, his jaw was so tense. "And if you want to pass it on to your sister, that's okay too."

* * *

I parked in the open air lot on O'Connor and walked a couple of blocks to the joke shop. Not as fancy as wherever Stan gets his stuff, but it took my mind off the Benning brief for a little longer, and gave me a chance to chuckle my way out of the chill created by Rudy Wendtz.

The office phone was ringing when I returned with my purchases. Someone persistent enough to keep trying while I fiddled with the key and let myself in.

"Where the hell do you go in that little office that it takes you seventeen rings to answer the phone? Just tell me that."

"Temper, temper, Merv. You don't want to have a stroke."

"Right. If my doctor knew about you, he'd put you on a list with cheap whisky and cigarettes and french fries. Health hazard."

"My secret ambition, Merv."

"I'll bet it is, too. Listen, I didn't call you just to chew the fat. There's a point."

"Get to it then, Merv."

I could hear him exhale.

"This guy Wendtz. He is major bad news. Remain as far away as you can from him. Do not meddle. He is connected. He is into some very bad stuff. Capish?"

"Point taken. Of course, you're a bit too late."

"Christ, Camilla. You got a death wish or something? Half the police forces in this country, including our own, have an eye on this guy, and there's you sticking your little pointed nose in."

"Don't exaggerate, Merv. My nose is not pointed. And if so many police forces, including our own, have so much interest, how come they don't nail him for Mitzi's murder, which he committed? Tell me that."

"They'd sell their souls to nail him for Mitzi's murder, they just happen to know he didn't do it."

"Yeah, right, and how do they know that? Were they with him at the time?"

"Jeez, that's just it. They were. The guy was under surveillance the whole night. He's been the subject of a major drug investigation. He wasn't out of their sight for two minutes. Some alibi, eh? Half the members in this town can swear he didn't do it."

It was my turn to be quiet, and when I spoke again it was through clenched teeth.

"I don't care what your mounties saw or think they saw, Merv, this guy's involved in this killing. Maybe he didn't do it himself, but I bet he made it happen. The local boys never even followed up properly on that blow-up he had with Mitzi the night before she was killed. I saw his face today when I mentioned Brooke Findlay. There's a connection. And according to my sources, Mitzi was about to do a real number on Brooke. That's why Robin's reacting the way she is."

"What did Robin ever do to end up in a family like that?"

"Unlucky, I guess."

"Can't you talk some sense into her?"

"I'll try, now that I have a bit of ammunition."

But I had two calls to make first.

*   *   *

Lunch at the Harmony was an experience to soothe your soul. The music soothed. Chopin's *Nocturnes*. The wine soothed. California chardonnay. The food soothed. Shrimp and scallops, with basmati rice and four perfect bitsy witsy vegetables. Richard Sandes didn't soothe, although he might have wanted to. Just the opposite. I could feel my heart going boom-bitty-boom underneath my teal suit.

"You look different today. What's up?" he asked.

I smiled at him and kept my dirty thoughts to myself.

"Just excitement, I guess."

"Excitement?"

I looked into Richard's brown eyes. This was a man you could bare your soul to. I explained about Wendtz and Large-and-Lumpy and about McCracken and what Merv had said, leaving out the bitchy things that I, myself, had said. But he didn't react the way I wanted.

"For God's sake. Why do you want to take these chances?"

I looked at him in surprise. "Because I want to end Robin's involvement once and for all by finding out what really happened."

He sighed. "And if it turns out that her sister, as miserable as you say she is, is involved, do you think your friend will thank you?"

I shot him a black look, because, of course, he had identified my greatest fear.

He laughed.

"What are you laughing at?" I snapped. "You're not supposed to laugh when someone looks at you like that."

I expected him to stop at that, but he didn't. After a minute of shaking, he picked up the soft apricot napkin and wiped his eyes with it.

"Hehehehehe!" he said.

"Oh shut up, you remind me of a set of teeth I once knew."

"I'm sorry," he said, giving his eyes one last wipe, "I know I shouldn't have laughed like that. If anyone knows this horrible case is serious, it should be me. I'm still dealing with the brass over it. God knows if I'll even keep my job from one day to the other. So I'd like the whole thing cleared up just as much as you would."

"Oh, good," I said, "so why are you laughing then, if it's so goddam serious, as far as you're concerned?"

"It's just the thought of you, in your little teal suit, with the bit of cat hair on the sleeve," he reached over and plucked it off as he was speaking, "it's just the thought of you backing these guys into a corner. I mean, I've seen Wendtz, the guy's huge, and these other guys, Large and Lumpy and McCracken…" He started to laugh again.

"Large-and-Lumpy," I said, with a great deal of dignity, "is only one person."

But I had lost him again.

I sat there with my lips pursed until he was finished.

"Sorry, sorry," he wheezed a bit later. "I can't help it. Maybe it's the tiny little pumps. I just see you standing there waving your fist and barking at these guys, and they're huddling…"

"Size six," I said, "not tiny little pumps. And none of these guys were huddling. Richard, I thought you were on my side."

"I am. Oh, I am. And once I get past the funny side, I have to make the point that you should leave it to the police. They know what they're doing."

"They do not know what they're doing, or they wouldn't be so interested in Robin as a suspect. They would not be denying that Wendtz was involved, and they would not be sitting on their butts."

"Whoa," he said. "I agree they're off base about Robin. You

only have to see her once to know that. She reminded me a bit of my wife, totally incapable of hurting any living thing. I bet she opens the door to escort spiders from the premises."

I had seen Robin do that. But what was this wife thing?

I stared across the table at Richard, his Belgian chocolate eyes, still a bit damp, his lean brown hands that I usually couldn't stop watching, his bony good looks and gentle manner. I felt a sharp pain behind my rib cage. It was time to face the music.

"Your wife?"

"Mmm," he said.

"I have to know about your wife. I have to know, are you still married? As we speak."

Richard stared into the crumpled peach napkin in his hand as if the answer were printed there. It took a while for the words to come.

"Yes," he said, "we are."

I felt my head swimming. The small, smothered rational part of my being tried to tell me it didn't matter. I wasn't over Paul yet. I'd only known Richard a short time, he was too old, the circumstances under which I'd met him had been too gruesome, I'd known all along he had a family. But none of it helped.

I clutched the tablecloth and held on. I kept telling myself it didn't matter.

"I'm sorry, God, I keep saying I'm sorry today. I should have told you our story right from the start. But I thought you were just passing through. And I still find it painful to talk about. Still, that's no excuse for not being straight with you."

I waited, my fingers white.

"I am still married. My wife is in a psychiatric institution suffering from profound depression. Her state is catatonic. No one knows if she will come out of it. But if she does, we will be together again, so I guess I should be upfront about that. I love her and I miss her."

I nodded, hoping my mouth didn't twist too much.

"The doctors don't hold out too much hope. But I hope anyway. Her facility is a good one, and it's a little bit closer to Ottawa than to Toronto, which was why I asked for this transfer. It's also why I'm usually out of town on my days off."

"I'm sorry to hear about your wife. Has she been sick long?"

"A year and a half. She never got over our daughter's death. She just couldn't admit it happened."

You could feel the pain emanating from him. The lines in his face that I'd found so sexy, I now realized were mementos of anguish. I hated to ask him anything else. And yet, I knew that this moment of candour wouldn't come again with Richard.

"Your daughter…"

"She was so beautiful, just like her mother, but she had some medical problems that affected her heart, and one day it just gave out. Twenty-four years old and everything ahead of her. Beautiful. Masters degree from University of Toronto. Engaged. A wedding planned. And one day, it just stopped."

"I'm sorry."

"Look, I should have told you this right away, but I had no idea that there would be anything between us."

"Don't worry about it," I heard myself say, "it's not like we made some kind of commitment or anything. A couple of meals together doesn't make a relationship."

"I hope we can still have lunch from time to time."

"Of course," I said, reaching out to pat his hand, a most un-Camilla-like gesture. "I knew you had a family, Richard, right from the start, from the photo in your office." I didn't bother to mention that I had hoped they'd been sliced from his life by divorce. A part of the past. "We can have lunch anytime you want. Nothing's changed."

But something had changed.

"Good," he said.

"Look, before I get back to work, which is piling up, I just want to know if I can talk to the maid who was in the hallway the day of Mitzi's death."

He started to say something negative, I could tell.

"Maybe she heard something or saw something. Oh sure, I know the police probably questioned her, but I'd like to try again."

Richard's grin returned.

"Well, good luck. I hope you do better than the police. That particular employee is a very recent refugee from El Salvador. She speaks very little English, just enough to follow her instructions for work, and even there I think the housekeeper has to use a little show and tell."

"I'm one hell of a mime."

"I bet you are. Well, I'll get you her name and work schedule, and you can give it a shot."

We said good-bye in the aqua foyer, and I stepped outside and waved. Richard stood and watched me go. It wasn't until I was out of his sight that I let myself slump a bit.

Sure, Richard would continue to be a friend. Kind of a Merv with manners. But the easy comfort with the sexy underpinnings had been destroyed. And let's face it, I told myself, friendship was not what drew me to Richard in the first place. Anyway, if I wanted companionship, I had the damn cats.

Eleven

It had been quite a full day, what with meeting Wendtz under his rock and Richard's revelation about his wife. My head was full of whirling information, and I wanted to flake out right after work.

But first I had to endure dinner with the family. And the cats were restless. Not only swarming me as soon as I got through the door, but causing me trouble even before that.

As I fumbled with my key, I heard my neighbour, Mrs. Parnell, coming out of her apartment.

Hurry, I urged myself, hurry, hurry, hurry, hurreeee, but I wasn't fast enough.

"Ms. MacPhee," she said, leaning forward on her walker in a menacing way, "meowing sounds continue to be heard coming from your apartment." She took a triumphant drag from her cigarette in its majestic holder.

"I don't know what you're talking about," I shouted, hoping to drown out the cat noises. "We've had this discussion before."

"I think you do know what I'm talking about."

"Meowing sounds? That's very peculiar, since I dislike animals."

"Sounds like cats to me."

"Cats?"

"Yes," she snapped. "Cats, not a difficult concept to grasp

139

for one with seven years university education, Ms. MacPhee."

"Well, Mrs. Parnell, I've been leaving the TV on to discourage burglars. Perhaps that is what you heard. Unless, of course, it is, as I suggested before, certain musical numbers you choose to play which have distinctive…um, feline tones to them."

Mrs. Parnell didn't rise to the bait this time. Perhaps because a long, low cat yowl drifted from behind the door, accompanied by some scratching.

"Are you in the habit of keeping your television by the doorway, Ms. MacPhee? No, don't bother to make up some pathetic premise to explain that sound. But allow me to remind you that this is a building with a policy that pets will not be allowed to disturb tenants. You have agreed to that in your lease, which, correct me if I'm wrong, is a legal document." She banged her walker as she spat out the last two words. "And somehow I doubt that the sound of cats yowling and scratching will be an effective deterrent to burglars." With her distinctive, pointed chin held high, she teetered back into her apartment, showing a lot more dignity than I did.

I managed to open the door and slip in before any cats flew into the corridor, confirming my guilt. Then they were all over me, rubbing and yarling and jumping on the furniture to get a little closer. I went straight to the kitchen, opened the last few tins of Meow Mix and scooped it into their dishes. They dived, whooshed and, in the case of the little three-coloured one, waddled to the dishes.

That gave me a breather to soak in a very deep, very hot apricot-scented bubble bath. After their dinner, they more or less ignored me, which was fine with all of us. Except the calico, who decided to join me in the bathroom. She swayed in, took a long look at the tub and somehow managed to fly through the air and land just on the edge, where she promenaded back and forth, her belly swaying. She took the opportunity from time to time to swipe at the bubbles and give me long, meaningful looks.

"Don't look at me like that," I told her.

I ditched the teal suit in favour of a casual aqua cotton knit top and skirt Donalda had given me for my birthday. Of course, I had to lift the calico cat off and give the top a shake before I could put it on.

"You're eating too much, you weigh a ton. Get any bigger and you'll need your own apartment. Not that it's such a bad idea."

She just settled down on my bedspread and purred at me.

I finished off my look, if you can call it that, by yanking a comb through my hair and slashing on a bit of pinkish lipstick. Just enough to keep the family off my back about my appearance.

I picked up the bag from the joke shop and I was ready to go. The little three-coloured cat rubbed against my ankles, purring. The others were dozing on the newspaper, snoozing on my teal jacket and lounging on my pillow.

* * *

"Stan," I said, with a shark-like smile, "wonderful to see you."

He shot a little glance of surprise at my unfamiliar good mood.

"Good evening, Camilla."

As I slid into the passenger's seat of the LeSabre, clutching the bag from the joke shop, I neglected to check for strange bulges on the seat. Too late. Rude noises from the Whoopee Cushion filled the car. Tears of joy filled Stan's eyes.

"Your diet, Camilla," he said, chortling, "you've got to do something about your diet."

I just sat there, thinking, I'll give you something to chortle about, Stan.

"Your sisters," Stan said, when he managed to get a grip on himself, "your sisters are very, very concerned about you. You're never in your office. You're never at home. You're cranky and distracted. They're going to want to talk to you about it. Please try to be mature and understanding," said Stan, as we drove south to Nepean.

Mature and understanding? Fine words from Mr. Whoopee Cushion, I thought.

"Sure," I said, "just watch me."

The highlight of the evening was Edwina's reaction when she saw the fake cigarette burn on her newly upholstered sofa. The package directions instructed: Place the cigarette burn on the table or other places and watch the fun. Great joke at a party. The package directions did not lie. Stan's the only smoker, and he picked up a few bruises before Edwina caught on to the joke. Let's just say, there was a chill in the air for the rest of the evening. Even the rubber chocolates I seeded in the candy dish weren't quite such a hit afterwards.

*   *   *

Stan drove me home and waited while I opened the main door to the foyer. I was still smiling to myself over the way dinner had gone.

Stan seemed a bit aloof, even if he did his duty and made sure I got into the building safely.

"Don't worry about it, Stan. Your bruises will fade. And nothing much can happen to me here."

A look of what seemed like regret flicked over his face.

I was humming as I walked down the corridor to my apartment. Until I saw the cats in the hallway.

The door was open. Just an inch or two. But enough. I scooped up the black one and the ginger tom and tossed them through the door. How the hell did they get the door open? I hoped it hadn't been opened by the Super, following a complaint from you know who.

I tossed the two cats through the door and went back for the white one with the black paws and the grey Persian, who showed remarkable energy in escaping from me. Once I had captured them, I looked around. No more cats in the hallway. The three-coloured one and the tabby must be still inside, I decided. Unless. Unless they had oozed into someone else's apartment or gotten on an elevator.

The calico was snoozing on the sofa. It was only when I got to the bedroom that I spotted the tabby lying on the pillow, her neck at a strange angle.

No, it can't be, I told myself, edging closer, heart thudding. But it was.

The tabby was dead. Still warm but dead, her neck snapped. A note was attached to her collar.

"Butt out," it said.

My hands shook as I picked up the phone to call the police. McCracken was off duty. I dug around in my suit skirt pocket for the number he'd given me.

McCracken's phone rang ten times before he picked it up. It gave me time to watch my hands shake and to feel the pulse in my ears. Someone had violated my apartment. Entered my space and contaminated it. Killed a defenceless, trusting animal to make a vicious point. Now I had something else not to butt out about.

I was about to slam down the receiver when McCracken answered, breathless and hopeful.

"Sorry to let you down, Sergeant," I said, "but I think I'll take you up on your offer of help."

Fifteen minutes later he was sitting on the sofa, looking tense as a high wire.

"Sorry," he said, "they just make me nervous."

"You'd better be careful. You keep stiffening your neck like that, and you'll be at the chiropractor's tomorrow."

"Can't you do something with them?"

I looked at the five remaining cats. They didn't appear to be grief-stricken. The black one was leaning against McCracken's calf, I guess because the Persian had already captured his feet and seemed to be dozing on them. The ginger Tom was facing McCracken on the sofa, purring at him aggressively. As I watched, the white cat with the black paws made a leap for his lap. Meanwhile, on the back of the sofa, the little three-coloured one paraded back and forth, making sure the tip of her tail brushed the back of McCracken's neck every time she turned around.

The rich sound of purring resonated in the room.

"I'm sorry," I said, "nothing I can do. They're out of control."

"I think I'm about to go out of control myself," said McCracken.

"Maybe if you had a drink?"

"Yeah," he muttered, "that might help."

McCracken had earned his drink. He'd already checked under my bed and in my closets and shower, where a murderer might hide. I didn't have the heart to tell him I'd already checked for murderers. But I appreciated the attempt.

"So," I said, after handing him a double dose of scotch.

I had one myself.

McCracken was sipping his scotch with a small smile on his face, showing no sign of wanting to pursue the required conversation.

"So," I said. Firmly, this time.

McCracken looked up from the scotch and gave me his full attention.

"I don't know what to tell you," he said. "My guess is that you stirred up a certain amount of trouble when you started nosing around in the whole mess."

"Thanks for the advice."

"That's not advice. The advice is, stop looking for trouble and let the police handle the investigation."

"Well, I can't do that, can I? Since the whole reason I'm investigating is to clear my friend's name and the police seem determined to arrest her."

He cleared his throat.

"We are pursuing other inquiries now. There's a lot of forensic evidence from the crime scene that should soon be available. That'll speed things up. Get some action."

Neither one of us believed him. I would have felt a bit sorry for him if he hadn't let Robin get dragged in to the station.

"We have some action," I said, pointing to the small corpse covered with my plaid wool winter scarf. "We have a dead cat. Now I know dead cats don't make The National the way Mitzi did, but whoever did this thought he was delivering a powerful message."

"Or she," he said. "These are modern times."

Or she?

I thought about this for a minute while McCracken polished off his scotch.

"Anyway," he said, breaking into my thoughts, "we've

145

disturbed a crime scene here. You'd better spend the night somewhere else, and I'll get a team in here tomorrow."

"I'm sure they'll be thrilled to investigate the murder of a cat."

"That's why I'm not calling them out tonight. Still, it's pretty obviously related to the Brochu murder, so we've got no choice."

"I'll stay here."

"I think the scene's been disturbed enough by both of us. It's better if you don't. Besides, you should get that door fixed. Do you want to sleep in an apartment where the front door's been kicked in?"

Normally I would spend the night with Robin in an emergency, but I couldn't face telling her about the cat. Edwina and Donalda would drive me crazy lecturing. That left Merv, who was as bad as Edwina and Donalda. And Alexa.

What the hell, I couldn't keep them apart forever.

*   *   *

Half an hour later we pulled into the driveway at Alexa's place. McCracken was still tense. Maybe it was because we were headed for Alexa's. Maybe it was because there were five cats prowling and howling in his car.

"Well, we're here," I said unnecessarily, since we were stopped in Alexa's driveway. "You'd better stay with them while I check that she's ready for them."

"Don't be long," he whispered.

"Who is it?" Alexa asked from behind her door.

"It's your sister who called you and said she was coming right over. Remember?"

"Yes, I remember," she hissed, as she opened the door.

146

"And I'll thank you to remember if you're asking to spend the night at my house with your five cats, that you can at least be civil to me."

"They're not my cats. And I'm sorry, you're right. I'm just tense and bitchy because a murder was committed in my home."

Alexa gasped. "A murder!"

"Yes. The tabby. The reason I'm here."

"Oh, the cat. Really, you scared me. I thought you were talking something serious. A person. Not a cat." She pulled her silk housecoat a bit tighter.

"Well, it was serious to me. I found the cat murdered on my own pillow."

"I'm sorry. But I didn't even know this cat."

I heard my voice go up an octave. "That's not the point. The point is somebody killed the cat to give me a message. And the message was to stop investigating Mitzi Brochu's murder."

"Well, I hope you're going to. Leave that to the police," she said, peering down the driveway. "Who's that in the car?"

"McCracken. Where do you plan to put the cats? Somewhere special or is it okay for them to make themselves at home on the furniture?"

"Conn McCracken? Here?" I hate to say it, but her hands flew to her face. "I don't have any make-up on, and I'm in my bedclothes!"

"Well, it is bedtime. So where should he put the cats?"

"He can't come up here. Not while I look like this. God, I haven't seen him for twenty-five years. I want to be prepared."

"Okay. But where will the cats go?"

"I don't care where the cats go. You just make sure that he doesn't come up here when I'm like this. Understand?"

Years of being a mom had given Alexa the training she

needed to talk tough when necessary.

"Right," I said.

Back at the car, I told McCracken, "Hand me those cats, two at a time please, and I'll put them in the house."

With some difficulty, he managed to pass the ginger Tom and the black one through the window. "Doesn't she want to…" he said.

"I'll be back in a tick," I told him.

I tossed the felines into the laundry room and jogged back for the next two.

"Wait a minute," McCracken whispered as I picked up the grey persian and the white-and-black.

"Hold your horses," I said to him, "till I get them all put away."

"For heaven's sake," Alexa said, as I rushed by her on my way to the laundry room. "Why is he still sitting out there? I look a mess." She stared at herself in the gilt-edged hall mirror.

I don't know what she saw looking back at herself, because her sigh indicated some sort of desperation. I saw a woman, tall, blonde, elegant, wearing a three hundred dollar silk housecoat and still finding something to sigh about.

"One more trip."

"Don't let him in here!"

When I took the last cat from McCracken, I asked him to pass me my overnight bag. And my camera case.

"I can take it in for you."

"Not tonight, Conn. You don't want her to see you looking like that."

"See me looking like what?"

"Covered in cat hair. And if you'll pardon my saying so, smelling like a distillery. Another time would be better."

It seemed to me Conn McCracken had a distinct slump as

he backed out of Alexa's driveway. I'm not sure if she got a real good look as she peered from behind the curtain.

*   *   *

Alexa still likes playing Mom. That meant at seven o'clock the next morning, I came face to face with two eggs, perfectly poached, bacon, crisp and fragrant and whole wheat toast, with a choice of marmalade or jam in little crystal bowls.

Alexa was bustling around in an off-white silk blouse with a pair of taupe twill pants.

"Anything else I can get for you?"

I wasn't sure how I would get through what was already there.

Alexa arrived at the table with a steaming pot of fresh coffee. Up close I could see she had on her pearl earrings, a nice light make-up, a smile and distinct traces of cat hair around the ankles.

"So," she said, sliding into a chair and smiling at me, "do you think he'll come back and pick you up?"

I shook my head. "I don't imagine he ever wants to see me again."

The smile dipped, but Alexa is a trooper. "I hope you'll spend a couple of days here, at least until the police are through with your apartment. I don't know how you can even consider going back there."

"It may not be much, but it's home," I said. "But I would appreciate you taking care of the cats until the new locks are on."

I thought I heard a meowing sound from behind the laundry room door.

"Oh sure," said Alexa. But I could tell her day was already

ruined, whether from the absence of McCracken or the presence of the cats was hard to tell. "So," she added, "I guess you won't be talking to him."

"Why don't you call him yourself?" I said, breaking down. "I have his number. I think he'd be very pleased if you did."

"I can't throw myself at him!"

I gave up at that point. Twenty minutes later, I was on my way out with the camera case slung over my shoulder.

"Are you taking up photography again?" Alexa asked.

"Just temporarily."

"That's good. It used to drive us all crazy you snapping pictures every two minutes and catching people with their mouth full. I guess that was before..." She stopped.

"Before Paul died" is what she stopped herself from saying. Back when I was playful and frisky and had a life. I'd put away my Nikon and lenses after he died. But now was a good time to dust them off again.

Alexa dropped me off at my building to pick up the car. I didn't even go upstairs to change. No time to spare. I spun my wheels out of the garage and made tracks toward my quarry. Starting with the early birds.

I clicked the zoom lens and waited for Deb Goodhouse to emerge from her fashionable brick townhouse along the canal, in the part of town real estate people call the Golden Triangle. She took the time to check the front garden, for signs of new life I suppose, and never glanced my way. She looked good for that time of the day. A little red cropped blazer and a long navy skirt. I could see her red lipstick from the car. On the other hand, I was blending into the scenery. She didn't see me snap a very good series of shots of her.

From there, I drove out along the Parkway and crossed over the Champlain Bridge to the Chateau Cartier Sheraton on the Quebec side. I hung around the parking lot waiting for Jo Quinlan to show up for her workout. It took half an hour before the silver Toyota Supra pulled in and parked three cars away from me. Jo didn't pay any attention to the drab little blue Mazda and its occupant and she didn't hear the shutter clicking.

So much for the early risers. My next stop was the Queen Elizabeth Driveway. I parked where I couldn't be seen from the windows of Rudy Wendtz's big place, but close enough to spot the great man coming or going. I made a point of checking around for signs of the local constabulary. But wherever McCracken was this morning, he wasn't there.

I got to hear a bit of *This Morning* on the radio while I waited. In the middle of the third interview, Wendtz emerged from the door, looked around and gave me an opportunity to zoom in on his nasty face with the three day growth of beard and the black ice eyes.

I put the camera down and opened the city map over it to plan my route for the next stop.

The knock on the window made me hit my head on the roof. Something that would leave a dent. Large-and-Lumpy leaned in when I opened the window.

"Shouldn't be here," he said.

I knew what he meant.

"Mr. Wendtz won't like it."

"I thought we were friends. Don't feel you have to tell him."

He smiled, displaying the few teeth he had. "Take a hint," he said as he lumbered back toward the huge house.

I crossed my fingers and prayed he couldn't see what I was doing as I slipped the camera out from under the map and got a couple of nice clean shots of my buddy.

Everything was going my way. The last of the targets, Sammy Dash, showed up at his favourite market café just as I finished a tricky bit of parallel parking in front of it. I was sweating when he stalked past the Mazda.

Click. Click. I enjoyed doing this. Stalking the stalker. He looked around to see if anyone was watching, then scratched his bum. I captured the moment for posterity. And a few other moments, too. Sammy lighting up. Sammy giving passing women the once over. I felt quite at ease. It's amazing how invisible you are in a middle-aged blue Mazda, when the world wants to look at Porsches.

I was glad I was so invisible when I saw who Sammy's date was. Brooke Findlay, in an outfit that showed a lot of leg, moved up next to him, smiling and allowing her bottom to be stroked in a way that indicated they'd met before.

I was smiling too, as I lifted the camera.

Twelve

Thank God," said Alvin when I trooped into the office, after lunching on a very dangerous pair of burritos. "I thought you might be dead or something when you didn't show up for such a long time."

He was working on a guilt-inducing look. You've hurt me and I don't expect to ever get over it, his body language said. I'd seen Mrs. Findlay pull the same routine on Robin more than once. No doubt Alvin had picked up the technique from his own mother. It was one of many things I'd missed out on.

"Who the hell are you to talk? You vanished for days without any word at all." The burritos put a little extra venom into my words.

"That's different," he said, with his long, pointed nose in the air. "You gave me assignments, which, might I add, I completed in record time. I can't be in two places at once. And anyway, don't you want to know what I found out?"

I did.

His almond-shaped black eyes glittered as he filled me in.

"So you can imagine," he said, "what kind of career Brooke Findlay would have had, if Mitzi had gone ahead and printed her piece on the 'Walk in the Woods' woman as a serious cokehead."

A serious cocaine user. That explained something about Brooke's behaviour. And her choice of friends.

"'The Walk in the Woods' people would yank little Brookie's contract in a nanosecond. Adios fame and fortune." Alvin's pixie smile twinkled.

"And Mitzi knew it."

"You bet. And enjoyed knowing it, from what I hear. She was so pissed off about Brooke and Rudy Wendtz, she would have done anything."

"So Brooke had a real motive," I said.

"So did Wendtz."

And Robin, I thought, as I tried to concentrate later, how much had she known about all this? At least it was beginning to make sense. If Robin had any suspicion that Brooke was involved, there was nothing she wouldn't do to draw attention away from it. Complete collapse, for instance. "I saw nothing," she'd told me. And told the police. It was probably true enough as far as it went. But what did Robin think had happened in Mitzi's room?

Alvin seemed to take a certain pleasure in reminding me of outstanding chores.

"A lot of people are hot on your trail," he said, waving stacks of little yellow messages in my face.

He was right. It was imperative that I call my contacts at the Department of Justice, at two separate provincial offices and at the City. Funding depended on it.

"Some of those people are getting impatient."

"What have you been telling them?"

"I've been telling them the truth, that I have no idea where you are or if or when you're coming back. And I've been offering to take messages."

"Offering to take messages? Well, well. That is a distinct service improvement. But may I suggest that you varnish the truth somewhat when dealing with real and potential funders and supporters of Justice for Victims. Tell them something compelling, that I'm in conference, that I'm at meetings, that I'm out of town on business. Use your imagination."

"Fine," he sniffed.

"And, while I return my stack of phone calls, can you slip over to the Rideau Centre and get a film developed? And get some cat treats from the pet shop." I fished out a fifty dollar bill from my secret money stash, in the Miscellaneous file. I reminded myself to hit the ATM for a bit more cash, and to find a new spot for the secret stash, since Alvin seemed to file just about everything under Miscellaneous.

"The Rideau Centre? Now? Can't it wait until I'm on my way home?"

"No, it cannot. But here, let me get a shot of you to make it worth your while."

I snapped it, hoping he hadn't had time to replace the look of petulance with one of supreme nonchalance before the camera caught it.

None of the real or potential funders were at their desks when I called back. I left messages. At least the ball was in their court.

I tried to return Merv's call, but he hissed into the phone that he couldn't talk just at that moment.

Ted Beamish just wanted to catch up on the news about Robin.

"Not much change," I told him, "except someone killed one of her cats."

He listened without interruption as I explained about the tabby's demise.

"Don't tell her," he said. "Wait till it's all over and I'll help you."

"Thanks," I said, thinking he was not too bad.

"How did you manage to sleep there last night, after that?"

"I didn't. I spent the night at my sister's." I felt, somehow, that this was a declaration of extreme cowardice.

"Good," he said. "That was sensible. Let me know if you want me to go over there with you when you go back. I could hang around until you feel comfortable again."

Seemed like a good idea to me.

Richard Sandes had left three messages. But I saved his call to the very end. After the locksmith. After the Mary Kay lady. When I got up the nerve to return it, I checked myself in the little mirror Alvin had installed on the desk. It didn't cheer me up.

What do you care, I told myself, it's not like he can see you or anything. Even so, I combed my hair and slapped on a little lipstick. There was nothing to be done about the sweater and skirt, now on their second day.

But it didn't matter, because he wasn't in his office.

I slumped in Alvin's chair and gave myself a lecture. Richard Sandes had a wife. And he was waiting for her to get better, to come back. Anything else was just a filler.

You don't want to get into a relationship with that kind of possible outcome, I said to myself. You're just getting over the worst thing that could ever happen to anyone. Don't ask for trouble.

Of course, a civilized little drink every now and then couldn't hurt. As long as I kept it to that.

I was arguing with myself about the dangers of a civilized little drink, when Alvin flung himself into the room.

"Boy," he said, "someone should tell these people about the notion of service. They keep you waiting, they have hidden charges, they're surly and snotty."

"Why don't you open up a training school?"

"Maybe I'll do that," he said. "Just maybe."

While he pondered the vast career potential in Alvin's School of Customer Service, I dug through the photos, smiling to myself. I dropped the cat treats into my purse. Then I held out my hand for the change.

Alvin was just grumbling and digging for it, when the phone rang.

Richard.

"I feel like I still owe you an apology," he said.

"You don't. However, if you feel like grovelling, why not do it over a civilized little drink?"

We settled on seven, in the bar at the Harmony. With hints of dinner to follow.

I hung up and looked over at Alvin, who was immersed in some very important work at the back of the office.

"Alvin," I said, "don't let the smile on my face lead you to believe that I've forgotten the change."

*   *   *

"So, Mrs. Parnell, let's see if I understand. The police came. And you didn't let them in."

It was after work and we were seated in Mrs. Parnell's living room. But where were the doilies, the knickknacks, the dozens of family photos? Where were the cushions and the afghans? Mrs. Parnell's living room did not conform to known standards for little old ladies living alone in apartments. For one thing, the furniture consisted of a caramel leather sofa, a matching easy chair and ottoman and a massive glass coffee table. A small glass table by the side held Mrs. Parnell's coffee cup and a hardcover book by Doris Lessing.

A serious sound system dominated the room. Records,

compact-discs and cassettes filled the shelves. A modern metal sculpture was the only decoration. Unless you counted the three sets of hand-weights in jelly-bean colours. Three, four and five pounds, as far as I could tell. A pair of leg weights in matching lilac lay next to them.

The dining area was set up with a computer and printer, one chair, and a double bookcase, jammed with volumes. That left just enough room for the cage containing the peach-faced love birds.

I would have preferred the room to be more traditional. I was nervous enough sitting here with Mrs. Parnell. If I'd been wearing a tie, I'd have loosened it.

Mrs. Parnell considered my question about the police as she popped another cigarette into the holder.

"Well, I'm not sure they were the police. They seemed to be saying that they were, but anyone could say that, couldn't they?"

"That's right."

"One of them looked too much like a rodent for my liking, so I decided against opening the door."

Mombourquette.

"A good move, Mrs. Parnell." I sipped my Harvey's Bristol Cream and beamed at her. "So one of them looked like a rodent. By any chance did the other one look more like a middle-aged Labrador Retriever with a bit of a weight problem?"

"Just the ratty one was there. With a skinny young fellow, reminded me of a Blue Heron. I didn't see the Lab," she said before taking a healthy swig.

"Mrs. Parnell…"

"But I think I saw you last night leaving with someone who looked a bit like a Saint Bernard, carrying cats which looked exactly like cats. And I do have to tell you, young lady, that

158

you will have to do something about those noisy beasts."

Behind her, a bird peeped in agreement.

"What about birds?"

"If you mean Lester and Pierre," she said, nodding towards the cage with purse-lipped satisfaction, "birds, Ms. MacPhee, don't disturb anyone."

"I don't know, Mrs. Parnell, that persistent chirping gives me migraines."

"Very funny, but don't try to change the subject. I knew those cats were there. And now look what's happened. The police are asking about it. I didn't like to turn you in, but I won't be able to hold out forever."

I looked at her with astonishment. "But, Mrs. Parnell, the police don't care about cats in the apartment. That's a civil matter."

"Not too civil if you ask me," she said, with a glance at the love birds.

"I mean, not criminal. You see…"

"Depends on your point of view," she sniffed.

"Mrs. Parnell, one of those cats was murdered last night. To my knowledge, the occasional loud meow doesn't merit the death penalty in this country." I leaned forward with fire in my eyes. Perhaps it was the Bristol Cream taking effect.

"Murdered!"

"That's right, its neck was broken," I snapped my fingers.

"Dear me," she said. "It's the disintegration of society."

"I don't really see it as the disinteg…"

"How shocking for you. Goodness, you need that drink topped up." She was spry enough to hop up and get the Harvey's bottle. She filled her own glass to the brim right after mine. "So what are you going to do with the other three, now that this one's dead?"

"The other five."

"Five! I only spotted three, I must be losing it." She polished off half the glass. "Oh well. May as well be hanged for a sheep as a lamb."

"Mrs. Parnell, this is a serious business. I need your help. From time to time you may accidentally see something from the peephole in your door." That was the kindest way I could think of to mention that Mrs. Parnell's eyes were rarely far from that peephole. "When you're checking up on suspicious noises." I didn't want to alienate her by adding that she was the nosiest woman I'd ever encountered.

She nodded at me and leaned forward. This Bristol Cream is the secret to promoting neighbourliness, I thought. I dug out the package of photos from my purse.

"Did you see any of these people going into my apartment last night?"

She kept nodding as I showed her each one of them. We went through them twice.

My heart banged a bit when she pointed to my new friend, Large-and-Lumpy.

"Are you sure?" I asked, hoping she wasn't.

"Pretty distinctive, don't you think? Looks like a bear. I thought at the time he must have been a boxer or something. He didn't seem to be your type, but..." she shrugged her shoulders, "who can tell these days."

I was clutching my sherry glass so hard the crystal pattern dug into my palms. Large-and-Lumpy, not my oldest buddy, but I'd felt a rapport with him, and now, to find out he'd been in my apartment the night the tabby was killed. On Wendtz's orders, I was sure. It told me something I wanted to know: Wendtz was implicated, despite his alibi, and he didn't want me digging around in Mitzi's activities. It told me something

I didn't want to know, as well. Large-and-Lumpy would do anything he was directed to by Wendtz. Frightening me. Killing a cat. I swallowed the rest of the Bristol Cream and thought the next logical thought: Would he also have killed Mitzi on Wendtz's orders? Did Large-and-Lumpy have an alibi for the time of Mitzi's death?

Mrs. Parnell poured another healthy dose into my glass and added a discreet amount to her own.

"Well," she said. "Well, well, well. Isn't this exciting?"

Exciting wasn't the word I was searching for.

"That explains, I suppose, that man who was working on your door today. And that the Super was up too. Good thing you and the Saint Bernard took the cats away last night."

Two and three-quarters glasses of sherry were enough to make my head spin, and I still had to drop in to see Richard for a civilized little drink. Mrs. Parnell was good enough to call the Super to bring up my new keys. She must have a way with him. I've never gotten action that fast.

While we waited, I took a couple of shots of her peach-faced love birds for her. And got a nice one of her standing next to the cage.

"The police said something about cats, Mrs. Parnell," said the Super as Mrs. P. opened the door and whisked the keys from his sweaty little hand.

"I think they said bats," she told him. "The burglars were out of there like bats out of hell."

I waved to him from the sofa.

As I staggered across the hallway to my empty apartment, I turned and asked her, "Promise me, Mrs. Parnell, that you'll let me know if anyone comes to my apartment in the next few days. Here's my office number. Thanks for the drinks. And for keeping my secret."

"My pleasure," she said, with what might have been the beginnings of a smile.

* * *

A bath, a nap, a change of clothes and the intervening three hours weren't enough to get me back to normal before I hit the Harmony. It had been a busy and distracting day even before the sherry.

It was the first warm evening of the season, and a frisky breeze ruffled my hair. Climbing out of the cab, I smoothed my deep green jersey dress and gave it a little tug. I wasn't used to having things end above my knees, and I wasn't sure what I had been thinking of when I bought it.

I was steady enough on the high heels though, plus I had clean hair, face and teeth and, best of all, I was fifteen minutes early. I also had my camera and plenty of film.

I recognized Naomi by her big hair and chirpy voice. She was working with Brad, who had lots of teeth set on perma-smile.

"Hmmm," chirped Naomi, "no, I've never seen him." She pointed to Large-and-Lumpy in the photo and gave a little shiver, "how could you forget someone like that?" She took a look at Rudy Wendtz's brooding expression. "Oh yes, he was here often when Miss Brochu was in town, wasn't he, Brad?"

"Sure was," said Brad. "Remember the night of the big fight? When we had to call in security?"

"Who could forget it?" Naomi rolled her eyes.

"And this one, too. I've seen him before." She pointed to Sammy Dash. "I think he used to accompany Miss Brochu, too. Kinda cute, isn't he?"

"These two women look familiar," said Brad. I put it down

to an attempt to change the subject. "I've seen them both before, but I'm not sure where."

"One of them does the news and the other's a politician, I think," Naomi added. "But the one who does the news, she was here the day of the murder, I remember her with a camera crew and everything. But I think she might have been in earlier too."

"Can you remember when?"

"Sorry," said Naomi.

"But she's been here all right," said Brad, not to be outdone. "Who could forget a face like that?" He pointed to Brooke.

"Big deal, she didn't look that great the day she was here." Naomi was prepared to sulk a bit.

"Upset, maybe. But still beautiful."

"When was that? Do either of you remember?"

Naomi shrugged.

"Well, this is the first day I've been back from my holidays," said Brad, "so it must have been just before I left. That would be the twelfth of May."

May twelfth, the day before Mitzi's murder.

"Who cares?" said Naomi.

"Great," I said, ignoring her and focusing on him, "any idea what she was doing here?"

They both shook their heads.

"She came in looking like a million dollars and headed straight for the elevator. She knew where she was going, all right," said Brad.

"And she came out again, a bit later, looking real upset. I think she'd been crying. Her mascara was running." Naomi offered the comment with some satisfaction.

Okay, Brooke. Gotcha now.

I tucked myself behind a pillar, snapped on the zoom, bagging a good shot of Brad and Naomi still arguing about Brooke. For good luck, I caught the bell captain and two bell boys.

Then I sashayed into the bar to meet Richard, right on time. "Smile for the birdie," I said, getting a nice image of him telling the waiter to give me special treatment.

* * *

I arrived at Alexa's place that evening with a grin on my face and what was left of my Catholic conscience locked in the basement of my mind.

Alexa opened the door the second Richard's car drove into the driveway, eliminating any mushy stuff. Just as well. After all, it had just been a civilized drink followed by dinner.

As I walked through the door, I sniffed L'air du Temps. I turned to wave good-bye to Richard.

Alexa was wearing very subtle yet effective make-up, creating a dewy, youthful appearance. An appearance bolstered by her soft, cream cowl-necked angora sweater and black pants with little patent flats. A very nice effect, but wasted on me at eleven in the evening.

"Is that him?" she whispered, watching the car pull out of the driveway.

"It's a different him."

"Oh. So who is he?"

"A friend."

"How nice," she said, sinking into a chair in the living room.

I could tell she wanted to talk, but I had to make a stop in the laundry room. I was feeling guilty about the cats. Maybe I could buy my way back into their favour with the cat treats.

"It's very hard to keep them in the laundry room," Alexa pointed out as she came up behind me. "They seem to want to get out and sit on the furniture."

"I think I can understand that."

"Yes, well," she said, "they're staying in."

Ten eyes glowed with reproach when I opened the door. It would take a hell of a lot of cat treats to get back in their good graces.

I closed the door and faced Alexa, who was slumping against the wall.

"I'm sorry. I still think you should just give him a call. Save yourself all this stressful self-torment. I've got to go to bed now. Big day tomorrow."

When I snapped her picture from the top of the stairs, she was sitting in the living room with the lights off. Mooning over McCracken.

Go figure.

Thirteen

C'mon, Alvin, you can do it." He looked across the desk at me, arms crossed, mouth a tight little knot, ponytail in full droop.

"Oh sure," he said, "get me to do all the real scruffy stuff that you don't have the taste for. Other Duties As Required. Give it to Alvin. The underclass."

"That's not true. I very much want to go to the Harmony and prowl around the delivery entrances and the back hallways. But I can't. The manager there knows me, and he told me he'd call the police in a flash if he caught me snooping."

Alvin had no way of knowing what Richard had said over dinner the previous night. But I remembered it well.

Be careful had been the underlying theme.

"I just want the name of the 8th Floor maid, Richard."

"Okay, here it is. But…"

"Thanks," I said, leaning over and looking at the card with the name Maria Rodriguez written on it. I had to touch his hand to pick up the card.

He was still talking.

"…this is a dangerous situation. Someone knows where you live, knows you have been investigating and wants you to stop. Dead cat, remember?"

"I remember. How would I forget?" It was hard to concentrate with his hand touching mine like that. Hard to keep my mind on our civilized little drink and dinner. And his civilized little warning.

"When does she come on duty?"

"She stopped working here, right after the murder. A lot of these refugees went through some pretty gruesome times in their own country. They want to feel safe in Canada."

"Where does she live?"

"The address is there, for all the good it will do you. This woman only had a couple of words of English. But, listen, why not give it to the police and suggest that they interview her? They'll find a translator from the community. One of these rocks you turn over in your investigation is going to have something pretty ugly under it."

"You're right," I'd said, smiling into those chocolate eyes and picking up the card with my free hand. "Why buy trouble?"

So Alvin, not I, would be nosing through the back halls of the Harmony with an armful of photos, trying to pin down just who might have been sneaking in the back way to see Mitzi Brochu before her death. For his own protection, I sent him over to the Rideau Centre to get the roll of film with Richard's picture developed.

"Alvin," I said, by way of convincing him of the wisdom of the Harmony mission, "the way I see it, we're partners, each with our own role to play in solving this gruesome crime. You've brought me a lot of useful information."

"Yeah well, I…"

But I'd had enough of Alvin's stalling at this point. "Time to hit the road. A rolling stone gathers no moss and all that. We need those photos ASAP. Now get going, partner."

"But Camilla…"

"Look, my day started with my sister sulking at me over the

corn flakes. Then things got a bit more exciting when I transported five, count 'em five, cats in boxes back to my apartment in the world's most anti-cat building. Now, here I am, it's nearly noon. I have to be on the alert for the beautiful suspect and now, instead of being a cooperative partner, you're getting your back up."

"Fine," he snapped, "wait for it then, partner."

He was out the door before I could clarify just what it was I would be waiting for.

I put in another call to Merv, who also has a tendency to sulk for unexplained reasons.

"Try the city police. I can't dig up a lot of information without people starting to notice."

"It's a situation I understand well, Merv, but I don't want you to dig up information on a lot of people, just one. Just one person, and I have his picture. And I would rather avoid talking to the city police since they don't seem to take me seriously."

There was silence on the line. I shook the phone. "After all, it's for Robin, in case you're forgetting, Merv."

"Yeah, all right. One picture. Drop it by. At the desk. Don't come in. You'll just give people ideas."

"Thank you, Merv." I stopped short of slathering him with all that partner bullshit.

My last call was to set up a meeting with my old friend, Elaine Ekstein. Elaine was hard at work setting up a support network for refugee women. She was glad to talk to me.

"Sure," she said, "I'll find her for you. She's probably scared to death. Especially if she's a new arrival and she doesn't speak much English. I'll translate for you."

I just had time to hop into the car and hightail it back to Elmvale Acres. My little visit with Robin confirmed what I'd hoped. Brooke was still home, but preparing to go out. Her mother was parked in front of the television watching *Days of Our Lives* and steaming Brooke's going-out outfit. She didn't even glance over when I snapped a picture of her.

"Be careful," Brooke called down, "it's new and it's linen. I don't want anything to happen to it, Ma."

"My God," said Ma, "can you believe Marlena would let him do that?"

Mr. Findlay followed me up the stairs with fresh sandwiches, chicken on brown bread, cut in little triangles and some lemon custard for dessert. Hot tea, too. That man knew how to put a tray together.

"Say cheese," I said, capturing the moment on film.

He grinned. "Just like old times, you and that camera."

From the sounds of preparations and shouted instructions, Brooke was quite a way from take-off. I could enjoy my lunch and try to get Robin to enjoy hers as well.

"Don't even think about taking my picture," Robin said.

I knew she meant it.

"How are the pussies?" she asked as we settled in with our little sandwiches and tea.

"Great! They miss you! But they seem to be enjoying life."

Robin put down her tea cup and stared at me.

My God, I thought, could she tell what had happened to the tabby just by looking at me? Did the words DEAD CAT appear on my forehead?

"They communicate with you?"

"No, but they…purr. And then every now and then they get a faraway look in their little green eyes, and I know they're thinking about you and about how they want you to get well and go home and be with them again." I folded my hands in my lap.

Until I noticed that tears were streaming down Robin's

169

cheeks. She also appeared to have stopped breathing.

"My God, I'm sorry, I'm only trying to…"

"Hahahahahah." At least she was alive.

"Stop laughing, or I'll eat all the sandwiches. Then you'll be sorry."

"You can tell all that from their eyes? You should go on Oprah."

The door shot open and Brooke bellowed through: "Keep it down, will you, I'm trying to catch something on the radio."

Robin's laugh was cut off mid-whoop.

"Don't mind her. She can't help it. She's under a lot of career pressure lately."

Nothing like she's going to be, I thought as I ate my sandwiches.

When I left the Findlay house, still ahead of Brooke, I pulled away from the curb, rounded the corner and pulled in again. I had a few minutes to sit there and admire the trees leafing out in the warm weather.

I was fiddling with the car radio when Brooke drove by in her fire-engine-red BMW. I wasn't too worried about following her, not even when she checked her rear view mirror. She was far too self-absorbed to notice anyone else.

I drove along with a smile on my face, wondering where she'd be meeting Sammy Dash this time. And what they'd get up to.

It wasn't always easy trailing Brooke, since she showed a disinclination to signal lane changes or even turns. We wound along Alta Vista and down Pleasant Park to Riverside Drive, and then followed Riverside to Bank. Except for having to keep an eye on Brooke, it was a pleasant drive, water, lots of green space. Brooke turned right on Bank, drove to the Glebe and parked on Fourth Avenue.

I watched, slouched down in my car, as she headed for the ATM. I had to admit, she would make a first-rate representative for "Walk in the Woods". Her blonde hair just cleared her shoulders and fluttered in the breeze. The vanilla-coloured linen suit with its elegant wrinkles showed off Brooke's slim shape. The cut of the skirt above the knees confirmed my long-held suspicion that Brooke was eighty percent legs.

She smiled into the sunshine. Her public smile. A middle-aged man stopped walking and stared.

Too bad she's such a bitch, I thought. Some of my reaction may have been related to my short legs. Who knows.

I almost lost her as we edged onto Bank Street again. Brooke headed for the Queen Elizabeth Driveway, which winds along the canal on the opposite side to Colonel By.

It's amazing, I thought, this beautiful woman in her red Beamer is cruising along this beautiful road, and her activities are somehow tied to a murder.

I'd been keeping well behind her, and yet I still had to stand on my brakes to avoid her as she whipped, without a signal or a brake light, into Rudy Wendtz's driveway.

I pulled over to the side of the road and crouched down again.

Seconds later, Wendtz pulled in after her and parked his black Mercedes.

I don't suppose they see that many passionate clinches on Queen Elizabeth Driveway. But this one would have made up for any lack. Two tall people, pressed together, for all the world to see. Of course, the world wasn't looking. Only me.

They deserve each other, I told myself, glancing away towards the front door of the house. That's when I noticed Large-and-Lumpy watching back.

Elaine kept talking as she ran the red light. I just pressed myself to the back of the seat and tried to remember my Act of Contrition. The Jeep, which accelerated at the green light, missed us by an inch.

"You have no idea," she said, "how often these people faced death. And how that must feel."

"I think I do."

"It's very difficult for them to find themselves in such a different culture. They're frightened a lot."

"I don't want to frighten her, Elaine. I'm not very frightening, in case you haven't noticed."

Elaine took her eyes off the road.

"You believe that, don't you?"

"Well, yes, Elaine, I do."

She was still watching me, shaking her head.

"On the other hand, you, Elaine, are terrifying and should not be allowed on the road."

"Don't be silly," she said. "I'm serious. You can be quite intimidating for such a small person. You come on strong and, if you'll pardon me mentioning it, you can be quite ruthless."

"I'll pardon you mentioning it, if you'll make an effort to avoid getting us decapitated by that truck ahead."

A squeal of brakes followed.

"Don't exaggerate, the truck was a good foot away. And back to the topic. These people are sensitive and fearful. They don't need to be hassled by the police."

"May I remind you that I'm not the police, Elaine."

"I realize that. But if Maria has some information, then you may be forced to inform the police, and you know what stormtroopers they can be."

"I do, indeed."

"Maria was quite upset by the whole thing with Mitzi Brochu. I mean, she was so close to that dreadful murder. Can you imagine how traumatic that must have been?"

"Yes. I was there myself. So I know only too well."

"Well then, you understand that we don't want her to relive that trauma."

Elaine stood on her brakes as if to punctuate her point. We stopped for seconds at a red light and then screeched away the moment it turned green.

"Let me repeat, Elaine, that I only want to show her some photos and ask if she has ever seen these people near Mitzi's room. With particular reference to the day of the murder, when she was working right there on that floor."

We pulled off Scott Street onto Parkdale and Elaine stopped under a No Parking sign.

"Here we are," she said, opening her car door without looking. A passing driver swerved and turned back to shake his fist. Elaine didn't notice.

I got out on the passenger's side and considered mentioning that two wheels of the car were up on the sidewalk, but it didn't seem worth it.

* * *

Was it just the language barrier? Did she not understand the question Elaine had translated? Elaine and I watched Maria Rodriguez give an affirmative nod to almost every photo. Even the ones that didn't belong in the set of suspects. Like me, taken at a family dinner.

"You were there," Elaine commented.

We were sitting around the dinette set in the dining ell on one of the few bits of furniture in Maria Rodriguez's apartment. Even the sounds of her husband and children laughing at Bugs Bunny in the next room couldn't lift the tension in the air.

You could see it in Maria's black eyebrows and the lines around her mouth.

I'd seen it too in the stiff shoulders of both the Rodriguez adults and in the huge, dark eyes of their children. As Elaine said, these were people who'd already had enough trouble.

Maria studied the photos I'd spread out on the beige, formica-topped table. They were a mixture of business and pleasure, friends and family blended with my own crew of suspects.

Deb Goodhouse, Jo Quinlan, Rudy Wendtz, Brooke Findlay, Large-and-Lumpy, Sammy Dash all got the nod from Maria. So did Robin.

She didn't recognize the rest of my family. Only me.

Maria wasn't sure about Mrs. Parnell, but after some thought decided she hadn't seen Mrs. Parnell at the Harmony.

"Sorry," she said.

"It's no problem. I'm glad somebody wasn't there."

I wasn't sure how much it helped my investigation to have every suspect confirmed as a visitor to Mitzi Brochu's suite at the Harmony the day of the murder.

"You sure you saw all these people, Maria?"

Elaine shook her head at me. "You're pushing too hard."

I decided to lighten up a bit and pointed to a picture of the cats.

The cats got a clear no.

At least it let the three of us laugh.

*   *   *

"She recognized all six suspects," I said, accepting a refill. "So I have to ask myself, did she really recognize them or was she just unclear about the concept? And to think I risked Elaine's driving, and I still don't know whether Maria understood the questions or not."

Richard smiled and sipped his Sambuca.

"It is not amusing," I growled, before sipping my own.

The Sambuca was just the way I like it, with three coffee beans in the bottom of the snifter, still warm from being flamed. It took the edge off the growl.

"You know, I think I'd like to meet this Elaine."

"Good idea, I'll fix the two of you up for a Sunday drive sometime."

"All kidding aside, any danger you might have been facing from Elaine's driving is nothing compared to what you're exposing yourself to if you continue to stalk this killer."

"I can see you haven't been in a car with her."

"Listen to me. You're dealing with someone who crucified a woman. Talk to the police."

I was bathed in irritation. This was like lunch with my sisters.

"Sulk if you want. But I like you much better alive," he said.

I could feel his hand on mine as he spoke. I remembered his daughter. And his wife. I jerked my hand away.

"Or I could talk to the police myself. Tell them you have this interesting stuff and they might like to chat with you about it."

"You wouldn't."

He tapped my nose with his finger and smiled. I would have gotten up and stomped out of the bar at that point except my knees were wobbling.

And of course, I didn't have my car. I had to ask myself why

I managed never to have my car when I was with Richard, so he always had to drive me home. For that matter, why was I wearing a knit dress instead of my chunky suit? And lipstick, for heaven's sake.

We ended the evening by driving around before heading back to my place. Down Wellington Street and Sussex, past the glass sculpture that is the National Gallery and across the Interprovincial Bridge to Hull, admiring the lights shimmering on the green roofs of the Parliament buildings and the sensuous curves of the Museum of Civilization.

As we crossed back into Ottawa on the Portage Bridge and drove along the Parkway to my apartment, the river glistened in the surrounding blackness. When we stopped in front of my building, I felt disappointment that the civilized dinner and drink were over.

"Okay, I'll talk to the police. I'll show them the photos and suggest they might want to have a word with the subjects." After I've had a word with them, of course, I added to myself.

Richard squeezed my hand. "I love it when you're sensible."

"You do not."

"I do," he said, watching my mouth.

Usually I'm not even conscious of having a mouth. But at that moment, it seemed like the supreme erogenous zone. I was surprised he couldn't hear my pulse pounding.

I don't know how long we sat there like that, stopped in time.

Then I remembered his wife.

*   *   *

I couldn't sleep, and it wasn't just the cats lying on various parts of my body either. I lay staring around the room. The eggshell walls were stark in the moonlight. I tried to keep still, because when I didn't, whatever cat was disturbed by the movement dug its claws into whatever part of my body had moved. And I didn't feel like kicking cats off the bed. I was already too much of a bad guy.

So there wasn't much to do. I could think about Richard if I wanted and get up and take a cold shower. Or I could think about Mitzi's murder and get up and have a drink. Or I could think about dead cats.

For as long as I'd lived in the apartment with the eggshell walls, I'd thought about Paul when I couldn't sleep. I saved that time for him. Picking up each memory from my mental safety deposit box, touching it, admiring it, feeling it. Remembering the time we first met on campus with the leaves crunching under our feet, remembering sipping cheap wine and munching stale crackers in our first lumpy bed, laughing about crumbs, remembering...but memories of Paul, always so fresh and alive, playing like a new videotape in my head, no longer filled every space in my mind and no longer left their trail of pain. Why was that?

I stared at the walls. Maybe it was time to get a few pictures.

My thoughts drifted to Richard. Although they were not the kind of thoughts you share with other people, the images were real enough for me, and as disturbing as our last conversation in his car. Richard and me. Richard and his wife. There was no way to make it work out right.

Moonlight filled the room, lightening the walls and the bedclothes and me, lying there. The fat little calico cat snuggled into my side.

Maybe it was time to buy some curtains.

*   *   *

In the morning, I snapped awake, remembering the Benning brief still had to be dealt with. Traces of the moon still hung behind the sky, just to haunt me. Five cats were haunting me, too.

It was a world filled with flashing tails and accusing, pointed ears. Cats leapt from floor to counter and from counter to floor as I opened the Meow Mix. The calico rubbed herself against my legs.

"Watch it, you guys, I'm not sure I'm cut out for family life."

No one paid attention.

When I pushed my way through the office door an hour later, a man's shape became visible. I came close to dropping my coffee and muffin and then exhaled in relief. Who else did I know with a brushcut?

Merv. His leggy presence took up most of the available room. He was sitting in one visitor's chair with his feet up on the other one, sipping coffee from a jumbo styrofoam cup. An immense bouquet of flowers lay on my desk. Daisies, mums and ferns mixed in with lilies and statice.

Merv was not a happy man.

"I don't know how you can get anything done in here. It's like a closet."

I refrained from saying that it was even more so when Merv squeezed his six-foot-three frame into it.

But he wasn't done yet. He looked at me with the same critical gaze you might direct at a head of broccoli that's been in the fridge too long.

"Look at you," he said. "You look wrecked. Yuck, what's that on your suit?" He reached over and brushed off a patch of cat hair.

"What can I do for you, Merv?" I said, unwilling to get caught up in personal grooming issues.

Amazement, or something like it, washed across his face and settled in around the eyebrow area.

"What can you do for me? I love it. Little Miss Busybody sends me on half a dozen errands and then says…"

"Can it, Merv. Three things, that's all I asked you. And may I remind you that you did them for Robin's benefit, not mine."

The hard line of Merv's jaw always softens when you mention Robin.

"It's still what I can do for you. What I've done for you." He fished a paper out of his pocket. "It's the scoop on your new friend."

Large-and-Lumpy.

"Denzil Hickey. Let's see," said Merv, "long history of criminal lifestyle. Couple convictions. Armed robbery. Assault with a deadly weapon. They were a long time ago. Served a couple terms in maximum security. And that's not counting the charges they couldn't make stick. Stuff like intimidating witnesses, trafficking. Well-known to police here and in Toronto. They know he's still active. He's a goon for Rudy Wendtz. I imagine he picked up a few nasty tricks in Kingston Pen. I would not join his bridge club if I were you, Camilla."

"I love it when you use the subjunctive, Merv."

The back of Merv's chair reverberated as the door to the office hit it.

"Sorry I'm late," said Alvin, squeezing in past Merv. He edged around me and hung his best black leather jacket up on the oak coat rack, flicked his pony tail back over his shoulder, realigned his right row of earrings and sat himself down at the desk. He regarded the flowers and Merv with interest.

Merv looked back at him with astonishment. I looked at

both of them and thought I would rather be elsewhere. But Merv was pretty well blocking the exit.

"Merv, Alvin. Alvin, Merv." I hoped that would be all there was to it, but the looks on both of their faces indicated they would be making evaluative remarks about each other when the time was right.

Merv sipped his coffee.

I remembered my own cup and opened it. It was still hot enough to drink, and I felt I needed it.

Merv must have decided that the best way to deal with Alvin was to ignore him.

"So my point is, stay the hell away from this guy. We have reason to think he may be involved in the disappearances of several people. People who were of great interest to the Crown. In the sense that they were potential witnesses and in the sense that nobody knows anything about their whereabouts as we speak. In the sense that they are no longer among the living. Do I make myself clear?"

"As clear as you ever do, Merv."

It didn't seem to bother him.

"Took the day off," he said, unfolding out of the chair and making the room look even smaller. "Planning to visit Robin for a while."

Well, at least that explained the flowers.

"And don't forget what I said about that guy. He is vicious. Stop your meddling. Leave the investigation to the police."

"May I remind you, Merv, that when the investigation was left to the police, they focused on Robin."

"You won't be much good to her if you're dead," was Merv's parting shot.

I whipped my camera out of its case and captured a shot of Merv with his bouquet, for future blackmail.

"Delightful meeting you," said Alvin. The morning sun glinted off his cat's eye glasses.

But the glass in the door was already rattling from Merv's exit.

I had managed to catch Merv's bad mood and add it to my own, and therefore was glad Alvin was in the office. At least I could pick on him. I looked around at the piles of paper.

"For God's sake, don't you ever get any work done?"

Alvin looked up from his magazine in surprise. A hurt look settled on his bony face.

"What are you talking about? What about all the sleuthing I've been doing for you? Do you think you're going to find out who murdered Mitzi without my help?"

"Yes, I do. It's just a matter of time until I figure out what happened there. I know that Brooke Findlay's big ambition was to be the 'Walk in the Woods' woman. I know she has a fondness for nose candy. I know that she was Rudy Wendtz's part-time girlfriend, and I know Mitzi was jealous and planning to fix Brooke but good. And I know Mitzi and Wendtz had a huge fight the night before she died. I know that Wendtz employs someone who probably will kill on command. Yes. I think I can solve it while you're catching up on the filing. The other suspects look pretty unsuspicious next to Wendtz and Company."

"Fine," he sniffed, "then you won't be interested in knowing that Jo Quinlan and Sammy Dash were high school sweethearts, and even lived together for a while, back when Sammy was plain old Sammy Dashchuk."

We looked at each other.

"I think I'll keep any other information I might happen to have to myself," he added.

Half an hour later he was still at his desk, doing nothing as far as I could tell, his scrawny shoulders tense.

I found it hard to concentrate on the Benning brief with Alvin in the room, oozing resentment. I also suspected he was making paper airplanes instead of filing, but confirming that would have meant walking over and checking on him, admitting defeat in our contest of wills.

I said, "Okay, I give up, what other information?"

A paper airplane drifted by.

"Well, I don't know, but I think you ought to treat me more as a partner and less as an indentured servant if you want information."

"Don't push me. What information?"

He couldn't resist telling.

"Well," he said, crossing his legs, "the scuttlebutt is that Sammy very much wanted to be Mr. Mitzi." He watched me through those cat's eye glasses, waiting for a reaction.

"Mr. Mitzi?"

"Right. He wanted to replace Rudy Wendtz as Numero Uno. He wanted a spot in the Brochu bed. He wanted..."

"I get your drift."

"So you see what that means."

I didn't.

Alvin leaned forward. "Some people say that he was setting up the whole thing. Stringing Brooke along, flirting with her. Finding out her secrets. Making sure Mitzi found out about Brooke and Rudy's relationship. Letting Mitzi know about Brooke's problem with her nose. People think that after Mitzi wrote her planned spread about Brooke and her problem, that would have been it for the Mitzi and Rudy show. Brooke's career would have been ruined. And Sammy would be on the spot to ooze in and comfort poor little Mitzi. And Sammy's career would prosper as a result."

"But it doesn't change anything."

"What do you mean, it doesn't change anything?"

"Well, we already figured that Rudy Wendtz engineered Mitzi's death, even if he was elsewhere."

"So."

"So, it may give us a bit more on motivation or background, but it doesn't solve the murder."

"Who said it did?" He jammed himself into his leather jacket.

He was out the door before I could say anything else.

*　　*　　*

I was kicking around my apartment trying to figure out where the rest of the day had gone and why I hadn't gotten anywhere with the Benning brief and what the stuff Alvin had found out meant, when the doorbell rang.

"You see what happens?" I said to the cats. "You guys lounge around all day on the furniture, and now someone's here and there's not one clean spot for them to sit on."

They ignored me. They're only interested in conversations about cat food.

"Who is it?" I squawked into the intercom system.

Alexa squawked back at me. By the time she reached my door, I had managed to sweep the black cat off the only armchair and brush most of the hair off the seat.

"God, that woman's nosy," she said, pointing at Mrs. Parnell's apartment and at Mrs. Parnell, who was lurking in her door, propped up by her walker, the ruby tip of her cigarette glowing.

"It's for my own good," I said, giving a little wave to Mrs. P. and scooping up a couple of cats before they could shoot into the hallway.

"What is that smell?"

We both sniffed the air.

"You've got to change the kitty litter. Every day. With this number of cats, maybe twice a day. Have you been doing that?"

"Sure," I lied, adding kitty litter to the growing number of things I was behind schedule on.

"Well," said Alexa, sinking her black-covered bottom onto the part of the sofa where the grey Persian sleeps, "guess what?"

"What?"

"I called him!"

Just in time, I stopped myself from asking who.

"Isn't that great?" she added. "I never thought I'd have the nerve."

I decided to be adult about it.

"So, what did he say?"

"He didn't say anything. He wasn't there. But that's not the point. The point is I got up the nerve to call him."

"Did you leave a message?"

"Of course I didn't leave a message. You must be kidding."

"You baffle me."

"Look, it took enough to get up the courage to call him. I wanted it to look casual."

"Okay," I said, wondering what she wanted with me.

She smiled at me. "Let's have a little drink. I brought Piña Colada mix. I know you have rum."

A pyjama party, it turned out. A chance for the girls, in this case Alexa and I were the only two available, to lounge around for hours sharing their deepest secrets.

I wasn't in the mood to share my deepest secrets with anyone, but I didn't have a problem listening to Alexa's.

Alexa, it was revealed after three Piña Coladas, had always been in love with Conn McCracken, especially after what happened on the night of their Senior Prom. Conn, it turned out, had never been far from her mind all those years. From time to time, she had been Filled with Regret.

"You hid it well over those twenty-five years of a marriage that everyone thought was happy."

"I don't mean my marriage wasn't happy and that I didn't love Mike. It's just I never lost all my feelings for Conn," she said, before filling me in on Conn's many, many good points.

"But you haven't even seen him, for…how long?"

"Gosh, about thirty years. Since I went away to nursing school."

I wasn't sure how to break it to her.

"He's changed. He's not the football hero anymore. He's a middle aged man with a paunch."

"Sounds cute," she said, draining her drink.

I tried to feed her a few more Piña Coladas in the hope I'd get some specifics about what happened on the night of their Senior Prom, but no luck. At midnight, after a particularly vacuous remark about his noble spirit, she rolled over and began to snore.

I hadn't said a word about Richard. Somehow, it wasn't so romantic, having a crush on a man almost old enough to be my father, with a wife who could reappear at any minute. It was stupid and inconvenient and most unlike me.

I was grateful to Alexa who had kept me from thinking about Richard, Mitzi's murder and how much I had to fear from Denzil the Deadly.

Fourteen

McCracken looked at me calmly. "Alexa's worried about you poking around in this crime, and she thought I should try to talk some sense into you," he said.

It was only eleven o'clock. I'd left Alexa in my apartment, hung over and surrounded by hungry cats, to try to catch up on a little work at the office. She must have called McCracken on my own phone.

So that was why he wanted to meet me for coffee and doughnuts. On a Saturday, too. I could feel the steam puffing out of my ears as McCracken kept talking.

He was in a good mood. Maybe it was Alexa's call. Maybe it was the two jelly doughnuts.

"Apparently your whole family is very concerned about your mental health, since you're obsessing over Mitzi Brochu's murder."

"She said that?"

"She did."

"Well, for one thing, I'm not in the least obsessed about…"

"I bet Alexa still looks the same, blonde and beautiful. Does she?"

"She's all right, I guess, if she remembers to keep her teeth in," I said.

I don't think he heard me. He was eating his second jelly doughnut with a faraway and long ago look in his eye.

*   *   *

I puttered around in the office all afternoon, snarling rude remarks at Alexa, who was not present.

At five p.m., I arranged my half-done office work in neat piles and set out on my next challenge. Sammy Dash.

I figured by five, Sammy would be home from his afternoon activities and not out yet for the evening of wowing the ladies. I decided it would be better if he didn't know I was coming.

Merv's information had Sammy at a very snooty highrise just off Sussex Drive. Like my own building, Sammy's had security designed to let the good people in and keep the bad people out. I decided that for the purposes of this visit, I was one of the good people.

A small rental moving van was parked outside of the building in the circular drive. I looked around to see if there were any movers I could pretend to accompany. But no luck.

I didn't want to buzz Sammy's apartment, since a surprise visit seemed more likely to elicit useful information. I stood by the door balancing my briefcase in one arm and pretending to dig for my keys with the other. A couple in tennis gear smiled as they let me pass in with them.

"Bad enough to have to work Saturday," I said, "and now I can't find my blankety-blank keys."

"Isn't it frustrating," she said, "the way those blankety-blank keys always sink to the bottom of your purse and hide?"

"It never fails," I said, as we stepped into the elevator. "Sometimes I think if we had a system of personal access codes, it would be better. But I know I'd probably forget mine."

"I know what you mean," she said. Her male companion

smiled. No doubt he was enjoying the natural superiority of one who always knew where his keys were.

They pressed the button for the twelfth floor. Sammy was on the twentieth. I pressed twenty-two and decided to walk down two flights. I was enjoying the sense of skulduggery.

I hoped it would be worth it in practical terms, and that the visit to Sammy would yield at least one or two small pieces to fill in the puzzle. It didn't occur to me to be afraid of Sammy.

On the twentieth floor, the coast was clear. No one was in the corridor, but there was a movers' dolly in the hallway, near Sammy's door.

I knocked on the door of 2012, Sammy's apartment. The knock was brisk, businesslike.

The door swung open. No one stood there to welcome me or tell me to go to hell. I knocked again on the open door. After a minute, I called out.

"Hello, hello. Mr. Dash, important message for you. Hello."

There are times in your life when you behave intelligently and there are times in your life when your actions are about as stupid as they can be. I knew that. And yet I stepped into Sammy Dash's parlour, wondering who was the spider and who was the fly.

"Hello. Mr. Dash. I have something urgent to tell you," I called out, stepping along the foyer towards the living room. I passed a large corrugated cardboard box, with an illustration of a sofa on it. That explained the dolly, I thought.

My sensible internal voice was screaming, get out, get out, the man's probably in the shower, he'll probably call the police when he sees you in his apartment, get...

A smell like rotten broccoli grew stronger as I approached the living area, expecting to be set upon by an enraged Sammy

Dash, wearing only a towel.

Instead, I saw a pile of refuse. Dead vegetables, cans, meat wrappers, yogurt containers piled on a ruby red oriental carpet. Sticky stuff oozed out from under the debris. The pile was high, much higher than you would expect to find in one person's apartment. It looked like a year's worth of garbage.

I slumped into a leather armchair, held my nose and pondered the scene. Destructive, vicious. Someone must have broken into Sammy's apartment. Someone with a major grudge and an imaginative notion of revenge.

I'm not certain why it took so long to realize that having entered Sammy Dash's apartment without his invitation at the same time that the vandalism took place might look damned suspicious to some people.

Thanking God that no one had seen me enter the apartment, I stood up to sneak out. Still holding my nose. Someone else could report this, I'd be long gone when it happened. My sensible voice, which had been busy saying I told you so, starting screaming. This time I listened.

After a minute, I crossed the room to call the police and report the damage. It was only then I spotted the shoes sticking out of the pile of garbage. A banana peel dangled off one of the heels. A scoop of something, mashed potatoes with old gravy perhaps, was stuck to the other.

Couldn't be, I told myself, although my heart rate accelerated into the unsafe zone and goosebumps crawled up my arms. Not possible, I kept saying, until I saw the hand, lying in a sticky puddle, clutching a piece of paper.

I leaned closer, my hand covering my nose and mouth. The hand belonged to Sammy Dash. I could see the rest of him half-hidden by rotting food. His eyes stared past me, over my shoulder.

I staggered towards the phone, gagging. I never reached it. I didn't have time to swing around when I heard the step behind me. I was dimly aware of a pair of tan shoes before I marvelled at the explosion of light in my head and heard my sensible voice say, I told you so, stupid, as I hit the floor.

*   *   *

The story as I told it to McCracken had a few editorial changes. Notably, that Sammy had agreed to see me and was expecting my visit.

"How did you get in? If the guy was dead, he could hardly have buzzed you in."

McCracken was not an easy man to fool and I decided to keep the fabrications to a minimum. But I felt it was important to prevent any notion of unauthorized entry from edging into the conversation.

"A couple of tenants let me in with them. I must have looked respectable."

"The things people do," he said.

I was sitting on the sofa in Sammy's apartment, holding my head and trying to figure out what happened.

McCracken was sitting on the chair, watching me.

"Now you're telling me that Dash's body was lying here, right on this carpet."

"That's right."

"There's no body now," McCracken said.

Reasonable enough. There wasn't. Except for a lingering, light odour of garbage masked by something else, floral bouquet carpet shampoo and room freshener I thought, there was no sign of anything unusual in Sammy Dash's apartment.

"True," I said, "but trust me on it."

Mombourquette was lounging against the wall on the far side of the room, smirking rattily.

McCracken looked troubled. "Pretty weird story," he said. "But the lab boys will check out the rug. If there was blood on it, they're going to find it."

"Not if. Was."

McCracken looked at me with a strange expression. Concern?

"Whatever you say, but you've got to keep in mind that you've been hit on the head. That kind of injury can be…"

"Wait for the lab results," I snapped.

But I knew he was right. There were things that were fuzzy. Something I should have remembered but couldn't. Something that could help. What the hell was it?

"We'd better let someone in your family know what's happened to you, whatever it was."

"No," I said, "they get hysterical. They'll just make me worse. I'll be all right. I'll take a cab to the hospital and get checked out. Don't worry about it."

"Yeah, right," he said.

McCracken drove me to the Civic Hospital Emergency, to have my head examined. I leaned sideways with fatigue. Leaning back was out of the question. My stomach lurched and I closed my eyes.

"I'll make sure your car gets home," McCracken said, as he pulled into the Emergency area and parked. "You want to give me your keys?"

I wrestled my car keys off the key ring. All I wanted to do was sleep. But something else was bothering me.

"Blast," I said, "the cats. Somebody's got to feed the goddam cats."

"Okay," McCracken said, "if they keep you in, I guess I

191

could let your sister know. I'm sure she'll do it."

McCracken took the upper hand with the nurse in charge in emergency.

"Police," he said, flashing his badge at her. "Head injury."

When my medical information had been given, I was whisked into an examining room. McCracken, to my surprise, came with me.

"Just in case," he said. "I'm not taking any chances. Your sister might hold me responsible."

My sister. I remembered I was mad at her. It seemed very long ago and unimportant.

I didn't much feel like talking, and after about two minutes McCracken went off for a cigarette. Who could blame him?

I lay there on my belly, head resting on crossed arms, thinking about what had happened. Who had killed Sammy Dash and why? Why hadn't they killed me? Why had they moved Sammy's body? Had any of it really happened?

My eyes popped open as the door squeaked. The resident who entered had not gotten to the lesson where they teach you to smile at the patients.

"I'm Dr. Granger. What seems to be the problem?"

"Someone whacked me on the head with something. I don't know what."

"When was this?"

I had to think. Nearly eighteen hours earlier.

"Is that a long time to be unconscious after a blow?" I asked.

"It happens," he said, touching my head. "Does this hurt?"

I gasped and gripped the sides of the examining table.

"I think we need an X-Ray here."

McCracken knocked on the door and entered. He and the doctor exchanged looks, both used to being in charge. I'm used to being in charge too, but I lacked the energy at that moment.

It was all I could do to hang on to my self-control until I got through the X-Ray. This didn't get any easier when Alexa came scuttling around the corner of the Radiology waiting room, her face glowing with anxiety.

She stopped in mid-step the second she spotted McCracken. Her hand shot up to fix her perfect hair. A reflex, I guess. Once she glanced at me, the anxiety was back.

"Oh, Camilla," she said.

"I'm fine. You should see the other guy." It was a well-worn joke in our family. This time, it happened to be true.

A smile fluttered around Alexa's mouth. "Are you sure?" she said, hugging me.

"Yes."

"Well, we'll see what the radiologist has to say."

I took a look at her. She wasn't wearing lipstick, or even any makeup. Her hair was caught back in a pony tail, a style which was probably invented for her. If she still had her hangover, it didn't show. She must have been in the garden when McCracken called, because she was wearing faded jeans and one of her late husband's shirts.

McCracken was staring. For some reason, his collar seemed to be tight.

Alexa gave me a little pat on the arm, before she turned to him.

"Hello, Conn," she said.

I hated sitting there waiting for X-Rays while the two of them pretended to engage in normal conversation. But every now and then Alexa would turn her attention to me.

"Maybe they'll have to keep you in, as a precaution. You could have a concussion, dear. Do you feel sleepy? Nauseated?

Let me see your pupils."

McCracken gazed at her with admiration.

"I can't stay in," I said. "I have to get home and look after the goddam cats."

*　　*　　*

It was only after McCracken was gone and Alexa had squeezed every drop of information possible out of the radiologist and we were in Alexa's car driving home that I remembered to give her hell.

"You used me as bait to call up McCracken. You didn't have the guts to just call him. The man dragged me off to a café and gave me a lecture about sticking my nose in this investigation."

Alexa kept her eyes on the road. "Looks like that was good advice. Which you didn't take, and now look at you."

She had a point.

"Anyway," she added, "I'm glad I called him. So there."

My apartment is a five minute drive from the Civic, and we pulled into the driveway before I could badger her any more. Good thing. I didn't want to hear any romantic drivel about McCracken.

Alexa fussed all the way through the foyer and up to the sixteenth floor in the elevator.

"I'm all right," I said as we walked down the hallway toward my apartment. But I almost toppled over as I went to insert my keys in my apartment door and found it unlocked.

Images of dead cats flashed through my mind, and I felt a wave of nausea.

Alexa grabbed my arm. "I knew you weren't ready to come home from the hospital."

"The door," I whispered, "the door is unlocked. Did you leave it unlocked?"

"Don't be ridiculous. Let's get out of here," she said.

"No way. You take off and call the police. I'm going to stay here and catch the cat-killer."

"You can't stay here." Her voice took on the familiar desperate edge.

"Never mind, go call the police."

We heard a clumping noise just as the door swung open.

Mrs. Parnell stood there, leaning against her walker. Cats flanked her ankles. They rubbed up against her as she inhaled on her cigarette and blew a great deal of smoke in our direction.

"Well, it's about time you turned up. I thought these damn cats were going to starve, they howled so much. First you create a noise nuisance bringing them here, and then you neglect them. Not a great track record."

Alexa rallied, once she recovered from the shock of seeing someone in my doorway

"Camilla has been in the hospital having a head wound attended to. She was injured in an attack last night."

I liked Alexa's approach. It had the nose-in-the-air-and-you'd-better-remember-just-who-you're-talking-to technique that had always worked so well for the MacPhee sisters.

Alexa propelled me past Mrs. Parnell and into the living room, where I slumped on the sofa.

"And as for you, Miss," Alexa snapped, "what were you going to do to the cat-killer when he came out of your apartment? Hit him with your purse?"

She had a point. Having dumped me on the sofa, she bustled off to the kitchen.

Mrs. Parnell thumped back into the room, followed by her new friends. "Head injury? My dear Ms. MacPhee, I am so sorry to have accused you unfairly. But is it serious? Should you not be still at the hospital? And who attacked you? And why?" She slid herself into the armchair and squinted at me in concern.

"Not too serious, Mrs. Parnell. I got hit on the back of the head. The x-rays indicate I'm all right. But if I'm not, Alexa is watching me like a vulture. I have no idea who did it. As for why, I think I discovered a body before the murderer was willing to have it found."

"Tea, Camilla?" Alexa called from the kitchen.

"Tea would be lovely," Mrs. Parnell said.

"Yes, please," I said.

Alexa poked her head out the kitchen door and gave Mrs. Parnell a dirty look, wasted as Mrs. Parnell was facing me.

"I have a question of my own, Mrs. Parnell. How did you get into my apartment?"

Mrs. Parnell snorted. "Well, Ms. MacPhee, the wailing of your cats became so pronounced during the late evening and early morning that it disturbed my sleep. I had no choice but to conclude that you had failed to provide them with the necessities of life and that it was up to me to get some sustenance into their whiny little mouths before one of the nosier neighbours called the police."

One of the nosier neighbours?

Alexa fumbled the tea tray at that one.

"But Mrs. Parnell," I said, unwilling to let go, "how did you get into the apartment?"

"Ah," said Mrs. Parnell, accepting a china cup from Alexa.

"You should use these more often," Alexa said, turning and adding in a whisper, "instead of that moss-encrusted mug you keep in the sink."

"I'm very curious about it," I said to Mrs. Parnell, who

showed no signs of answering my question. "How did you get into the apartment?"

"Well," she said, and took a sip of her tea.

I waited.

"I felt I had no choice."

I nodded.

"I asked the super for a key."

"You what?"

"I asked the super for a key. I explained that you had asked me to water your plant and I had misplaced the key that you'd left me and I was in a panic."

"What plant?" said Alexa. "Camilla doesn't have any plants."

I motioned to her to keep quiet. "And he gave it to you?"

"Yes. Oh, he offered to do it himself. But I assured him that the plant had to be watered at 9 o'clock sharp because I knew he was tied up then."

"And he believed you?"

"Naturally. He's not exactly a rocket scientist."

"You weren't bothered by the fact that this was against the law?"

"Not in the least," said Mrs. Parnell. "As much as I dislike the idea of animals in our building, I didn't want the beasts to starve."

Four of the cats were clustered near her feet, basking in the warmth of their newfound friendship. Only the fat little calico waddled over to me. I had to lift her on to the sofa.

"Camilla thinks she found a body lying in a large amount of garbage. We're not certain that this idea did not come about as a result of her head injury," Alexa said in a conversational tone.

Mrs. Parnell nodded in agreement. "Very unsettling, head

injuries. I've had a few myself."

"There was a body," I snarled, "and I'm sure the lab boys are going to agree once they finish going through that apartment."

"Fascinating," said Mrs. Parnell, "and were you alone at the time? No other witnesses."

"That's right."

"Hmm. And how did you get into the apartment where the body was?"

"The door was open."

I shot her a glance. Sure enough, I saw a little glimmer of amusement. Point to Mrs. Parnell.

Fifteen

I had trouble sleeping after the incident in Sammy's apartment. I dreamed about tan shoes and garbage. I wanted comfort. I wanted someone to pat my hand. I wanted a shoulder to wipe my nose on. I think I even wanted to be cuddled. But I found myself alone.

Since we were kids, Robin's been the one who comforted me when I needed it. Now, of course, it was out of the question to go to her with my problems.

Richard, I thought, was suited to comforting, and I could see myself sniffing on the padded shoulder of his navy suit. Richard could have done a hell of a good job, but he was in Toronto doing something tedious at corporate headquarters.

That left my family.

Sunday dinner at Edwina's was their way of easing me back into normal life after my brush with violence. Even Stan refrained from practical jokes in the course of the evening, although he did have a suspicious bulge in his jacket pocket. The conversation was cautious. Everyone stared at me when they thought I wouldn't notice. My father looked more puzzled than usual. I was certain they were all convinced the entire Sammy in the garbage scene was a product of the blow to my head.

So no one mentioned it.

We spoke about the poached Atlantic salmon, which was

very nice, the parslied potatoes, which Edwina always did so well and the fiddleheads, which a friend of Stan's had picked and sent by Priority Post from the Restigouche. Praise was heaped on the dinner rolls and hollandaise sauce.

The Chardonnay was excellent. We discussed it for a while.

We might have been meeting for the first time at a dinner party.

"The weather's been lovely," said Alexa.

"Very nice," said my father.

"Great for the Tulip Festival. Tourists all over the place," said Stan.

"The tulips are spectacular. They really are," said Donalda.

"Is everyone ready for lemon mousse cheesecake and coffee?" Edwina prefers action to talk.

No one said much of anything while she and Alexa and Donalda bustled around in the kitchen.

I fiddled with my napkin. Stan patted his pocket. My father looked at me with his brow wrinkled.

For the first time in my life, I would have preferred to help out in the kitchen. But I'm never allowed to. Something about my track record with china.

By the time we were all settled in with lemon mousse cheesecake and steaming coffee, I'd had it with pussyfooting. "So," I said, digging into my cheesecake, "looks like I was right."

Everyone looked at everyone else, before everyone spoke at once. "Right about what?"

I pointed to my mouth to indicate I couldn't talk.

They watched me munch on my cheesecake.

Edwina drummed her fingers on the table until Alexa reached over and gave her a little nudge.

I took my time. When I finished, I dabbed at my mouth with a linen napkin.

"Well," I said, pausing for effect.

Everyone leaned forward.

"Sergeant McCracken of Ottawa Police Services phoned me this afternoon."

I looked around the table, beaming. "Do you all remember Conn McCracken?"

"Get on with it." Edwina has a hard time maintaining a gentle, nurturing pose.

Alexa blushed.

"Well," I repeated, "he called me today to give me the results of one of the tests taken at Sammy Dash's apartment."

I took another mouthful of cheesecake, savouring it.

"For God's sake, Camilla, what were the damned results!" Edwina exploded.

My father shook his head at her. It was enough to get Edwina to stop, but I noticed her fingers started drumming again.

"How did he sound?" asked Alexa.

That was sufficiently peculiar to direct attention away from me. Of course, that wasn't my intention.

"In this particular test, they use a chemical, which will cause blood stains which have been cleaned up to show under certain light." I smiled.

"And?" asked Donalda.

"Well," I said, smiling around at everyone, "the results were very interesting."

"Get to the point," Edwina barked.

"The test showed, and I must say I feel vindicated by the results," I paused for a breath, during which there were definite signs of rebellion at the table, "the test showed what must have happened."

"Camilla," said my father, in the voice he'd perfected as a

school principal, "stop teasing your sisters."

"Well, the test showed large quantities of blood at the spot where I told them the body had been lying. It must have soaked through the carpet."

Everyone gasped at once. Most gratifying.

"My God, you were lucky…"

"You must have interrupted the killer."

"You could have been murdered."

"It must be a maniac."

I leaned back and enjoyed the reaction for a minute.

When they started to settle down, I added, "There was something else Sgt. McCracken said."

I took the expectant silence as an indication of interest. "They found blood stains all over the place. On the walls and even on the ceiling."

Stan said, "Somebody must have really hated this guy."

"Or else, it was someone completely ruthless, without compassion," said Donalda.

Exactly. And with the kind of psychotic sense of drama needed to lug in a pile of garbage in a packing box just to add substance to the sentiment. I wondered if Sammy Dash had had one encounter too many with Denzil Hickey, acting on behalf of Rudy Wendtz.

"You were in real danger." My father could always cut through to the real issue. "I regret that we didn't believe your version of the events, the first time. It is not like the MacPhees not to take each other seriously."

I spent the rest of the evening smirking at my sisters and making faces at Stan when no one was looking.

*　　*　　*

"I don't know where your photos are," Alvin said.

It was Wednesday before I was pronounced ready to go back to work. Alvin was still peevish when I walked in. I put it down to jealousy, since I'd gotten closer to a murder than he had.

"You just don't remember where you put them," he added.

"That's right, I don't. But I know they were either in my apartment or in my briefcase or here in the office."

"Yeah."

"Yeah, and they're not in my briefcase."

"Umhum."

"And they're not in my apartment. I've been through every inch of it."

Alvin shrugged.

"Soooo, they must be here. Let's get moving and find them." By this I meant, you get moving and find them.

It was a distressing thought, searching through the piles of paper in the office. Paper was piled everywhere. The twin disasters of Alvin's arrival and my preoccupation with Mitzi's murder looked like the undoing of Justice for Victims.

"I already looked through everything. They're not here," he whined.

I stared at him, long and hard.

"Maybe someone, the murderer I guess, stole them from your briefcase in Sammy's apartment. When you were out cold."

Maybe, indeed. I couldn't even remember if the photos had been in my briefcase. My head was still fuzzy enough to blur the events just before my visit.

"Maybe someone broke into your apartment and stole them." This was said with enthusiasm on Alvin's part.

"Nobody broke into my apartment."

"Yes, they did. Remember the dead cat?"

"Of course I remember the dead cat. How could I forget the dead cat? However, I still had the photos after that."

"Oh."

Of course, I knew Alvin was right. Someone had stolen the photos. From me. From my apartment, my briefcase or my office. No question about it. Someone who had been in one of the photos. Someone who didn't want me going around asking questions. But I hated to give Alvin the satisfaction.

I also hated to go around snapping the suspects again. And one of them was dead.

Alvin's face lit up a bit. "Of course, I have the negatives."

"Good, where are they? We can get copies made and you can head off to the Harmony to do your back hall investigations."

"They're here somewhere."

"What do you mean 'they're here somewhere?'"

"I filed them."

"Well, get them out of the file."

"Give me a minute. I need to think of what I filed them under."

I glared at him while he stared at the ceiling as if the file title might be written there. I thought about how much I wanted to file Alvin under Employees, Former.

The blast of the phone startled both of us. I grabbed it before Alvin could.

McCracken.

I gestured to Alvin to get his head back into the files.

"So," said McCracken, "looks like you were right."

When Alvin pulled the negatives out of the Miscellaneous file, I was caught up in what McCracken was saying. I pointed in the direction of the Rideau Centre and hoped that Alvin would understand that meant take them in to get printed again.

McCracken was saying Sammy Dash had turned up in a dumpster, outside a renovated building. He had been punctured, many times, by something very sharp. And he'd been there a while.

Underneath him, a poem was clutched in what was left of his hand. McCracken read it to me, over the phone:

> *Here lies Sammy Dash*
> *Who sold trouble for cash*
> *Now he's where he belongs*
> *With the rest of the trash*

I heard about it again on the evening news as I passed through the Findlay living room on my way up to see Robin.

"Oh, look," said Mrs. Findlay, "they've identified that man they found last night. Isn't that terrible? We're not even safe in our beds anymore. Even Camilla here found another body. What is the world coming to?" she asked Brooke.

But Brooke, who'd been slumped on the sofa, surrounded by Holt Renfrew bags, choked on her cigarette. She took the stairs two at a time and slammed the bathroom door.

I could hear her retching as I passed the door on my way to Robin's room.

"What's wrong with Brooke?" Robin asked.

"Reality struck too close to home this time, I guess."

Robin is used to my more oblique remarks and she let that one slide.

"My mother says you found a body. Is that true?"

She was looking better. A little more pink and white, a little less yellow. And she was sitting up, with her hair combed and her eyes clear.

"It's true."

"My God," she said. "What happened?"

I hesitated, but it was time to talk straight.

"Yes," I said, "while crawling around town to investigate the murder which caused you so much psychological distress, I visited one Sammy Dash. Mean anything?"

I watched her face. Sammy Dash was a new name to her.

"He was Mitzi's Brochu's photographer. And some people say he wanted to be more than that."

She shook her head.

"I wanted to talk to him about his relationship with Mitzi and a few other things, and I went to his apartment. Someone hit me over the head when I found his body." I rubbed the sore spot.

Robin gasped. She leaned forward, grasping my arm.

I hated to do it, but I said, "He was a good friend of Brooke's."

Her head hit the pillow with an audible plop.

I pressed on. "That's why she's in the bathroom throwing up. He was her friend. And now he's been killed and dumped in a pile of garbage with a little note."

Robin was shaking her head, trying to keep the words out.

I grabbed her shoulder. "It's the same person. The same person killed them both. You've got to tell me how Brooke's involved before something else happens."

But Robin had covered her face with her hands. "Stop, please," she whispered.

I put my face next to hers. "I can't stop. You're my friend and this is destroying you. And people are being killed, even if they're not very nice people."

"Oh, God, don't try to find out any more. Please."

I was attempting to shake some sense into her when the door jerked open and Mrs. Findlay stuck her head in.

"My heavens, girls. The news is enough to…what's wrong? Why are you crying? What have you done to her, Camilla MacPhee? For God's sake, don't you think she's been through enough without you upsetting her? And she was just starting to get better too. Get out of here."

I stared. Robin snuffled something incomprehensible.

"You heard me," said Mrs. Findlay, "and don't come back until you're willing to behave in a civilized fashion."

Mr. Findlay was just starting up the stairs with a plate of brownies when I stormed past. I know it was childish of me to slam the door. But I got a lot of satisfaction out of the way the glass rattled.

*   *   *

Lucky for Alvin when I swung open the door of Justice for Victims on Thursday morning and opened my mouth to snarl at him, he said the right thing.

"There's a message from that guy."

"What guy?"

"You know, what's his name from the hotel. Richard. You talk about him enough."

"Richard called? When?"

"Just a few minutes ago. He lost his cool when I didn't know where you were or when you'd be back."

"But you did know. You knew I was at Robin's and…oh never mind. Why don't you go check if the copies of those photos are ready yet?"

"Why should I go over when I can just call?"

"Because," I said, lifting the receiver, "I'm on the phone."

Richard's reaction was enough to make me feel comforted. He asked all the right questions.

"I couldn't believe it," he said, "when I got in and saw this message from you. The office should have called me in Toronto. Bit of bad judgement there. That won't happen again. And then I called your place and got that twit. He told me he was not at liberty to tell me whether you had been seriously injured. And furthermore, he was unaware of your plans for the day and could I call back. Tomorrow."

"He sees his job as shielding me from a demanding public. Perhaps he'd be more suited to a large corporate office."

"Oh sure. I'll see if I can get him something at Harmony Corporate."

"Richard?"

"Yes."

"I'm glad you're back."

"Me, too."

* * *

I left work early. Alvin had been assigned to take the reprinted photos and prowl through the back passageways of the Harmony looking for anyone who'd seen our suspects moving around where they shouldn't be. My money was still on Denzil Hickey, but I wouldn't let Brooke Findlay or Jo Quinlan or Deb Goodhouse off the hook until I knew for sure. Even Sammy might have been there.

"Stop sulking. It's only one afternoon and evening," I snapped at Alvin, slamming the door to cut off any rejoinders.

I smiled all the way home, even on my many stops. Richard and I had plans.

It's annoying what you can buy when you put your mind to it. I managed to pick up herb-crusted poached salmon, rice, a medley of five blanched vegetables, salad and two slices of killer chocolate cake. And some lobster and asparagus dip for starters.

I hit the liquor store feeling smug and picked up two bottles of Pouilly Blanc Fumé and a little Armagnac, just in case.

I don't know what hit me, but I doubled back to the florist and bought a dozen tulips.

You're getting worse than Alexa, I told myself.

By the time I raced out the doors by the corner of Laurier and Bank, I was uncertain of my ability to get all the way home with my bags, bottles, containers and tulips. It was one of the few days when it would have made sense to take my car.

Now a taxi was in order. As I snagged a Blueline, still smiling, a familiar face turned to stare.

Ted Beamish was crossing Bank Street. A taxi turning right nudged him, but he didn't seem to notice.

"Camilla," he said, racing around and sticking his head into the cab, "you look great. I heard about your terrible experience. You seem to have recovered. What's all this?" he gestured toward the flowers, candles and food. "Planning something special?"

"Yes."

"Oh. I know you must have been very busy," he said, with his flush starting to spread from his neck, "but did you ever get my messages?"

"What messages?"

"No one answered at your apartment and your office line is always busy. But I did get through a couple of times and I left two or three messages."

"Sorry, Ted, I never got them. Maybe they're stuck in a pile of papers or something. Was it something important?"

The taxi driver took that moment to rev his motor a little bit.

"No, nothing important. I just wanted to know how you were doing." Ted said, with his entire face in full blush. "It's okay, but maybe you can give me a call when you have a couple of minutes."

"Sure," I said, as the cab pulled away.

I looked back as we moved along Laurier Street. Ted was still watching the cab. But I have to admit, I didn't give him another thought for the rest of the day.

*   *   *

When Richard arrived at 7:00, the apartment looked pristine. The reports and files, which had been stacked on the floors and on all available surfaces, were now stacked in the closets. Almost all the cat hair had been vacuumed up, and the felines were still a little miffed.

The furniture, what there was of it, was now in an intimate little grouping, and the lights were as low as they could go. I'd set the dining room table in the window by the balcony, where you could see the river.

I was wearing the kind of smile you might expect from a person who'd gotten everything done, right on schedule, and then soaked in a tub fragrant with Watermelon Foam Bath while sipping a glass of chilled Pouilly Fumé.

I was also wearing my red jersey dress.

I buzzed Richard through and waited by the door, my breathing a bit uneven. I was doing an excellent job of keeping my conscience quiet.

As I let Richard in, he stopped and stared. "You don't look like you need too much comfort," he said, handing me a bouquet of short-stemmed, peach roses.

"Try me," I said.

Behind him in the hallway, from Mrs. Parnell's open door, the red end of a cigarette glowed. I shut the door and forgot about her.

"You look great," Richard said. "Getting hit on the head is obviously good for you."

"I do like seeing those stars."

He hugged me. The old-fashioned kind of hug you don't plan, it just happens. Full of affection. Just like Paul used to do.

"You're funny," he said.

"And you haven't even had dinner yet."

I liked that hug. It reminded me there weren't enough hugs in my life. I didn't pull back until he did. We looked at each other for a long time, smiling.

"Mousse?" I asked.

We sat on the sofa, munching the mousse and crackers, talking, our thighs close enough to feel the heat from each other. Cats watched us from freshly vacuumed chairs, from the newspaper basket and from under the dining table. When the sunset turned the sky over the Ottawa River into a wall of flame, I remembered about dinner.

I got the salmon from the microwave to the table, turning down Richard's offer to help.

When I raced by Richard to put the first casserole on the table, I noticed he was trying to entice one of the cats to join him.

"Don't bother," I said, when I swung back into the room with the rice and veg. "Cats will only come to you when you don't want them to."

When I trotted out the salad, I added, "You're trying too hard."

"I think you're right."

Three cats had left the room. The fourth, the black and

white one, had turned its back on Richard and was watching the wall with great interest. The fat little calico was following me.

"This is it," I said as I made my last trip into the room with rolls and the wine.

"Kitty, kitty, kitty," said Richard.

The black and white cat jumped from the chair and stalked into the bedroom, tail twitching.

"They're all in there now," Richard said.

"Not true, the calico's still in the kitchen. And don't feel bad about it. It's the nature of the cat to be in charge."

"I suppose."

"Trust me. When it becomes inconvenient to have cats around, they'll be all over you."

"If you say so. I've always had dogs, myself."

"And who can blame you?" I said, fluffing the tulips and lighting the candles.

In the course of our dinner, the last traces of raging sunset disappeared. Not that we were paying attention.

By the time we were through our chocolate cake, the sky was dark and starry. We took our coffee and Armagnac on to the balcony and sipped it in the dark.

"You can see the dippers," said Richard.

I wasn't paying a lot of attention to the dippers, because our knees were touching. Richard watched the stars, and I watched Richard. I didn't think about his wife. I didn't even know her name.

The night was mild, with a sensuous little breeze. A taste of summer to come.

We talked. About the Harmony, about Justice for Victims, about his hobbies, about why I didn't have any, about the Tulip Festival, about the weather. About my friends. About my family. About what it's like to relocate in middle age.

I don't know when we stopped talking. The silence that replaced the talking was intense, almost noisy. It was full of watching and tentative touching.

I need this, I thought, as we moved back into the living room, wrapped around each other. I need to feel together. I was tracing the outline of Richard's ear as we sank onto the sofa. Two cats exploded off the cushions. We didn't care.

I felt a bit catlike myself, stretching and purring.

"We might be more comfortable elsewhere," Richard whispered in my ear after a long time.

"The cats are, um, elsewhere."

"We could ask them to stay and that should get rid of them."

I was enjoying the sensation of laughing when a blast from the phone knifed through our mood.

"Don't answer it," he said, very close to me.

"It'll just take a second. It could be Robin."

He nodded, leaning back.

"Yes," I breathed.

Squeaking sounds surged through the receiver. Richard leaned forward again when I gasped. His face creased with concern.

"Arrested? Where? For what?" But, of course, I knew. "Okay, calm down. I'll be there. I said I will be there."

"What is it? Has Robin been arrested?"

"Not Robin. Alvin."

"Alvin?"

I nodded. It was going to get worse.

"What was it, drugs or something?"

I took a long, assessing look at Richard before I told him.

"He was prowling around the back corridors of the Harmony, and someone called the police."

Richard nodded, approving. "We don't take any chances with theft or attacks on guests."

"He was just asking a few questions. But I guess someone had seen him there before, and he looked suspicious."

"Well, I don't know what the hell made him decide to do that, but I'll bet he's in hot water now."

"Right. And I have to get him out."

"Why? He's not your responsibility."

I took a deep breath before I started in on my explanation.

* * *

I hadn't thought that Alvin could get any paler, but he managed it. I hadn't thought he could get any snippier, but he managed that too.

We were crossing the Portage Bridge to Hull at the time. Close enough to the Peace Tower to see the time was 11:30 p.m.

"Okay," I said, turning around to face Alvin in the back seat. "May I remind you that I was prepared to post bail for you? If necessary. But the charges have been dropped, haven't they? You can thank Richard for that." I pointed to Richard, who was driving.

Richard seemed a little on the stiff side to me.

Alvin sniffed. "I guess you should have been prepared to post bail for me, since you were the one who sent me on a criminal expedition in the first place."

"Hardly criminal. Just asking a few questions in the hotel."

"Then why did you ask me to be discreet?"

I could feel Richard's eyes on me.

"So as not to scare off any potential witnesses. And I thank you for what was no doubt a very thorough and effective job."

"I notice *you* didn't have to sit in the slammer waiting for someone to bail you out, even though you were the brains behind the whole operation."

I sighed. "There was no operation. And I'm beginning to think, no brains. I just need some kind of information that would ensure the police don't come hounding Robin again over Mitzi's murder."

"Sure, let them hound poor old Alvin."

"How did I know you were going to draw so much attention to yourself that you'd get arrested?"

I turned to Richard before Alvin could respond. "It's not far from here," I said. "Turn left, and then first left again, and then first right."

As we stopped in front of Alvin's place, he and I were still swapping recriminations.

"I'll walk in with him," I said to Richard. "He's a little shaky."

Alvin shot me a look that could have melted metal.

"It's no trouble. Just want to make sure you're all right."

I hopped out of the car, grabbed his arm and propelled him to his door.

"Let go of me," Alvin said, jerking away, "you're going to leave bruises."

"I'm just trying to help you."

"Yeah, right," he said.

"Okay, fine. I'll leave you alone now. But tell me," I stole a look back to the car where Richard was waiting, "what did you find out when you were in the Harmony?"

"You astound me," said Alvin.

"Come on."

"No. I've just spent the worst night of my life and all you can think about is your stupid investigation."

"Not all, not all. Haven't I been concerned about your welfare tonight? Didn't I race to the police station with the one person who could get the charges quashed?"

"Big deal."

"So, what did you find out? Had any of them been there?"

Alvin leaned against the door to the apartment building. He pulled out the key to the front door. I could tell he was trying to decide whether to tell me or not.

Finally, he broke.

"Yes."

"Which one for God's sake? Don't tantalize me."

Alvin's eyes glittered. He inserted the key into the lock and turned it. The door swung open. Alvin stepped through.

"They all were," he said, just as the door closed in my face.

Sixteen

As I shlepped along the corridor to my apartment, I had time to reflect on the evening.

I could still feel the nip from Conn McCracken's look when he had told me what he thought of Alvin's investigation and my part in it.

Richard and I had decided the visit to the police station had been enough to take the magic out of our evening. I felt that Richard had taken Alvin's prowl through his hotel too seriously. And worse, he had his doubts about my motivations for our date.

"How could you even suggest such a thing?" I stared at him, astounded.

"What am I supposed to think?"

"Not that!"

We were pulling up in front of my building, when he dropped this bomb.

"Well, it seems kind of funny, we have this very nice dinner and romantic evening on the same night your hired help goes snooping around my hotel. And, of course, I'm not there to catch him, because I'm all snuggled up with you on the sofa. What else could I think?"

I felt rage rising and bubbling. I could hear my anger buzzing around my ears. The first time I'd let myself relax with someone since Paul, a man I felt I could trust, maybe even love, a man who made my knees crumble. And he reduces it to a scheme to get my own way. I bit my tongue, grabbed my purse and jumped out of the car as fast as I could.

"Go to hell," I said and slammed the door.

*   *   *

"What did you mean, they all were?" I snapped at Alvin the next day.

His back was turned to me, bony and repellent. His ponytail drooped. He yawned.

"I'm on my break," he said.

"What do you mean, you're on your break? You just got here and it's three o'clock in the afternoon."

"First, it was time off for overtime. You remember last night? Which I spent in the slammer after doing research for you. Now it's my break. I always take my break at three o'clock." He didn't turn around.

"Fine," I said, "I'll wait."

I picked up the Benning brief and stared at it. I'd been staring at it all morning and most of the afternoon. It hadn't gotten me anywhere so far.

When the phone rang, I snatched it on the first ring.

"Hi," said Alexa.

"Hi."

"I just thought I'd let you know how things are going."

"How are things going?"

"Oh, they're wonderful."

They are not, I thought. In fact, they couldn't be worse.

"That's great," I said.

"Conn and I went out last night. To dinner. We were having such a nice time, until he got a call about a case

218

he's been working on."

"Oh."

"Quite an exciting life he has really."

"Indeed."

I already knew about Alexa's date. I'd seen Conn McCracken the night before. He hadn't been too happy at the time.

"Well," he'd said, "I was enjoying a very nice dinner with a very nice lady. We were comfortable and relaxed when the call came in that a suspicious character was prowling around the same hotel where we're investigating a nasty murder. I had no choice but to come downtown and see for myself."

"I know what you mean," I'd said.

"And what do I find? You again."

He had me.

"Where you shouldn't be."

"Right."

"Because two people have already been killed, and you have already been hit on the head, and you might have been killed. Because this is a serious business."

"I agree."

"And because your sister wants me to make sure nothing happens to you."

"She does?"

"That's right. And I want your sister to be happy. So, for the last time, I will ask you to leave this to us."

"Sorry," I said.

He ignored that. "And don't think sending your weirdo sidekick is going to be just as good. We know him now, too."

We both looked over at Alvin. Alvin looked back at us, misery obviously flooding his being.

Alexa held me personally responsible for the unplanned

end of her evening, and she wanted to make sure I knew it. It was three fifteen when I got off the phone, and Alvin's break was over by my calculations. I could resume questioning him.

"So, just what did you mean, they all were?"

"They all were. What's ambiguous about that?" Behind the cat's eye glasses, his eyes were slits.

"Explain, please."

"Every single one of the people in your photos had been seen by someone or another behind the scenes at the Harmony."

"Even Deb Goodhouse?"

"Even her."

"Even Jo Quinlan?"

"Yup."

"Even Brooke?"

"I said all of them, didn't I? All of them. Even the dead guy, Sammy Dash."

"Wendtz, too?"

"Right."

"What about him?" I held up Denzil's picture.

"Him, too."

"Really?" I said, smiling for the first time in eighteen hours. "That's great."

"It is?"

It was. My life was in ruins. I was not welcome back to my best friend's bedside. My relationship with Richard was in the toilet. My business was dying of neglect. My sister had Conn McCracken on my back. I had five cats in my apartment and Alvin in my office. I was thrilled to have some people to take it out on.

"I can't think of a single reason for a Member of Parliament to skulk around the back halls of a hotel, can you?"

Alvin shrugged, but I knew he was intrigued.

"Did you happen to note just which hotel employee saw which of our suspects when?"

"Yes, I did." He extracted a semi-shredded notebook from one of his many pockets.

I smiled some more.

"I got their names, who they saw, where and when, as far as they can remember."

"Did you give this information to the police?"

He shook his head. "They thought I was some kind of burglar. They didn't believe I was investigating anything, so I didn't tell them anything."

"Well, that'll show them, I guess."

Alvin shot me a look.

"So, now we have witnesses."

"I can't go back there. They'll call the cops in two seconds. And I don't think you'd better go there either."

"We don't have to go there. You have the names of your witnesses."

"Right," he said. "I knew that."

"Okay," I said, "let's get on with it. So, what were they doing there?"

"Fighting mostly."

I was going to enjoy this. "Let's hear it."

"Where do you want me to start?"

"Let's start with Deb Goodhouse. I'm very curious about her."

"Well," said Alvin, "it was very strange. One of the bus boys was delivering room service to Mitzi Brochu's suite. Just as he gets to the door this woman bursts out, practically knocks him over, bites his head off..."

"And?"

"The woman was Deb Goodhouse. He said he'd recognize her anywhere. He described her. Even her size, which you don't get a sense of from this picture, although I guess you did your best."

"All that from just a glimpse as she came out of the door?"

"Well, no. He saw her again. On the staircase. He, my source, was taking the staircase because he wanted to have a cigarette, and employees aren't supposed to smoke around the Harmony. But he was in a bad mood because La Brochu didn't give him one red cent for a tip. They all say she was too cheap to tip anybody for anything. So he felt like a smoke, and he thought the stairs would be safe. But Deb Goodhouse was there. Hanging on to the stair rail. And shaking. Of course, my source doesn't want to be identified, because if they find out he was smoking on the stairs, maybe he could lose his job."

"Shaking from what?" I asked. "Was she frightened?"

"No, she looked very angry. If looks could kill, he said he'd have keeled over on the spot."

"Well, well." I felt like one of Robin's cats after a bowl of half-and-half. I may have even licked my lips. "Isn't that interesting."

It almost killed Alvin to ask, but he did anyway. "Why?"

"Because the Hon. Deb Goodhouse told me that she'd never met Mitzi Brochu. Now what do you think the chances are that she got into and out of Mitzi's room without meeting her?"

"Not so hot. Mitzi was there, according to my source."

"Good, very good. What else do you have?"

"Well, there's more. Your friend Robin's sister. She was in and out. Couple people saw her on different occasions." He looked at me coyly.

"Go on."

Usually I have to drag every little fact out of him, but in

this case his desire to tell the story overcame his desire to string me along for a while.

"I guess Brooke's problem is even worse than we thought. One of the cleaners saw her doing a line of coke in the washroom outside the big ballroom on the mezzanine. Cut it and snorted it right on the fancy counter where the ladies fix their make-up. This source was cleaning the cubicles and Brooke didn't even bother to hide. Like cleaning people don't count, and you could do anything in front of them."

"Sounds like Brooke."

Alvin was getting coy again. "That's not all," he said, looking at his watch.

"What else?"

"Well, she stayed in the ladies room for a while, and then when my source was coming back with replacement tissues and paper towels, she saw Brooke come out of the washroom, and he was waiting for her."

"Who?"

"Rudy Wendtz."

"Bingo."

"And that's not all. He belted her right in the chops."

"What?"

"Slammed her back against the wall. My source pretended to be polishing the water fountain so she wouldn't miss anything. You know what he said?"

I shook my head.

"He told her he didn't want her anywhere near Mitzi, and she'd better get the message. Then he belted her again. My source said there was blood running down the side of Brooke's mouth, and she was crying."

Whoa.

"And then Brooke said, don't mark my face, it's my career.

And he said, what do you think Mitzi will do to your career if she finds out about us. Don't be a stupid bitch, Brooke. You're going to ruin everything."

"My, my."

"And then there was the other one. The TV lady, Jo Quinlan."

"What about her?"

"Everybody seems to have seen her. More than once too. Trying to get some dirt on Mitzi. She talked to the chambermaids and the kitchen staff. I heard she even tried to get her hands on the garbage that got taken from Mitzi's room. She tipped people so they didn't mind telling her stuff. Mitzi didn't tip anybody, and she treated everybody like dirt, so no one minded shafting her."

"How did they shaft her?"

"Well, they didn't because I guess they didn't have enough dirt on her. She was cheap, cheap, cheap. And they figured she did a bit of coke on the side herself too. But there wasn't anything really, um, newsworthy about what she did when she was at the Harmony. Except for the politicians."

"What politicians?"

"Lots of them. The people I talked to didn't know too much about it, but Jo Quinlan got pretty excited about some of the people who went there."

"How did she know who went there if they couldn't tell her?"

Alvin looked down at his Docs. There must have been something fascinating about them, but I couldn't see it myself.

He sighed.

"What is it?"

"Well, it's just that these people didn't want to tell me all this. Their jobs could be at stake, you know. So I had to give them a little something to help out."

"How much of a little something?"

"Jeez, there were a lot of people. About eighty or ninety dollars." He looked at me through his eyelashes.

"Fine."

"More like a hundred, really."

"I'll give you your alleged hundred dollars. But in return I want to be able to talk to any one of your sources, whenever I need to. That means names, Alvin. Names."

"Jeez, I forgot a couple guys. It cost me more like one twenty-five by the time I was through."

"You're close to being through again."

"Like, I really hate it when you don't even trust me."

I'm afraid I snorted.

"What does that mean?"

"Where did you get all this money you so generously gave to your sources?"

He drew himself upright. "I work here. You pay me. I got other things going on the side. I get by. You can't go around trying to get information in this town without a bit in your pocket to help people relax."

"Hmmm. Okay. I'll write you a cheque. You start by giving me the list of who saw whom do what at the Harmony."

We were both in the middle of writing when a black shadow loomed against the door and Merv barged into the office, without knocking.

"Whoa," he said, "you sure know how to get yourself in deep doo-doo."

"Why, Merv, how poetic."

He shrugged, "If you got it, flaunt it."

"Why am I in doo-doo?"

"Well," he said, lowering himself into a visitor's chair and giving Alvin a nasty look, "a couple of reasons."

I nodded to encourage him.

Merv was still narrowing his eyes at Alvin.

"Alvin," I said, "you've been working pretty hard. Why don't you take a little break, get some air?"

Alvin picked up his half-written list, slithered past Merv and vanished out the door.

"Gives me the creeps," Merv said.

"Merv, Merv, you've got to learn to broaden your horizons. It's a whole new world out there."

"Yeah, well."

"Back to the topic, Merv. Why doo-doo?"

"Ho. I've been over to Robin's. You are most unwelcome there. Do not darken the door and all that."

"According to whom?"

"Jeez, you know I hate that whom shit. According to everybody, that's whom. Mrs. Findlay and Brooke are pissed off. Maybe even Mr. Findlay, who knows. You'd never get past the front door." Merv took out a cigarette and lit up. He kept watching me for a reaction.

I didn't even tell him to put it out.

"There's no way to get to her."

"We'll see about that, Merv."

"And anyway, that's not all. I heard that you screwed up your sister's date with McCracken, and that everybody's pissed off about that, even your family."

"Who told you that?"

"Bit of police gossip."

I thought for a minute. "That didn't take too long to get around."

"Hey, you just got to have coffee with the right people." Merv heaved his shoulders. "Anyways, I can't hang around here chewing the fat with you all day. Some of us have to work." He lumbered through the door, leaving me with an additional set of problems.

The first one rang on the phone while Merv was still thudding down the stairs. Alexa.

"How could you?" she said.

"How could I what?" I said, knowing perfectly well.

"You know perfectly well. You're the one who ruined my date."

There was nothing to do but take my lumps.

"I'm sorry. I had no idea that Alvin's investigations would ruin, I mean, interfere with your date with Conn McCracken."

"You never wanted it to work out. Admit it. All those nasty remarks about him having a wife. All those little digs. I have a right to be happy. Sometimes you are a selfish brat and I wouldn't put it past you to set up Alfred or whatever his name is to commit that burglary just to get Conn to go down to the station and leave me there to get home on my own."

"I'm sorry, I…"

"We didn't even get to say good-bye."

"I know what you mean, my own date didn't work out either."

But she'd already hung up.

It was only when peace descended on the little office that I remembered. Alvin hadn't told me about Large-and-Lumpy. Who had seen Denzil Hickey behind the scenes at the Harmony and when?

Of course, Alvin was gone for the day.

Seventeen

I spent the early part of the evening puttering around the apartment. I had a lot to do, mostly involving making sense out of what I knew.

It is easier to concentrate in an apartment that does not house five cats. Not only did the kitty litter need to be emptied and the cat dishes filled, but the cats wanted company.

I ran into Mrs. Parnell while I was putting out the garbage.

"Home alone tonight, Ms. MacPhee?"

I didn't want to get into my social life, disastrous as it was, with a neighbour whose nose just wouldn't quit.

"All work and no play, Mrs. Parnell," I said, opening the door of my apartment and scooping up two escaping cats. I closed the door behind me without looking at her again. One more second and she would have been asking me about Richard. I wasn't ready for that.

"Now, buzz off," I said to the cats. "You've been fed, you've had something nice to drink, you've got clean kitty litter."

But they were all over me. Jumping up on the table where I was laying out my notes about the Mitzi Brochu case. Sitting on the nice, fresh pad of lined paper. Batting my pens and pencils onto the floor. And just getting between me and anything I wanted to do. The fat little calico had trouble jumping up and cried until I sat her on my lap.

"Behave, or I'll never solve this case and get you back to Robin's where you belong."

That brought me back to earth. I had to convince Robin to tell me what she knew about Brooke's involvement. But how was I going to get past the dragons?

I think it was watching the ginger cat, washing his paws perched on my writing paper , that gave me the idea.

I put the calico down and fished out the phone book. She followed me to the sofa.

"No wonder you're so fat," I said, lifting her again.

I was just a little edgy as the phone rang in my quarry's home.

"Camilla MacPhee here. I wonder if you can do something to help Robin?"

Ted Beamish muffled the surprise in his voice.

"Anything," he said.

No questions asked. I like that in a man.

"Good. Here's what I need."

I was smiling when I hung up. Let Ted deal with the dragons. It would develop his character.

I had other fish to fry. Such as, how to confront my suspects with their presence in the Harmony without getting myself hit on the head.

The doorbell rang before I had made any progress.

Mrs. Parnell. I guessed that closing the door in her face wasn't quite subtle enough.

She clomped past me into the living room, where five cats greeted her like a long-lost relative, although there was nothing catlike about her. If you had to liken her to an animal, it would be an elderly elkhound.

"I know I'm butting in," she said, taking the chair and looking around with interest. "But I couldn't help but notice you seem to have more than your fair share of troubles. Break-ins, assaults, and last night I believe you had to race out of here with that nice man and go to the police station."

Was she at that goddam door every minute of every day and night? Didn't she ever sleep? I had to admire such unrelenting, unabashed nosiness.

Even as I was admiring it, she pulled herself to her feet and moved toward the balcony door using her walker. She had excellent upper body strength, as far as I could tell. Just one leg seemed to drag a bit.

"Nice view you have on this side of the building," she said. But I could see her eyes stray to the notebook and the other materials on the dining room table.

She looked over just in time to catch me catch her. But there were no hard feelings. When I'm her age using a walker to get around, I hope I'll have the energy to annoy people too.

"So," she said, "is there anything I can do to help?"

"Like what?"

"Like watch your apartment. Like notify the police if you don't come home. Like help you rig up booby traps."

"Booby traps?" I couldn't suppress the laugh.

"Fine," she shrugged, "you're the one with the dead cat, not me."

She had a point. But I still couldn't imagine her having the strength to construct booby traps. On the other hand, there were those weights back in her apartment.

"Mrs. Parnell," I asked in a dizzying departure from the conversational track, "those weights in your apartment, what do you use them for?"

"Why Ms. MacPhee, I bake cakes with them, of course. I expect more intelligent questions from you. What do you think I use them for? Weight training, of course. Trying to get back a bit of the old get up and go. After this damn stroke. Trendy kind of treatment for us old crocks now."

Stroke. And I hadn't even known it.

"Sorry, Mrs. Parnell," I said, putting my hand on her shoulder, "didn't mean to get you all steamed up. Let's forget the booby traps and weights and all that. What I need now is someone plugged into the gossip at the House of Commons."

"What makes you think I'm not?"

I gave her a second look. "Let's have a drink, shall we? I have some very good Armagnac that's just going to waste."

I waited until we were well into our drink, before I mentioned it again.

"So do you have any contacts there?" Maybe there was a bit of truth in the neighbourly speculations about Mrs. Parnell's powerful past.

"The Senate. Close enough. Well, used to. Most of them are dead now. Or in Florida. Same thing if you ask me."

"That's too bad," I said, sipping my drink with regret. "Lovely weather we've been having."

"Of course, I might have a few connections left. *I'm* not dead yet."

"Or in Florida," I said under my breath.

"Is it about that Goodhouse woman?" she asked

So much for any idea I might have had that she didn't get a good look at the notes on my dining room table.

"Right. I'd like to know what the late Mitzi Brochu might have had on her. Something publishable, anything from embarrassing gossip to something nastier.

"Oh, I think we can find that out," Mrs. Parnell smiled, putting her empty glass back on the table between us, next to the bottle, where I could not ignore it.

* * *

Robin and Ted were just visible at the end of the outdoor café as I strolled up to the Canal Ritz the next day. Summer weather at last and Robin's pallor was highlighted by her flowered sundress. Her hair was in a French braid and she'd put on a bit of make-up. I stood and watched for a minute, searching for more signs that she was getting better. She sat facing the water, shaded a bit by the large umbrella. Her eyes were hidden by sunglasses, but she was smiling as she listened to Ted tell what I expected would be some tedious work tale. The smile became a laugh. They were drinking Coors Light, and neither one of them noticed me.

"Gosh," I said, "what a nice surprise." I reached over to hug her. "Imagine seeing you here."

The smile slid down Robin's face, and her Coors light teetered on the table. I could see her face crumple, all the nice effect of the pink lipstick and other stuff lost.

"Don't let yourself fall apart here." I slipped into the chair that would shield her the most from the view of other diners. "This is a place you want to come back to after all your problems are over. Just keep telling yourself, Camilla's my best friend and she wants to help. Maybe I should trust her."

She turned to Ted, the poor sap.

"You were in on this, too?" The note of betrayal in Robin's voice was unmistakable, and Ted didn't mistake it for one minute.

He turned the tables on me. "She didn't tell me you wouldn't want to see her. I'm sorry."

I had to restrain myself from reaching over and belting him. "Excuse me," I said, "but let's use a bit of logic here."

"I don't want to use a bit of logic. I want to go home."

"You heard her, she doesn't want logic. She wants to go home," said Ted.

"So, twenty-seven years have passed since that first day in Grade One when we shared the red crayon. I may not be the nicest person in the world, but in that entire twenty-seven years have I ever been anything but a friend to you?"

"It's okay, it's time to go. I'll take you home now. I didn't know she was going to ambush you like this."

"Time to shut up, Ted. Robin and I have something to discuss. What about it, Robin? Have I ever been anything but a good friend to you?"

She shook her head, fighting for control now. I knew she'd never made a scene in a restaurant in her life, and she wasn't about to start.

"It's okay, Ted, I'll talk to Camilla and then you can take me home. Would you mind waiting over there? Some of this is quite private."

Once Ted was settled two tables over with another Coors, we eyed each other with caution.

"Look," I said. "I know this is painful…"

She shuddered.

"…and I don't want to hurt you. Believe me. But you're hurting yourself. Let me help find out what really happened. The police or the newspapers are going to dig it up soon enough. I think I can help to minimize the damage to you…and to your family."

I knew the time was right, and Robin needed to share her fears. I waited. Finally she said, "You know, I wanted that red crayon all to myself. You just made me so nervous."

Good, I thought, I hope it still works.

I signalled to the waitress for two more Coors Light. "Tell me," I said, "what happened."

I waited while Robin paused to try and control herself.

"Well, you know I tried to reach you that day," she said

with a shudder. "She, Mitzi, had called Brooke and told her she would never get her big break, because Mitzi was going to splatter terrible things about Brooke all over the papers. Mitzi was furious because Brooke was seeing this Wendtz person." She shuddered and looked at me. "Brooke would have lost the 'Walk in the Woods' account. They would have dropped her."

I nodded. We didn't have to talk about the terrible things Mitzi was going to write.

"Brooke called me from Toronto the night before. She told me all about what Mitzi was planning to do. Write an exposé on recreational drug use by certain top models, with Brooke being one of them. Brooke was hysterical. Completely out of control." She paused to blow her nose in the paper napkin. "First she wanted me to get an injunction to stop the story."

"Not good," I said, "even if you did, a street fighter like Mitzi would get her story out of the injunction. So would a lot of other people who might not pay attention to Mitzi's write-up in the first place."

"Exactly what I said to her."

I should have known.

"Then she wanted me to go and see Mitzi and tell her that we would sue her for libel the minute she published anything detrimental to Brooke. I spoke to Mitzi on the phone first, and she more or less told me that she didn't give a shit, the pleasure of seeing Brooke get hers would be worth any legal repercussions. I couldn't believe it."

I could believe it.

"But she agreed to see me that afternoon."

"Right," I said, "she was looking forward to twisting the knife."

"I imagine," said Robin.

I looked at her with surprise. Now that she was telling the story, she was calm. I could see the old Robin swimming to the surface again. Calm, articulate, practical.

"I called you to come along because I thought you would be tough enough to support me if I got upset. I wanted to talk to you first and fill you in, but I figured you could just wing it if you had to."

"I was right behind you."

"I know that now. But Mitzi told me that I'd better be on time, because she had just fifteen minutes for me. I was flustered. I guess I should have waited for you."

I shrugged. "She'd still be dead."

"You're right."

But perhaps Robin was thinking that if she had waited for me, we would have either found Mitzi together or left when there was no answer, leaving the nastier bits of dealing with a suspicious police force to someone else. But Robin still would have had her problem.

"And when you found the body?"

She shuddered and pulled back. I grabbed her hand.

"Robin, we have to get through this. I am not the enemy."

After a long time, she nodded.

"It was horrible."

I knew. I'd seen Mitzi myself.

"And I thought, I thought…"

I kept a steady pressure on her hand.

"I thought…" Robin was having trouble with her breathing.

The hand I held was shaking.

"You thought," I said, not letting go of her, "Brooke might have flipped out and killed Mitzi before you could get there to fix things."

She exhaled. Shuddered.

"And you preferred to have the police badger you and make

you miserable, rather than have them find out about the connection between Brooke and Mitzi."

She nodded.

It was out on the table now, between us. I'd suspected and even known this was the problem. At least now we could discuss it, develop a strategy.

"You were making yourself sick over it."

"I was sick. I was terrified, my mind just imploded thinking Brooke must have been there. That she might have…"

"You saw her, didn't you? Leaving just before you went in?"

I thought back to Maria Rodriguez, pointing to Brooke's photo with such certainty. "Don't lie to me any more."

Robin gave up. "I saw her slipping out the stairway exit just as I was heading up to the room. She must have seen Mitzi and panicked. I had to protect her. She's my sister."

"Does she know you saw her?"

"I don't think so."

"You don't think she should feel obligated to protect you?"

"Please, Camilla. That's why I couldn't tell you. I know the way you feel about Brooke. I knew you wouldn't help her. Poor Brooke, she…"

"Okay, enough about Brooke," I said.

The little witch, I thought. She'd hightailed it back to her expensive condo in Toronto and sat there for the better part of a week while her sister held off the police. On the verge of a complete breakdown. Even when she finally sashayed home, she didn't seem concerned with Robin's well-being. If ever anybody deserved to lose an account with a major cosmetics company and be pilloried in the press, it was Brooke Findlay. The "Walk in the Woods" witch.

"It would have killed my parents to have Brooke involved in this. They're so proud of her. They just adore her."

I knew Robin expected me to understand. But I didn't. I thought about my own peculiar family and realized that what happened to Robin would never have happened to me. None of us would be expected to sacrifice so much for the others. We would all stand together no matter what. Bitching and complaining, but together. I decided to call Alexa, soon. I didn't like to think there might be a bit of Brooke in any of my behaviour.

Robin was watching me. "I had no choice."

"You have choices. You are a useful, productive, compassionate member of our society. Consider when you make your choices the effect your breakdown had on your workplace, your volunteer activities, remember the Food Bank, the Humane Society, your clients. You could have chosen to protect yourself. We'll get to bottom of this, believe me. And we'll try to keep Brooke's name out of the papers, but if it comes down to the crunch, it will be you, not her, I'll be protecting. That's my choice, like it or not."

It was a minute before she nodded.

"And what's more, one of these days your parents are going to have to wake up and smell the coffee."

"I'd still like to spare them."

"Well, I'm going to need to stay in touch with you on all sorts of developments, so you'll have to let your family know that I'm a welcome visitor at the Findlay's again, or they'll get an earful of reality from me."

"Okay."

I reached over and gave her a hug, glad to have the old Robin back. She smiled.

"How are my kitties getting along? I miss them."

I was able to dodge the tricky question of how the kitties were getting along, because Ted inserted himself back into the group at just the right moment.

It seemed to me, as I watched them depart, that Robin was steadier, happier, better off after our meeting. I sipped a cappuccino as I watched Ted collect his car and come back to pick up Robin. But I was the only one who noticed the other silent observer. A man with a great deal of misery drawn across his face.

Merv. Watching Robin like a lovesick Great Dane. All this goddam romance. It was enough to make you throw up.

Eighteen

Gee, hi," I said. "Imagine meeting you here. I was just on my way over to take a look at the tulips. Aren't they great?"

I might have been a maggot on the stem of one of those tulips the way Deb Goodhouse looked at me. It wasn't just that she was splendidly casual in a full patterned cotton skirt and matching blouse that I thought might be from Suttles and Seawinds while I had on my ancient blue jeans and an oversized tee-shirt that said "I'm With Stupid". Maybe she just wasn't used to people sneaking up on her right in her own neighbourhood.

"Mind if I walk along with you?" I asked, walking along with her.

"I'm in quite a hurry."

Deb Goodhouse had been meandering along until I sidled up behind her. A typical Saturday stroll for someone lucky enough to live in a fashionable townhouse smack in the middle of the Golden Triangle.

"I'll try to keep up," I said, picking up my pace to match hers. "I'm not sure if you remember me...."

"Of course I remember you."

"Oh good, that makes it easier. I have a couple of questions for you."

Her mouth compressed.

"Well, just to clear things up. You see, you told me you had

239

never met Mitzi Brochu. The funny thing is there are people who claim they saw you visit her in the Harmony Hotel. People who could not help but notice you were upset."

I looked at her with what I hoped was a guileless expression. She was two shades paler after I dropped my little bombshell. Of course, it didn't do to underestimate Deb Goodhouse. I gave her one more little push.

"I'm not sure what the police will make of this information," I added.

"I don't intend to stand around listening to you slandering me," she snapped. "I have nothing to say to you on this or on any other subject. Now if you don't get out of my way, I will call the police." She stepped onto the street to pass me, stepped back onto the sidewalk again and kept going toward Elgin.

"That was an incorrect use of the term 'slander'", I called after her, but she didn't seem to hear me. "Bingo," I added to myself. Everything about Deb Goodhouse's body language and expression told me I had gotten what I had come for.

Jo Quinlan was the next name on the list I fished out of my jeans pocket. Alvin had provided me with an address along with a very interesting tidbit of information. Luckily for me, Alvin had also put in a little map, because Jo Quinlan lived on the Quebec side, over in Chelsea.

I retrieved my car and double checked the map. I was still chuckling over Deb Goodhouse as I crossed the Portage Bridge five minutes later and spun along towards Highway 5.

Jo Quinlan, according to the notes left in Alvin's back-handed scrawl, lived in the country and kept horses. Alvin's directions were better than his office skills, and not long after, I found myself pulling into a tree-lined driveway with a mailbox marked Quinlan/Belliveau.

A man in a pickup truck was pulling away as I nosed my

car into the driveway as far as it would go and stopped.

I stuck my head out the window and bellowed. "Jo Quinlan around?"

"She's out back," he hollered. "You might need to yell a bit to get her attention."

The German Shepherd beside him in the cab sat there assessing me.

"Thanks."

"No problem." His pickup was already rolling down the drive.

"Hello?" I yelled a few times as I walked towards the back of the house. "Hello?"

The house was one of those modern cedar designs with floor to ceiling windows and skylights. In back the property took a spectacular slope, a view well worth looking at.

Another German Shepherd came loping across the lawn.

"Hello?" I continued to holler as I approached the nearest of the two barns.

The Shepherd was in front of me and seemed to be considering if I would be tastier with or without mustard.

"Hello!" I roared as loud as I could.

The Shepherd barked back at me, moving forward at the same time.

Jo Quinlan took that minute to walk out of the barn.

"What is it, Maggie?" Behind her, horsy sounds emerged through the barn door.

"Hello," I breathed.

She looked at me for a long minute, running me through her own internal computer.

"Health Club," she said. "You were asking questions about Mitzi Brochu."

"Exactly. I wonder if you could spare a couple of minutes.

There are some things I need to understand. I'm trying to help my friend, the one who found the body."

"Sure, why not?" she said. "You want to come inside? Have a coffee or something?"

Saturdays seemed to agree with Jo Quinlan.

I followed her across a large deck, though a large door into a large country kitchen. With a wood stove and a lot of pine furniture.

Maggie stayed outside, whining through the screen.

"This is a wonderful place," I said, settling myself in at the large kitchen table.

"Yep." I could see this was an understatement on her part. Her colour was high, her eyes were bright.

"Sorry to bother you on a Saturday. A nice man told me you were in back."

"That'd be Dan. My husband." She laughed a bit. "I still find it sounds a bit strange. We've only been married for six months. You want to make that cappuccino?"

Aha. No wonder Jo Quinlan seemed to shine. She was living happily ever after with a new husband, a spectacular place in the country and a cappuccino machine.

"Sammy Dash," I said, after the cappuccino was in my hand.

"What about him?" she said, the smile slipping.

I took a little sip, to help rid myself of the sudden chill. "I understand you were very good friends for quite a long time."

"Yes."

The quintessential interviewer knew how to clam up when it came to her own personal life. She looked at me for quite a long time, her hazel eyes cool.

I felt a surge of relief when she started to talk.

"We grew up in the same area, we met in high school and I guess we were inseparable from that point until...we broke up."

"You must have felt terrible about his death."

She hesitated. "Well, you have to be repelled by the way he died. But, if you'd known Sammy, known how manipulative and cruel he was…"

"You mean you were expecting something like that?"

"No, of course not, not exactly like that. But something, for sure."

"Mind telling me why?"

She exhaled, and I noticed she was pale. The effort of talking about Sammy Dash had undone all the good of her Saturday in the country with the horses and the dogs.

"He was always asking for trouble, all his life. When I was a teenager, I thought he was great. A real rebel. Smart but undisciplined. He brought me a lot of trouble too. My parents hated him, and when I stuck with him it weakened my relationship with them. All my relationships."

"Why did you stick with him?"

Her smile held a bit of self-mockery, I thought. "Because he was powerful and sexy and I was caught in his net. He liked to have women caught in his net. And once you were caught, he didn't like to let you go."

I considered what I knew of Sammy Dash. The lazy arrogance, the macho stances, the way that women's heads turned when he was around. The public way he'd touched Brooke Findlay outside the restaurant in the market. It fit.

"By the time I got through Journalism at Carleton and landed my first job, I began to realize not every relationship was like ours, with one top dog and the other one the snivelling slave."

It was hard to imagine Jo Quinlan as a snivelling slave. I said so.

"I know. I seem in charge, I guess, but it was a long, hard fight to get away from him and become a bit tougher." She looked at me. "Okay, a lot tougher. At work anyway."

"How did you do it?"

"Well, for one thing I felt I had to. He was not only treating me like dirt, screwing around, slapping me, drinking too much, hassling me at work, but he was getting more and more implicated in the whole drug scene. Getting involved with the big guys."

"Like Rudy Wendtz."

"Like Rudy Wendtz."

"So you left him."

She nodded. "And he hassled me until the day he died."

"How?"

"Calls at work, calls at home, threats, embarrassments. Sammy didn't like women walking out on him. He didn't handle rejection well."

I thought about the story that Sammy had been after Mitzi. Could he have killed her because she mocked him? And then who killed him? Wendtz for revenge? What a tangle.

"The photos and stories about you in *Femme Fatale*?"

"I'm pretty sure the stories were orchestrated by Sammy. I never had any dealings with Mitzi Brochu at all. I was stunned when she first started to make fun of me in the press. Until I figured out the Sammy connection."

I thought back to the photos, nasty, sneering invasions of Jo Quinlan's privacy. "You must have been pretty uptight, not knowing when he was going to stick his head out of a bush and snap."

She shrugged. "By that time I had my job as an anchor, I had self-esteem and I even had Dan. Sammy had sunk to nuisance value."

"What about your career? Didn't all this sneering commentary hurt that?"

"On the contrary. It seemed to help. I started to get calls and mail in support. That's how I met Dan. He picked up a copy of *Femme Fatale* by mistake in a dentist's office. It was the first one where Mitzi and Sammy took a real shot at me. Dan was outraged. He called me at the station to tell me he thought I was," she flushed, "beautiful the way I am. I think I fell in love over the phone."

"Dan must have hated both of them then."

Just what I needed, a new suspect to up the confusion level. But the more I thought about it, the more it worked.

"Don't even think that," Jo said, her eyes hard. She reached into a basket on the table and tossed a business card at me. "He was at work that afternoon. Easy enough for you to confirm."

Maybe, I thought, deciding to dig further. Tan shoes, I reminded myself, were all I knew about whoever attacked me and killed Sammy. To my satisfaction, Maggie started a ruckus outside.

"Mind if I use your bathroom?" I asked Jo as she moved to the door to check it out.

"Go right ahead. The one downstairs isn't working right, try the one at the top of the stairs."

I scuttled up the stairs, pausing to peek into the downstairs closet. No luck. Upstairs, I ducked into the master bedroom, not paying attention to the country style decorating, sticking my head into the walk-in closet and checking out the men's shoes. I couldn't see any tan ones. I peeped under the bed. Nothing.

I ducked into the hall bathroom just as the front door slammed. Dan was back, standing at the foot of the stairs, when I emerged one loud flush later. I could only pray he hadn't seen me explode out of the bedroom.

I smiled at him when I walked into the kitchen. Jo was

giving me facial signals I interpreted to mean don't talk about Sammy, don't talk about the murders.

"Well," she said, "I don't know what got into that dog today."

Maggie whimpered from the deck.

I accepted the offer of another cappuccino, because it gave me a chance to check out Dan.

He was not as tall as he looked in the pick-up truck. I think it was the heavy shoulders and large upper body that led me to expect a near-giant. Standing, the top of his head reached Jo's ears. From the look on her face, that was just fine with her.

I smiled at him in a way I hoped wouldn't let him know I had just added him to my list of possible murderers. Close-cropped grey hair, silver-rimmed glasses. Wearing jeans, and, checked, running shoes.

"Camilla," said Jo, "is looking into Mitzi Brochu's murder and she was wondering whether I could…give her some insights into what Mitzi was like."

He flicked a glance at me. It was a lot chillier than the way he looked at Jo. The room, which resonated with Jo and Dan's feelings for each other, was an uncomfortable place for me.

"Terrible woman," I said, having no qualms about speaking ill of the dead. "Everything I hear about her confirms it."

"You getting anywhere, um, looking into her murder?" he asked.

"No," I said, "nowhere at all. I seem to be wasting my time. Everybody disliked this woman. I'm probably going to have to give up."

"What's Mitzi Brochu's murder to you?" His eyes behind the metal-rimmed glasses were as grey and cold as the Atlantic.

"A very good friend of mine found the body. The police are giving her a hard time."

He watched me as he inhaled the cappuccino.

"I told you about that, honey," she said.

I couldn't wait to get out of that room.

Jo walked me to my car.

"I don't imagine you'll find out who killed them. But I kind of hope you do. It would make a hell of a story."

"Right."

I climbed into my car and bumped down the long drive. As I turned on to the main road, I could see Jo Quinlan still standing there. I waved.

Ten minutes later, I pulled up outside Alvin's apartment in the centre of downtown Hull. I was skipping through the front door when two children selling candy bars stepped out. It only cost me two dollars. Banging on Alvin's door gave me a certain satisfaction. I was almost sorry when he answered, standing there in his jockey shorts squinting, without his cat's eye glasses.

"You look like death," I said, slipping past him. I didn't say a word about his belly-button ring.

"God, it's not even noon. And it's Saturday," he said, leaning against the wall.

"Get dressed, I need you to come with me."

Another ten minutes passed as I sat in the black living room, staring at the blenders and electric frying pans painted on the floor and covered with about eight coats of high-gloss plastic. From the rest of the apartment came sounds of flushing and brushing.

Five minutes later, the Alvin I knew emerged, tucking his tee-shirt into his jeans, the fake leopard skin vest in place. His pony tail was slicked back, and he picked up his best leather jacket from the coat rack, although it was the hottest day so far in the year.

As we walked out the front door, a girl with long red and

blue hair emerged from the bedroom. She was wearing a carelessly wrapped sheet and smoking something illegal.

"Alvin?"

"Go back to sleep," he said, closing the door behind us.

We were back in Ottawa and zooming along the Queen Elizabeth Driveway, before he spoke.

"I'm thinking about going back to Cape Breton."

"That's a great idea," I said. "I'll help you make your arrangements as soon as we finish this little chore."

The little chore was my impending visit to Rudy Wendtz and his tame gorilla, Denzil Hickey.

"You stay here, in the car. And if I'm not out of the house in twenty minutes, you call the police. Do you have that? Twenty minutes."

"I forgot to put my watch on."

"Use the clock on the dash."

"I don't think the time's right. You didn't adjust it after Daylight Saving Time, did you?"

"It doesn't matter," I said, through my teeth. "Just twenty minutes after whatever it says. Got that?"

"No need to be snotty," Alvin said under his breath.

I left him there and marched up to the tall and wide front door of Rudy Wendtz's big house.

"Hi," I said, shaking Denzil Hickey by the hand as soon as he opened the door. "Good to see you again. I can tell by the car in the driveway the man himself must be home. This'll just take a minute."

Denzil looked at me with eyes that reminded me of ball bearings. I tried not to think about him murdering the tabby. I intended to deal with him on that matter later. He shrugged and I followed him down the hall to the conservatory. His shoes, I noticed, were black.

Rudy was working out with a set of hydraulic weights. He kept going without a pause as we entered the room. This was good, because I wasn't sure what I was going to say to him.

It must be nice, I thought, to have enough money to have a house that overlooks the canal, and to have all the time in the world to develop your deltoids while watching the water ripple in the warm spring breeze. Wearing fashionable workout clothes and some kind of black running shoes.

I waited. Denzil lurked in a corner. After a while, I cleared my throat. Patience is one thing, but I didn't have all day. And Alvin was set to call the police if I didn't show up in twenty minutes.

"I just popped around to mention that you and Brooke Findlay were observed and overheard arguing over her intention to speak to a certain recently deceased media type and people are beginning to gossip. And also, since your friend here," I gestured to Denzil, but he seemed to have stepped out, "was seen lumbering around the Harmony Hotel, the police may wish to reconsider your involvement. I thought I'd mention this to you, since we hit it off so well the last time."

He didn't seem to have heard me at all. Just kept on pumping that iron.

I waited for a while, checking out the plants, touching the equipment, before I glanced at my watch.

"Oh God," I said, "will you look at the time. Gotta run. Keep in mind what I said though."

"The police," said Denzil as I passed him in the hallway, "are not interested in little things like that. Or little things like you and your friends. They're not going to bother Rudy. So you can save your concern."

"Great," I said, "I can sleep tonight."

I skipped through the front door, down the stairs and past

the black Mercedes, hoping that Denzil hadn't been able to see my heart thumping through my tee-shirt.

Alvin was slumped over on the seat, snoozing. "Some lookout you are," I snarled, giving him a shake as I climbed into the driver's seat. I gasped as he toppled over onto me, his eyes closed, blood matting the back of his head behind the ear.

I sat there in the car, struggling to get my breath before I thought to lock the doors and drive poor damaged Alvin to the hospital.

*　　*　　*

The police were less than helpful.

"Rudy Wendtz. In front of his house. This happened in broad daylight in front of his house. Are the citizens of Ottawa not safe in their own cars?" Perhaps I'd raised my voice a bit with this. Other people in the emergency area turned to stare.

Mombourquette leaned against the door, smirking his ratty smirk, staying removed from our crisis. At least they took our statement.

Then I took Alvin home. I was left with the impression that since Alvin had not been attacked inside Rudy's place and since Alvin never knew what hit him, there was unlikely to be a riot squad attack on Rudy Wendtz's home to capture him and protect the decent people of Ottawa from scum.

By the time I pulled up in front of Robin's place late in the afternoon, my stomach was growling. But at least Alvin was all right, resting at home, no doubt smouldering at his memories of me. So I was cranky when Mr. Findlay's face appeared.

"Oh hi, Camilla," he said, holding the door open.

Surprise. I was half expecting to be a pariah among the Findlays.

"Robin's upstairs changing. Excuse me, I have something to take care of in the kitchen."

I walked through the living room. The TV was off. I'd never seen that in all the years I'd been coming to the Findlays.

"Mother's at a funeral. I thought I'd better stay here in case Robin needed me." Mr. Findlay's voice drifted out of the kitchen. Although I was sure I hadn't asked the question.

Robin's room was empty. Shower sounds were coming from the bathroom. Good. I tiptoed down the hall to Brooke's door and knocked. She looked surprised to see me, and stunned when I plunked myself down on her bed and started talking.

"I find it interesting, Brooke, to know you had a major problem with Mitzi Brochu trying to ruin your career. And you were seen in the Harmony minutes before her body was discovered, although your family believes you to have been in Toronto, too busy to come to your sister's side. I also find it interesting you had a public battle with Rudy Wendtz, noted drug dealer and thug, about your intention to confront Mitzi, and I'm fascinated your consumption of cocaine is so well known. Not good news for the 'Walk in the Woods' image, I'd say. And while I'm talking, let me add, if you treat Robin with anything less than the care and respect she deserves, and if you cause her to take any responsibility for crimes, or if you attempt to have me kept away from this house, I will go to the newspapers. I'll ruin you, and I'll smile while I do it. The choice is yours."

I left her, white-faced and shaking on her bed, and walked back to Robin's room. Robin, wrapped in blue towels, including a blue turban on her head, was glad to see me.

"You look better," I said.

"I feel better. And you? Are you staying out of trouble?"

"Absolutely."

"Good. I think I can go home again, pretty soon. I talked to the people in the office. I might drop in on Monday."

"Great."

She reached over and grabbed my hand. "Thanks. Thanks for talking tough. I guess I'd made myself a bit crazy. Lost perspective."

"Hey, what are friends for?"

"Hmmm. I can't wait to see my kitties."

I took a deep breath. How long before I could tell her about the little tabby? Would it plunge her back into grief?

Mr. Findlay popped into the room behind us. "Hungry, girls?

"Yes," I said, not waiting for Robin's reply.

"Got a couple of Monte Cristo Specials in the kitchen. How's that sound?"

"Perfect."

Robin laughed. "Sounds good to me, too, Dad. We'll eat downstairs."

"Good." Mr. Findlay turned as Brooke brushed by in the hallway.

"What's the matter, honey? You don't look too good."

"Nothing," she said, "just a headache." The bathroom door closed behind her.

Mr. Findlay bustled downstairs to put the finishing touches on the Monte Cristo Specials. Robin started to change from towels to clothes.

"Tell me, Camilla, why you looked so guilty when I asked about the cats."

"No reason. Nothing to feel guilty about."

"Out with it," she said.

I hesitated, not wanting her to know about the cat in her fragile state.

She sat on the bed, turning white. "Oh God! You've let them all escape."

"No!"

"Tell me what it is before I flip."

"One is...I mean, one of them, um, died."

She sat down on the bed. "Died? Which one?"

"The little tabby."

"Dahlia."

I bit my tongue before I could say "whatever".

"How did she die?"

I looked straight into Robin's blue, blue eyes and said, "Natural causes."

She blinked. "Well, of course. But what natural causes?"

"I don't know. We're talking about a cat. I didn't have an autopsy done."

A tear trickled down her cheek.

"I'm sorry. I know you loved your cat. But maybe she had some congenital disease that strikes without warning. I don't think there's anything either of us could have done."

"You're right," she said. "She was just a little stray, but I loved her."

I patted Robin's bare arm.

"So sorry," I said.

"I'll be okay. I don't want Dad to see me crying. Let me pull myself together. But it's like losing a friend, you know."

I wasn't sure how I felt about that.

Later, as we hovered over the French-toasted cheese the Findlays all call Monte Cristo Specials, Robin had pulled herself together. But I could tell we'd be dealing with her grief for Dahlia for a while.

"What's the matter, Robin," Mr. Findlay joked as he served up chocolate layer cake, "cat got your tongue?"

Nineteen

It was Saturday night, but what the hell. I'd stirred up a little action with the various suspects and spending a night alone gloating with the cats seemed like just the thing.

As I rolled down into the parking garage, a man jumped from the shadows and loomed towards me. I stopped gloating and started backing up. He ran faster.

"Camilla," he shouted, "I need to talk to you."

Richard.

A wave of weakness swept over me, and some of it remained in my knees.

"Richard," was all I could say. But I did roll down the window.

"I want to talk to you," he said, bending over. "What's the matter? Did I scare you?"

"You bet," I said.

"Sorry, I didn't realize. I've been waiting, because you don't answer your phone here or at your office, and I wanted to talk to you."

"Talk."

"Here?"

"Here."

"Okay. I'm sorry. I'm sorry about the way I acted the other night. But I felt used and betrayed. I thought you'd gotten me over to your apartment so that your, um, your, um…"

"Employee," I said.

"Right. Your employee could scavenge around the Harmony without me catching him."

"Hmm."

"I can't stand that guy. He's caused me problems every time I've tried to reach you at the office."

"Right."

"So the point is, I acted like a jerk and I'm sorry, and I was willing to sit in my car in front of your apartment for as long as it took to tell you." He squeezed my hand, which was only slightly less shaky than my knees. "Can I see you again?"

"Okay," I exhaled. "But not tonight. I've got a commitment."

I didn't mention that the commitment was to myself. As much as I was attracted to Richard, particularly now that he was properly apologetic, I didn't want to spend an evening with him when I was distracted by having to develop a strategy to stay alive.

"Sure," he said.

"Maybe tomorrow."

He nodded.

"But listen, I have an idea. Walk me up from the basement, I'm a bit skittish, for reasons I'll explain later."

Richard hopped into the passenger seat and we drove down into the garage. A place I never give any thought to. Tonight, it seem filled with shadows and bad possibilities. Every square concrete column seemed large enough to conceal Denzil Hickey.

As Richard and I strolled toward the elevator, he was whistling. A creak in the corner caused me to jump.

"Relax," he said. "Maybe you should cancel your commitment and just rest tonight. You're very jumpy."

"You're right. Maybe I'll do that." I said as the elevator took us to the first floor.

He turned, smiling.

I melted under his hug.

"I'm glad you're back."

"Me too," he said, kissing my forehead.

"Tomorrow," I mouthed.

Still smiling, he waved back. Tomorrow.

On the sixteenth floor everything looked suspect. The strands of hemp in the wallpaper seemed to reach out and tug at my hair.

Pull yourself together, I told myself. You created this situation by stirring the pot, now you'd better cope with it without falling apart. I scuttled along the hallway with my keys held between my fingers like a weapon.

Relief, relief, relief when I reached my door. Until it swung open.

I found myself rooted to the floor, unable to move.

Mrs. Parnell humped out, using her walker.

"You stay there, cats," she said. "I told you I'd be back later to check." She pulled the door closed behind her and I heard a meow of outrage.

We both gasped in unison.

"There you are," she said. "We've been worried sick."

We?

She inclined her head toward my door, from which sounds of protest could still be heard.

"I've been busy."

"Pretty skittish, aren't you?"

I nodded. "It's been a rough day."

"Come on over and tell me about it."

I hesitated. "The cats..."

"The furry spongers have been fed."

"Ah." I followed her into her apartment, still worried about Alvin's head injury. What had I stirred up? I wanted to spend the evening thinking about a strategy to flush out a killer without creating a new batch of victims. I wanted to make sure Alvin didn't end up dead because of me.

Instead, I found myself perched on Mrs. Parnell's leather sofa holding a full glass of Harvey's Bristol Cream. I was still jittery, and it seemed to me that she was too. Behind us, the peach-faced lovebirds twittered.

"Here's to your health," said Mrs. Parnell, downing her sherry in a gulp.

I tried to sip and noticed my hands trembling.

"Well, Ms. MacPhee," she said, following a discreet burp, "now that you're sitting down, I have two things to mention to you."

"Mrs. Parnell," I asked, feeling a sense of *déjà vu*, "how did you get into my apartment again?"

"Ah, make that three things."

"Go ahead. Let's hear them."

"First things first." She topped up her glass.

I shook my head when she offered me a refill.

"Well, would you like the good news first or the bad news first?"

"The bad news." I always want the bad news first.

"Okeydokey. Then, remember when you had five cats?"

"Six cats. Not that they're mine. Five remaining."

I felt pretty stupid discussing cats when my life and Alvin's might be in danger.

"Not any more," said Mrs. Parnell. "That's the bad news. The little three-coloured one seems to have disappeared."

I don't even like cats, but my stomach clenched. The

little calico was an extremely naïve animal, capable of taking a liking to the worst kind of people, myself included. Could she have…?

"I spent hours checking your apartment, the hallway, everywhere. I knocked on every door on the sixteenth floor. No one has seen the damn thing."

"But how could it have gotten out?"

Was that a little flicker of guilt on Mrs. Parnell's grey face? She stuck another cigarette into the long holder and lit up.

My voice rose a bit.

"Did you come over to my apartment to snoop, and let the little cat escape?"

Her head drooped. "It is possible, I suppose, while I was tending to the others, she, er, slipped out the door."

"They didn't need tending. I left them plenty of food and clean litter too. What are you suggesting, I don't take care of them?"

"No, no. I didn't see you all day, and I thought that perhaps something had happened to you. I went over to see if you needed help. The cats were just an afterthought."

In a strange way, it felt comforting to have someone in the same building looking after my well-being, checking to see if I needed help. On the other hand, I value my privacy and I didn't want Mrs. Parnell exploding through the door every time she imagined things were a little too quiet in my apartment.

"You still have a key?"

She grinned.

"The Super didn't ask for it back?"

After a pause, she admitted: "I had a copy made."

I held out my glass for a refill.

"I'll make a little notice for the elevators and the laundry rooms. I don't think that cat could get out of the building, do you?" she said.

"No. Not unless somebody took her."

We looked at each other. Somebody had already killed one cat... Maybe the same someone had plans to use this cat to intimidate me or Robin in some way. We have your cat and if you don't... I shook my head. Too far-fetched.

"You never know," Mrs. Parnell said, as if she'd read my thoughts.

The lovebirds kept on twittering. Very edgy, those birds.

"The good news, though," she continued, "is I think I know what the Hon. Deb Goodhouse didn't want to make the papers."

I waited for her to tell me but it appeared I had to come right out and ask.

"What?"

"Well, seems she's been in and out of these places, fat farms, you know, where they try to program you to lose weight. Treat it as a psychological problem. Lotta bull if you ask me, but nobody ever does. Anyway, turns out she's had a couple of visits, paid for by the government, and she's a bit sensitive on the subject. The legitimate press doesn't cover that sort of thing. But the late Ms. Brochu would have made hay out of it. And apparently she'd intended to."

Bingo. I could just imagine it. Deb Goodhouse was still a large woman. Mitzi could have had fun with that. Before and After pictures, the same size. She would have included the costs for extra zing.

"Potentially quite humiliating," I said.

"You bet. Although I'm not convinced it's enough to send a sensible and successful woman, as Goodhouse appears to be, right over the edge. At least, we know she had a new reason to be upset with Mitzi." Mrs. Parnell rewarded herself with a healthy belt of Harvey's. "God, this is fun!"

I turned down another refill. It was time to head home and think a bit.

"I'm sorry about your cat," Mrs. Parnell said at the door. "I'll find her for you."

Back in the living room, the birds kept twittering.

"I don't know what's gotten into them," she said, turning back and leaving a trail of smoke.

As I crossed the hall, I wondered how I could tell Robin that she now had two ex-cats.

As the lights went on in my apartment, they went on over my head too. Did this have to be my problem? I called Ted Beamish, since he always wanted to help, and assigned him a chore intended to get me out of the situation.

The cats alternated between surrounding me and disappearing for the rest of the evening. When I took my bath, all four joined me in the bathroom. When I felt like a cuddle, they vanished. When I snacked on a tuna fish sandwich, they all tried to sit in my lap. So what else was new?

I sat at the table by the window and worked once more through the tangle of motives and clues. I knew one thing—Alvin and I had aggravated the murderer all right. Pushed him or her to action. But just which one of them was it? And what would he or she do next? Was I sure about Large-and-Lumpy? Could Jo Quinlan or her new husband or even Deb Goodhouse have followed Alvin and me?

I never would have noticed. A chill ran through my body. I'd never thought about who was stalking me. I'd been too busy playing detective.

The buzzer jolted me out of my chair. Edwina. I buzzed her in.

Two minutes later she stormed through the door, followed by Stan, who was lugging a cast-iron planter exuding vivid geraniums. I knew Edwina was there to give me hell. The geraniums were just a consolation.

Mrs. Parnell's shadow rippled behind her half-opened door.

"We must talk," Edwina said, gesturing to Stan.

Stan grunted on toward the balcony with the geraniums. That cast-iron container must have weighed thirty pounds.

"Great idea," I said. "Would you like a drink?"

"No," said Edwina.

"Yes," said Stan, returning from his chore, red-faced and puffing.

I went with Stan. Lowest common denominator.

Stan and I decided on rum and Coke.

"Tea for you, Edwina?"

"I might as well have one too."

When we had settled down, I noticed that Stan had a small, brown bag in his lap.

I smiled at Edwina. The smile I always used when I got caught with my fingers in the icing bowl. It didn't work as well as it used to.

"Well, the family has noted that we have not heard much from you lately," Edwina said.

"You saw me at dinner the other night. Anyway, I've been quite busy."

"I imagine, since you haven't called back and I've left messages."

"I figured you just wanted to give me hell over Alexa's date."

"I do want to give you hell over Alexa's date, and please do not think you can escape merely by not calling me. And may I add, it has been observed by more than one of us, you always have time to call when you need something."

"Well, yes," I said, "that's what families are for."

Edwina opened her mouth and shut it again. I thought I could detect a fizzling sound coming from her.

She tried again. "We were informed today that your employee, Albert, was attacked while you were harassing certain individuals around town."

"Alvin," I said.

"Not important," said Edwin. "Is it true?"

I glanced at Stan, but he seemed hypnotized by the cats.

"Who told you?"

"It doesn't matter who told me. Is it true?"

I knew why they'd selected Edwina to set me straight. She's the only one with the correct configuration of personality traits to have made a career as a Mother Superior.

"I suppose McCracken told Alexa. What a worm."

"The point is, whatever you call him was attacked, and it could have been you, and we are very concerned. That's the point."

"Here, kitty kitty," said Stan.

"Alexa is distraught. That nice policeman had to stay with her to calm her down."

"I've never heard it called that before."

"Be serious."

"I've been a lot of things, Edwina, but I think this is the only time I've ever been convenient for anyone."

Edwina's upper lip twitched.

"Pssss, pssss, pssss," said Stan, clutching his brown paper bag.

"All right," said Edwina, "I'll grant you that Alexa enjoyed being comforted by Sgt. McCracken. But even so, she was worried and so am I and so is Donalda and so is…" she looked over at Stan.

Stan was bending forward, grinning at the cats, some of whom were beginning to move toward him.

"…and so is the rest of the family. Except for Daddy. No

one has told him. If you would like it to stay that way, stop this Nancy Drew nonsense."

My father. What a nasty threat. Everyone knew my father is the one person I can't stand up to.

Edwina leaned forward and lowered her voice. "We are terribly worried about you. Two people have been viciously, violently murdered. You have been hit on the head. Alphonse has been hit on the head. You live by yourself in this isolated, vulnerable apartment…"

"I'm not alone. I've got Mrs. Parnell. And the cats."

I looked over to where the four cats were now very close to Stan.

"And that reminds me…"

"It reminds me, too, that your apartment was broken into and one of the cats was killed."

"That's just it. Do you have any idea of how to…"

The sound of a large dog, snarling and growling, cut through the air. Edwina and I jumped. The cats leaped and spun, their fur on full alert, claws out. They vanished as the growls turned to serious, loud barking. I held my chest, heart banging, head thumping.

"For God's sake, Stan, this is hardly the time for your stupid jokes."

It's not like Edwina to give Stan hell, and he had the grace to blush.

I picked up the tiny toy dog with the powerful bark from the floor and removed the batteries. I dropped the batteries into my pocket and tossed the stupid mutt through the door of my bedroom with full force.

"It's okay, you can come back now," I called to the cats. "As I was saying, Edwina, do you remember what Deb Goodhouse was like as a girl?"

"Why on earth do you want to know that? Don't you have

more important things to think about?"

"Indulge me."

Edwina narrowed her eyes. She seemed to feel I was up to something.

"It's hard to remember. She was kind of self-conscious. Worried about how people looked at her. She always had to shine at something, like Debating Society or Drama Club or some damn thing. She wasn't pretty and she wasn't popular, and she didn't have any decent clothes. I don't remember her ever having a boyfriend."

This didn't sound too bad. I'd been pretty much the same, except for the self-conscious and worried part.

"How come she hung out at our place? All of you were always popular."

Edwina shrugged. "I don't know. I think Alexa felt sorry for her. And she always wanted to be around us. It used to irritate me from time to time, but Alexa and Donalda always stuck up for her. Why don't you ask them?"

"Yes, well…"

"And please don't think that this inquiry will distract me from the main purpose of this visit. You are to stop all your ridiculous and dangerous attempts at detecting." She got to her feet with great dignity, marred only slightly by the clumps of cat hair stuck to her rear end.

I smiled.

"Come along, Stan," she said, "and forget about that silly toy."

"But, Edwina…" he said

We both knew he was out of luck.

Even after they left, no cats appeared, suffering no doubt from a crisis of confidence in the management of their current hotel. It was fine with me, I had things to do. I was whistling as I picked up the phone.

Twenty

Sunday morning I woke up early, my breathing laboured because of a great weight on my chest. The cats had chosen to forgive and forget. The black and white one apparently found me quite comfortable. All four of them were miffed when I had the nerve to get out of bed.

I bumped around the kitchen, yawning and fumbling. Cat food into the dishes, coffee into the coffee maker. Fragments of the night's dreams clogged my head and zoomed forward now and then, causing me to gasp. Robin and Alvin and Deb Goodhouse had filled those dreams, had been dead in them.

I was glad when the coffee was ready. I took a couple of sips and went to phone Alvin at home.

"Wha'?" he asked after a considerable amount of banging with the receiver. "Whoosis?"

"It's Camilla, merely checking on your well-being. I'm glad to see you survived the night. Well, good-bye now."

"I'm claiming overtime for this." He managed to slam down the phone before I did.

Still, he was alive and back to his old self. My second call got a positive response. I had another cup of coffee to celebrate. I had my feet up on the coffee table and was reading the Sunday paper when the doorbell rang. Another success.

Ted Beamish looked as furtive as a pudgy man with thinning red hair can look. The large doughnut box he was clutching seemed to have a life of its own, shifting and swaying in his grasp. From her open doorway, Mrs. Parnell peered at him with undisguised interest.

They both stared at me. Perhaps because I was still in Paul's old blue pyjamas, with the legs kind of rippling on the floor past my toes. What the hell, it wasn't like either one of them made much of a fashion statement.

"I got it," Ted hissed.

"Got what?"

He whipped around to stare back at Mrs. Parnell, who had asked the question.

I swear he made a peeping sound.

"The answer to our troubles, Mrs. P.," I said. "Come on over. It'll save you having to lean against my door with a glass in your hand and maybe losing your balance and hurting yourself."

"No need to be snotty," she said as she hobbled into the apartment.

"Well," I said, "let's have a look in that box. Have we solved the problem?"

Ted flipped open the top, and a small round calico cat hissed at him.

"Perfecto," I said.

"You found it!" said Mrs. Parnell.

"Not it, but one that looks just like it. What do you think? Robin will never catch on," I said

"Boy, that's a relief," said Ted. "I wasn't sure I could find one with a face like a pansy. I wasn't even sure exactly what a pansy looked like."

"You did well, young man," said Mrs. Parnell, whipping out a cigarette to mark the occasion. "It looks like the same cat to me. A little slimmer perhaps."

"Robin will probably attribute that to my cooking. I owe you, Ted. Was it hard to find?"

"My contacts at the Humane Society paid off. You're absolutely sure Robin won't catch on? She was pretty ticked off about the restaurant. I wouldn't want to have another strike against me."

"Let's show a little backbone here."

I thought I'd calmed him down, but he still jumped at the sound of the doorbell.

"You get a lot of company, for a Sunday morning."

Robin's voice chirped through the intercom and silenced us. By the time she arrived at the apartment, we were all sitting stiffly around the living room, trying to look like we had nothing to do with any conspiracy.

"Hello-o," she called pushing open the front door. "Here kitties."

"Robin," I said, "this is great. How did you get here? Do you feel well enough to drive?"

"Brooke dropped me off. She had somewhere urgent to go."

Kitties appeared from everywhere, showing great interest in Robin. She scratched behind their ears and snuggled up to them. The grey one, the black and white one, the Persian, the ginger. She looked at the little calico with surprise.

"Aren't you cute," she said. "Who are you? Don't tell me that Camilla finally broke down and got a pet."

My throat felt very, very dry as I said, "That's your little calico cat, Robin."

She stared at me, astounded.

"That's not my cat."

"Of course, it is," I told her firmly.

Robin's voice went up a notch. "This is not my cat. I know my cats, and this is not one of them. Where is my calico cat, Camilla?"

I blundered on. "Perhaps, Robin, the effects of your recent..."

"Enough bullshit. Has something happened to Myrtle?"

She looked around just in time to see Ted and Mrs. P. exchanging looks that any jury in the world would accept as a sure sign of guilt.

"Not really," I said.

"Then where is she?"

"She is not here right now. However, I'm certain she'll be back shortly. In the meantime, this lovely creature will permit you to return home with five cats."

"You tried to trick me, didn't you?

"Certainly not."

"And you," she said, turning to Ted, "were you in on this duplicity too?"

Ted uttered a strangled sound.

"What he means to say," I said, "is that he knows nothing about this. He merely came here in response to my request that he help me improve security in my apartment. He's what they call an innocent bystander caught in the crossfire."

Robin nodded. At least she accepted that.

"And Mrs. Parnell is an innocent bystander too. Just dropped in for a bit of tea."

"I should have known you could concoct something so ridiculous all by yourself."

"I'm not really innocent," said Mrs. Parnell, drawing off the enemy fire, "I seem to have let your little cat escape. It was not Camilla at all. She wanted to spare you any additional pain. I agree the idea was naïve, perhaps even asinine, but it was well-meant."

"Robin," Ted blurted, "I'm not really innocent either. I

found this cat and brought it here."

What is the matter with these people, I asked myself.

"It's okay, Ted, I understand you wanted to help."

She turned to me. I raised my chin.

"But you should have known better. You should consider the consequences of the things you do."

*   *   *

I was damned glad to be alone when they left, Robin to go back to her apartment, accompanied by Ted, Mrs. Parnell to spy on the rest of the neighbours, the cats to their castle.

I was slumped on the sofa, telling myself I liked the place better without cats anyway, when I had an idea.

"Camilla!," Richard said, when he answered, "Are you feeling rested or still jumpy?"

"A bit of both. Irritated too. How about if I tell you everything tonight? I really feel like spending some time with someone who won't lecture me and who will see the humour in my existence."

"That someone sounds a lot like me."

"Great. Do you feel like coming here?"

"What time?"

"Seven?"

It gave me something to smile about, and I considered not answering the phone when it rang two minutes later.

The woman on the phone sounded panicky, breathless and far away. A familiar voice, familiar because so many women who have been victims are frightened of being victims again.

"You've got to help me. They're going to let him out."

"Who is this?"

"Please help me. I'm afraid."

"I can't help you if I don't know who you are."

"My boyfriend. He's out on parole. He's coming after me."

"There are things you can do. How can I get in touch with you?"

"You can't. He'll find out. I need to see you now."

"Fine."

"Can I meet you in your office?" She sounded like she was hyperventilating.

Why not? Despite the pull of the Mitzi Brochu case, helping real or potential victims was my business. It wouldn't be the first time I'd spent Sunday with a terrified woman.

"Sure."

"When?

"In an hour." Long enough to change and walk.

"Please, I can't take the chance of anyone else knowing."

Who the hell else do you think is hanging around on a Sunday morning with nothing better to do than listen to our conversation, I thought.

"All right," I said.

I took time to shower and change into my jeans and a tee-shirt. I pulled on a light plaid blazer on top in case I needed to look the tiniest bit businesslike.

As I left the apartment and pulled the door closed behind me, I was humming. Even a trip to the office couldn't take that away from me.

"Good-bye, Mrs. Parnell," I said to her half-open door.

* * *

The walk to Elgin Street was wonderful, and I needed it. The combination of head injuries and high drama had played hell with my regular exercise program.

The smell of new leaves, grass and general spring aromas tickled my nose, leaving me with the wish that I could enjoy the sun, the grass and the water instead of barrelling on toward the office. With luck, I told myself, I could amble back, stopping to check out the tulips, which were tantalizing the tourists.

I took Wellington Street all the way, enjoying the strollers and amblers and the splashes of tulip colour up on Parliament Hill.

All down Elgin Street, people were heading to and from restaurants and parks. My turn will come, I thought, as I entered the little foyer that led to the empty stairs that in turn led to Justice For Victims. Too bad the woman I was meeting had been so terrified. She would probably reject my suggestion that we move to the Mayflower's open air café for our discussion.

I turned the key in the lock and gave a little push. Stuck. Must be the start of the damn summer humidity, I thought, banging against it. The door opened suddenly and I shot across the room and hit the desk.

"So glad you could come," Rudy Wendtz said from the other side of the desk.

The blinds were drawn so that no one from the condos in the next building could see in, and the lights were on. I didn't like that.

I also didn't like the look of Wendtz's smile. It hardly reached the ends of his lips, let alone his eyes. His eyes held something else. Anticipation? Whatever it was, I didn't like it either.

On the growing list of things I didn't like was the sight of Denzil Hickey lounging near the door.

They didn't even bother to close the door. No one was in

the building to see the gun Denzil pointed, very deliberately, at my head. I don't know much about guns, but this one looked like the type that could make a very large hole.

"Very fashionable, I'm sure," I said. As long as my bladder didn't betray me, I wasn't going to give him any satisfaction.

I think I managed to look cool, but my heart sounded like someone knocking at the door.

"Give my regards to Brooke, I appreciated her acting ability on the phone," I said.

Wendtz smirked.

"You may wish to recommend some additional coaching on the finer points. If I was able to see through her, think what the critics would make of such a performance."

"Cute," said Wendtz.

"Very," I chirped, feeling I had little to lose. "Cute enough for me to catch on. And get back-up."

He lifted an eyebrow and stared before his smile broadened, showing teeth.

"Let's see how much good your back-up does you against Denzil."

I took another look at Denzil and deduced that the long, cylindrical object he was attaching to the muzzle of the gun was a silencer.

"Keep talking, Mr. Wendtz, your threat to have Mr. Hickey aerate my head is being duly recorded by the police who know you are implicated in the murders of Mitzi Brochu and Sammy Dash."

Denzil caressed the weapon.

"Nothing personal," he said.

"I hope you got that, McCracken," I bellowed. "That should be enough to hold them."

Wendtz kept on smiling. "Nice bit of bullshit. I suppose if

you want to die with dignity, that's the way to do it."

He nodded to Denzil. Denzil raised the gun.

There was nothing I could do against the two of them. I kept my eyes open, expecting to melt into blackness, expecting to die.

Not expecting Wendtz to laugh long and loud.

I watched with my mouth open.

"I hope," said Wendtz, unbending out of my chair, "you get the point of this exercise. You are a little lady, and you are playing with the big boys. You are stirring up trouble, and you are upsetting a lot of people. Take a lesson and mind your own business."

I slumped against the desk, oozing with relief and resentment. My stomach felt like there was a dogfight going on in it.

He gave a lazy, arrogant stretch, secure in his power, knowing he had gotten through to me. Completely.

I glanced over to Denzil, who was showing his bad teeth. I did a double-take when I saw the third person. From behind the open door, a movement.

I whipped around to speak to Wendtz just as his head exploded like a pumpkin landing on the road. I dove for cover. From what? From whom? I didn't know. And from the frozen look on Denzil Hickey's face, he didn't either.

I suppose I shouldn't have been surprised when the office lights went out; after all, the switch was in the hallway outside, along with someone wearing tan shoes. I grabbed the side of the desk and crawled around it, trying to stay away from Wendtz's body. The room was deep grey rather than black. A deeper something moved on the other side of the desk. I could distinguish the shadow that was Denzil before the flash that finished him. With his last scream echoing in my skull, I lay

273

cowering behind the desk for an eternity. But it was really less than a hour. Time enough to think, though. Who had killed Wendtz and Denzil? Had I really seen the same tan shoes again? And was the killer coming for me too?

*   *   *

"Excuse me while I call somebody," I said to McCracken. "I'd like to use another telephone though."

Bits of Wendtz were splattered over my own phone, and I couldn't see myself picking up the receiver.

It was only after the police arrived with their sirens and heavy shoes that I began to shake. I could see my hands vibrating, and I stuck them in my jeans pocket. I tried to keep the wobble out of my voice, but didn't quite manage.

"I'll come with you," said McCracken.

I didn't know if that was procedure or some violation of it. But it suited me. Someone had killed Wendtz and Hickey, someone who knew about my involvement in the Mitzi Brochu case.

"How did you know?"

McCracken held my arm as we walked down the stairs together. He did it well, so that I felt supported and not diminished.

"We received a call from an anonymous source."

"Ah."

He nodded gravely.

"Perhaps whoever shot them?"

"Could be."

Across the street at the Mayflower, McCracken anted up for coffee and chocolate banana cake for two while I made my call.

When I finally reached Richard and told him what had happened, it was all I could do to keep him from coming over.

"No," I said, "I'd like you to be as far away from this as possible. I'll see you tomorrow instead. I'll enjoy the time with you more if we don't have the same images in our heads."

"I guess so," he said. "Will you be up to it then?"

"Yep. Come after dinner for drinks. I can't count on getting things organized."

"Tell you what, why don't I bring dinner? I've got excellent connections in the kitchen here. Think you could rustle up two plates and a bit of cutlery?"

"Sure. See you about seven."

I gulped down the coffee when it came, but pushed away the cake. The taste of dust from the office floor and the smell of blood had done bad things to my appetite. And even though Wendtz and Hickey had been bottom crawlers, I had still seen them die.

I went over and over the sequence of events with McCracken. So much better here than in the office. In the course of our discussion, we each had two more coffees and McCracken ate my cake.

I talked while he ate.

"Who do you think killed them? And why do you think they didn't kill me? And why did they call the police? Or if they didn't, who did? Could this be some kind of turf war between rival drug distributors? How were Mitzi Brochu and Sammy Dash connected? Who were Wendtz's rivals? And how did that link up with my office? Are you going to talk to Brooke Findlay? Her miserable life might be in danger too."

McCracken blotted his mouth with a napkin. "Do you really want me to answer, or are you just going to keep spewing questions?"

"And that poem," I said, referring to the scrap of paper McCracken had picked up by the door when he arrived, "that's the same motif as Sammy and Mitzi. What do you think about that?"

"I think that the deaths are most likely linked to the industry. After all, they all knew each other."

"Unusual to have poetry written to commemorate murders in the drug trade."

He shrugged. "You see a lot of real strange stuff in this business. C'mon, I'll drive you home now. Maybe get Alexa to come over and keep you company. Have a drink together or something."

"She'll be more upset about hearing this story than I was living through it. You have a drink with her. It'll do everybody more good."

"Maybe. But you better take care anyway. One good thing. Since you have no idea about any of this stuff, at least you'll stop playing detective. Wouldn't want you to run into those tan shoes again and get hurt."

"Don't worry about me," I said. "I've learned my lesson." For the first time since I'd met him, I felt good knowing Conn McCracken.

*   *   *

My phone rang at 8:30 in the evening.

"Camilla," Robin breathed. "Dad just called. The police took Brooke in for questioning as soon as she got in tonight. My mother's hysterical."

"Gosh," I said.

"She's going to need a lawyer."

"I suppose she will."

"Couldn't you…?"

"Robin, your sister took part in a plot to lure me into my office, where I was terrorized by two thugs, who are incidentally now dead. This will have the effect of depriving Brooke of her much-needed cocaine, but aside from that they will not be mourned. So let me make myself clear. Your sister is in much greater need of protection from me than from anyone else."

"She took part in a…?"

"She phoned pretending to be someone in great danger knowing I would present myself in my office, alone in a deserted building on a Sunday, to be met by two very dangerous men."

"Oh."

"'Oh' is right. And do you know why she did that? She did it because she let her relationship with Wendtz and her need for drugs override her resistance to anything. She was willing to have me threatened and maybe even assaulted. She's nothing but trouble, and more to you than to me."

"Even so, she's my sister."

I had to let it drop there. My own sisters had been calling all afternoon, trying to entice me to spend the night with them.

Edwina had ended up by slamming the phone down in my ear at my final refusal. But I'd felt safer sipping Harvey's Bristol Cream with Mrs. Parnell, which was what I'd been doing all evening.

I hung up after Robin's call and returned to my guest, who was amusing herself by coming up with new and unlikely suspects.

"Humph," said Mrs. Parnell, showing no sign of ever returning her peach-faced lovebirds. "Are you sure you trust that boy in your office?"

"I trust him to be Alvin, who, with all his faults, is not a killer."

"Tell me what the poem said again."

I managed to cover my sherry glass with my hand before she refilled it. I waited until she'd filled her own before I repeated it from memory.

> *Ruining lives and still unjailed*
> *It's time you bastards both got nailed*
> *Perfidy should be unveiled*
> *To let you live would mean I'd failed*

The police could make all the statements they wanted to about Denzil and Rudy being killed by underworld elements, but I knew it was the same person who had crucified Mitzi and perforated Sammy. The same person who had deliberately left me alive.

"Well, it's not Shakespeare."

"You're right, Mrs. P., but who is it?"

The phone rang again ten minutes after Mrs. Parnell had finally teetered home.

"You okay?" asked Richard.

"Yes," I said.

"Good. See you tomorrow night."

I found myself smiling into the phone, even after he had hung up. But the smile disappeared soon enough as I lay stiffly in my bed, replaying the day's events. The night was just as bad, drifting through dreams, flashes of gunfire, running feet, tan shoes. I woke up at three, sweating, remembering where I'd seen those shoes.

*   *   *

Monday was suitably grey. A decent follow-up to murder in the office. I decided to give Justice for Victims a miss, since it would have been impossible to concentrate on clean-up and insurance matters. Anyway, the police were probably still hanging around.

I read both the papers. The headlines were sufficiently gratifying to clip. "No Justice for These Victims" one paper chirped, while the other one screamed "Bloody Shootout in Refuge for Crime Victims Leaves Police Baffled." The shot of the crime scene added a jolting dose of reality.

I stood on the balcony and savoured the warm air. The hot-pink geraniums were flourishing in their cast-iron container. Summer was on its way. Too bad it was blighted by what I had figured out. Whatever thoughts I'd had on human motivations before were nothing compared to what I had now.

I took some satisfaction from waking Alvin.

"Whoa," said Alvin, once he figured out what was going on, "right in our own office? That is amazing. So, what about work? Will the cops still be there?"

"Probably in and out. It's best for us to stay away. I haven't really been thinking about work."

"Yeah, well, thanks, I could use a holiday. But I might want to get a look at the place."

"Not a holiday. Just a day or so away from the office. But, wait a minute, since you'll still be on the payroll, such as it is, I want you to find out something for me."

"What?"

I told him what I needed to know and by when. I tossed in how to find it, just for good luck.

"Call the neighbours, tell them you're a reporter doing a feature on the topic. Change your voice, sound like a woman.

Dig around," I said.

I could hear him squawking on the other line.

"I thought you had connections," I said.

This was a matter of pride to him. I assumed the silence to imply consent.

"And, Alvin."

"Yeah?"

"Be discreet."

Elaine Ekstein was next on my wake-up call list.

"Of course I was up," she claimed.

"I need to see Maria Rodriguez again."

"Why?"

"Another question."

"For Christ's sake. Haven't these people been through enough as refugees without you grilling them all the time?"

"I'm not grilling them all the time. I just want to ask one little question."

"I'll call you back."

I used the time to get dressed, not as easy as it might seem with the shortage of clean clothes. Finally, I found a navy linen skirt that looked all right with my aqua cotton sweater. Normally, I would team it up with the plaid blazer I'd worn on Sunday with my jeans, but I was never going to wear that again. A dry cleaner might get out the blood stains, but nothing could remove the memory of the savage scene in my office.

Alexa called while I was pushing my cereal around in the bowl. I didn't feel like putting any of it in my mouth. Yesterday and all its tastes were still too close.

"Camilla," she said, "are you all right?"

"Of course."

"That was a terrible thing yesterday."

"Indeed."

"But it looks like it's over."

"I'm glad you think so."

"Conn says that these people, well, I hate to speak ill of the dead, but…"

"Oh, go ahead."

"Well, Conn says they were all involved with the drug trade in some way. Even Mitzi Brochu was tied to those people. They played with some very dangerous criminals, and they were dangerous themselves. This is the way it is, they get killed in disputes over territory or settling accounts. It's not like they were innocent bystanders."

"Like Robin."

"Like Robin."

"And me."

"And you."

"I hope Conn's right."

But I knew he was wrong. These deaths had been more than a settling of accounts. It had been someone with a major axe to grind. Someone torn up by memories. Someone who hated all four victims. More than business, this had been pleasure.

At nine o'clock, I made my first business phone call. And got the answer I'd expected and feared.

Twenty-One

"You missed that pedestrian," I said to Elaine. "Do you want to try again?"

"Very funny," she said, swerving into the bus lane and jamming her foot down on the accelerator.

I closed my eyes until we pulled up in front of Maria's apartment building.

Maria was not happy to see us. I didn't blame her. This time her husband sat with us, the set of his shoulders sending a powerful message.

"I don't want her to be upset. She's been through too much already." He gave Elaine a look, like she should know.

Elaine hunched in her chair and translated the look into a glare. For me.

"Make it snappy," she said.

I had only one picture with me this time and only one question.

"Ask her how long this person was on the eighth floor the day of the murder, Elaine."

I guess my excitement was evident when I got the answer I wanted. Long enough.

Maria must have translated my smile into a potential visit from the police. Her husband covered her hand with his.

"It's time for you to go," he said.

"Thank you for your help," I said as we stood to leave.

"She doesn't want to talk to the police," Maria's husband said. The door closed behind us.

*   *   *

"Oh, it's you," I said.

My unexpected visitor stood at my doorway, holding a box.

"I'm really busy right now. Can we do this some other time?"

I gestured around the apartment, which I was cleaning up to pass the time while I waited for McCracken to call or show up. I still had to hide the dirty laundry in the closet and put the unwashed dishes under the sink.

"No, it'd better be now," she said, pushing her walker forward.

The box was precariously perched on the handles. Mrs. Parnell kicked the door closed behind her and it snicked shut. I could never figure out how she had such great balance in some directions and none in others.

"You'd better sit down," she said, blowing smoke in my face.

"Five minutes," I said, "is all I have. Do you want me to carry that box?"

"No, you sit."

I perched on the edge of the sofa, irritated. Mrs. Parnell inched her way to the armchair and settled in. But not before she had placed the box on the floor. I was relieved to note that she didn't have the bottle of sherry in the pocket of her walker.

"Well," I said, when I couldn't stand it anymore.

"Stick your nose in that box, why don't you."

I could think of a dozen reasons why I didn't want to.

"Go ahead," she said, her narrow, mud-coloured eyes watching me.

I inched toward the box.

Mrs. Parnell chuckled. The chuckle gave me goosebumps. "What are you expecting in there, a severed head or something? Go ahead, open it."

I couldn't stand being taunted. I flipped the lid up and gazed into the contented face of the little calico cat.

"Surprise," said Mrs. Parnell.

"Are those...?"

"Indeed," she said, heaving out of her chair and looking down at the calico cat in the box at her feet. "I'm lucky I didn't have another stroke when I found that animal in my linen cupboard. No wonder Lester and Pierre have been in such a twittery state."

The calico cat rolled over to give her four kittens a better chance at dinner. She licked her paw with barely concealed self-satisfaction. Top that, she purred.

"Good thing one of the kittens is a calico. You'll be able to return this amorous little creature to your friend Robin with interest."

I looked at the kittens. Two the colour of marmalade, one inky black one and another tiny calico. They looked just like rats.

After Mrs. P. left, I pondered what to do with four kittens and a cat while I chucked the rest of the junk in the apartment out of sight.

I put Ma Calico in the bedroom while I vacuumed. She was still there purring when I finished. The cardboard box added a decorative touch to my bedroom. The only other decorative touch was the little dog with the big bark. That would get a rise out of Alvin, I thought. Chortling, I tucked the batteries into it and took it to the living room to put it next to my briefcase. I didn't try to improve the look of the bedroom in any other way. Why bother?

When the phone rang, it was Alvin. I listened to his report.

"What are you yelling at me for?" he asked. "Wasn't that what you wanted me to find out?"

It was.

I called McCracken again and left another message: "Just tell him I figured it out. And tell him it's urgent, life and death."

"Excuse me, it's time to get myself fixed up a bit now," I said to the cat.

In the shower, I thought a lot. The key was to remain calm and dispassionate. I could manage that.

I towel-dried my hair and hunted around for something to wear. The red dress didn't seem right. But it was clean and even hanging up. I decided to sit down with a glass of wine to calm my nerves while waiting.

The doorbell jangled. I looked at the clock. Five to six. Richard wasn't due for more than an hour. No one had buzzed to get in.

It must be McCracken, I thought, and about time too. I whipped open the door and felt myself being shoved back into the apartment, the door slammed behind me. For once, there was no sign of Mrs. Parnell.

"What a surprise," I said. "But I thought you were bringing dinner."

Richard stared at me and began to smile, slowly.

"Well, anyway, I'm glad you're here, we can relax for a little while." I chattered. My voice was as close to normal as I could make it. "How about a little bit of wine?"

"It's not a social call," he said, invading my space, walking toward me.

I found myself backing up. And hating it.

"Of course, it's a social call, Richard. And if you want, we can go out to dinner. I'm feeling much better now. And the police believe they're about to locate the guys who killed Wendtz and Hickey. Underworld connections. So that takes a load off my mind."

"Does it?"

I looked at him, really looked at him. And, for the first time, saw behind the long lean body and the deep brown eyes, saw the fire that had been eating at Richard for years. And I knew that he knew that I knew that no underworld connections had been the killers. When I turned away, I tried not to stare down at his tan shoes. The shoes I'd first seen in the family photo in his office.

"Sure it does," I said.

"It was a mistake to phone around to find out what my daughter died of. I know it was you. You've been like a steamroller all through this. No respect for anybody."

Oh, Alvin. How ham-handed have you been, I thought.

"One of my old friends gave me a call," he said.

Now that I found myself alone in the apartment with the man who'd killed four people, I had to ask myself why I hadn't just told McCracken my theory instead of getting Alvin to check it out.

"And you did a little more snooping, didn't you? Calling Harmony Head Office to find out who offered Mitzi Brochu the special deal at the Harmony. Don't bother lying. I already got a call from Corporate. There was no special deal. Just me getting Mitzi where I wanted her."

Think, I ordered myself, while fighting to keep my face neutral.

"Mitzi was such a stupid, greedy bitch, she fell for it," he said, apparently not expecting any comment from me. "All I had to do was wait for the right time to make her pay. I wanted her to know before she died, just why she was dying. I told her the whole story. I watched her eyes."

I thought of Mitzi, tied and gagged, listening to Richard's explanation of her coming death. A shiver ran through me.

It was too late to pretend I didn't know anything, to hope he'd just go away. He hadn't made that revelation to someone he expected would live to pass the information on to the police.

I had nothing to lose by asking. Everything to gain by stalling.

"How did you get into Mitzi's bedroom without alarming her? How did you tie her up without her screaming the roof off the Harmony?"

His fists clenched when he talked about Mitzi.

"I told you she was stupid," he said. "Vain, too. She thought every man had to be interested in her. She thought I was coming on to her and she was willing. Imagine, a disgusting, ugly harpy like that." His face twisted as he spoke. Mitzi was dead, but Richard's hatred still burned. In his mind he must have been back at the scene, raging. "It made me sick to touch her. Before and afterwards."

Not before you wrote on the walls in her blood, I thought. I fought to control my shivering.

"You had your reasons," I said.

"Yes, I did. And I could tell my wife that the witch was dead."

I nodded, and he seemed to bring himself back to the present and me.

He shook his head.

"But as I said, it was stupid of you to go digging around."

"I disagree, Richard. It would have been stupid if I hadn't mentioned it to anybody. But I did."

He loomed in a little bit closer. Where I'd felt warmth and attraction just the day before, now I felt nothing but fear. Trickles of sweat soaked my hair. The red dress clung to my back.

"Really?" he smiled. "Who did you mention it to?"

I wasn't about to tell him about Alvin and Elaine and Maria who all had Richard's name. I didn't want them to find themselves with poems before they thought to take their information to the police.

"I told the police."

"I don't think so," he said. "The police would never have agreed to let me come here, if you'd told them what you knew."

"Exactly. It's not seven yet. McCracken will be here any minute."

"I'm afraid not. McCracken and Mombourquette got a message from you sending them over to search Jo Quinlan's farm in Chelsea. I imagine they're butting heads with the Quebec Provincial Police right now."

My heart beat wildly in my chest. He was telling the truth, I was sure. I'd played right into his hands all through my investigation, even telling him about the personalities of the investigating officers. There would be no reinforcements.

"But even so," I said, "they won't find anything there. And they'll be back here afterwards." I was surprised at how calm I could sound with my cardiovascular system in crisis.

Richard's smile hadn't changed. The emotionless grimace of the damned.

"But they will find something there," he said, "Sammy Dash's wallet. And a pair of Mitzi's shoes. Souvenirs from Wendtz and his stooge too. And they will come back here. But it will be too late for you. I'm afraid you'll be dead." Regret fluttered over his face and was gone. The chocolate eyes radiated pain for himself, maybe even for me.

He doesn't want to kill me, I told myself. Try to reach him. Keep talking.

"You don't want to kill me, Richard," I said.

"I didn't before. But you wouldn't stop digging."

"I thought you cared about me. I thought we had something special." I could feel my stomach heave as I said the words. "Didn't you feel it too?"

"I did. I felt it," he said. "But now it's too late. I have no choice."

"Don't be too hasty, Richard. I think we can get people to understand your actions. After all, your life was ruined by Mitzi, who promoted an artificial ideal of thinness and made life hell for anybody who didn't fit the mould."

At least he was listening to me. I forced myself to lay my hand on his arm without recoiling.

"It wasn't fair," I said, "a beautiful young girl like your daughter, struggling to make it as a model, fighting a slight tendency toward plumpness, reading fashion magazines, soaking up junk from people like Mitzi, soaking up ideas that sparked the anorexia that killed her."

"She wouldn't listen to us, her mother and me, everything was the fashion gurus. Mitzi..." he spat the name, "Mitzi was the worst. We heard about her all the time from my daughter. Mitzi Brochu this, Mitzi Brochu that. Even when we could see my little girl's ribs sticking through her clothes, Jenny kept on talking about Mitzi's latest witticisms about plump people. I wanted to make an example of Mitzi, with her vicious physical pronouncements on the right way for people to look. Mitzi and the scum like Wendtz who make money pushing drugs to kids like Jenny."

"But Richard, no one knows what your motivations were,

they don't realize you were making an example of Mitzi…and the others. If you tell them, and I'll help you, it will make people think about these things."

"I don't think so. There's still a lot of people out there who need to pay the price for what they've done. They'll lock me up and I don't want that to happen until I'm finished my work."

Shit. We had edged close to the patio doors to the balcony. The balcony I loved, where I savoured warm summer air. Now I caught the faint odour of death. Buy time, I screamed to myself, buy time, buy time.

"Did you kill Robin's cat?"

The man who had murdered four people looked offended.

"Of course not. I figure it was Wendtz trying to scare you off. The kind of thing he'd do."

"Hmmm. How did you know Wendtz and his muscle man would be at Justice for Victims yesterday?"

"I didn't. I was following them, looking for my opportunity. When they went into your office, I knew they were going to try to hurt you. I had the gun. I was waiting for my chance."

"And you probably saved my life."

He nodded.

"Then why the change now?"

"You know what happened. I have no choice."

"Really? And did you write a poem for me?"

"Of course."

"What, um, does it say?"

The little smile played around his lips. I watched it, horrified, wondering how I could ever have wanted to be close to him. His eyes had once reminded me of chocolates. Now they were cold, hard, dark and dreadful. Like dog turds in the snow.

"You wouldn't like it. It's a suicide note," he said. "It will

290

explain your guilty feelings about the other deaths. Your involvement in them. Your suicide note is next to the items they'll find in the woods."

All the time he was talking he kept shoving me toward the balcony door.

My wonderful balcony, where I could see all of Ottawa and no one could see me. Or us, struggling. Where a six-foot-two man could flip a five-foot-two woman over it. Where all traces of violent struggle would be obliterated after the sixteen-story fall. I tried not to think of what that fall would feel like. Instead, I decided it was as good a time as any to put up a fight. But the only weapon I had was distraction.

"Get him," I shrieked, looking over his shoulder.

In the seconds when he turned to look, I picked up the little dog by my briefcase, flicked the switch and flung it toward the other end of the room. A blizzard of barking filled the space.

Richard stared at me with contempt. "I can't believe you'd think I could fall for that. And what's that dog thing supposed to do? Scare me?" He had to yell it to be heard over the barking, but it didn't detract from his menace in any way.

I hollered and kicked as Richard pried my fingers away from the door. Just as he peeled the last finger off, I aimed a kick at his crotch. It stopped him, but not for long. As I streaked across the living room towards the front door, he brought me down with a body tackle. The boom must have shaken the ceiling fixtures in the apartment below.

The dog kept barking.

I was gasping for breath as Richard slung me over his shoulder and moved toward the balcony again. I grabbed at his hair, pulled with one hand and raked my fingernails across his face with the other. If he was going to kill me, there was goddam well going to be evidence of it on my body and on his. As I took a tearing bite at his earlobe, he slammed the side of my head and I slumped.

"Why?" I pleaded. "I understand why you killed the bad guys, but I'm one of the good guys. Why are you killing me?"

"You know too much. I'm not done yet. I owe it to my wife."

What the hell, I thought, it's a Sunday afternoon in a highrise apartment complex in peace-loving Ottawa. Someone must be going to call the police.

"But still," I yelled, praying I had an audience somewhere, "it must not feel right. You don't want to kill me."

"You get used to it," he said, just before I elbowed him in the eye.

I grabbed the curtains as we passed through the door and held tight. I felt the fabric tearing in my hands. None of me touched the balcony floor.

"Good-bye, Camilla."

I looked over his shoulder and shrieked, "Get him."

"You don't think that will work again," he said, too softly, as he lifted me higher. Over the edge.

I clung to the wrought iron railing of the balcony, screaming. My body dropped, and I could feel the skin on my palms shredding. I fought the thoughts of the sixteen-story fall as Richard pulled at my hands.

"Hang on, Camilla!"

I hung. Richard whipped his head around and slumped, half-stunned. Mrs. Parnell whacked him in the chest with the leg of her walker. He reached over to loosen my hands. I heard the sound of metal hitting bone as Mrs. Parnell loomed behind him.

I heaved and managed to climb back onto the right side of the balcony, my legs without bones.

Mrs. Parnell continued to slash the walker at him. He staggered and lurched towards her. He struck with both fists in her direction. Mrs. Parnell dropped her walker and tumbled forward.

I flung myself at him with enough force to throw him off-balance. I picked up the walker and hurled it at him, pushing him back to the edge of the balcony, striking the side of his head.

Mrs. Parnell crawled toward him. A woman who never gives up.

Richard lurched against the balcony rail and kicked Mrs. Parnell. She slid and lay still on the balcony. He picked up the walker and dropped it over the side of the balcony.

I could hear my breath in harsh rasps as he turned toward me. I stepped back and leaned down. With every bit of failing energy mobilized, I picked up the cast-iron pot of geraniums and heaved.

The thonk of metal against skull reverberated in the fear-filled air.

Richard's head snapped back. His arms flailed and he grabbed for the rail. Blood spurted from his forehead, washing into his eyes. He staggered, blinded, stumbling against the balcony rail. Crying and sweating and hardly believing he could still be conscious, I pressed myself against the wall.

He made a growling sound and surged forward, one final vicious lunge. Against the balcony rail, he reached and found only air.

I stared as Richard plunged tearing and grabbing through the sixteen story drop, his scream echoing back on the wind.

Mrs. Parnell's shrivelled paws shook as much as mine did when we locked hands. She leaned against the wall and gasped for air as I collapsed on the chair.

"You're pretty good with that walker, Mrs. Parnell," I said, when I could talk again. "Thank God for those weights."

"I never did trust that man." She closed her eyes.

Twenty-Two

O f course, I knew Camilla would never have that dog thing barking in her apartment with the mother cat and four kittens there. There had to be something terribly wrong," Mrs. Parnell said with a coy glance at my father.

"So, in a way, you can thank me you're still alive," Stan smirked.

July 1. Canada Day and also Edwina's birthday. My family and friends were jammed into my apartment swilling cheap Spanish champagne provided by me, gorging on an elaborate buffet prepared by my sisters and fussing over the Canada Day fireworks about to begin on Parliament Hill. From my balcony, you had one of the best views of the display in town. This would be the first time I'd ventured out on the balcony since May, when Richard had tried to hurl me over the side. I had to get used to going out there again. My knees wobbled and my knuckles whitened just thinking about it. No one was paying any attention to Stan or to me bantering. My sisters were more absorbed by Mrs. Parnell's habit of lighting up cigarettes between trips to the buffet. She was polishing off another plate of cold sliced rare roast beef with potato and bean salad and roasted red peppers in olive oil and garlic.

Conn McCracken gazed at Alexa like she was the winning combination for the Lotto 6/49. Whenever she glanced back at him, she glowed.

On the other hand, Robin and Ted were looking suspiciously solemn. The month of rest and the knowledge that Brooke hadn't been directly involved in Mitzi's death had been good for Robin. She was pink and white again, her blonde hair shining and from time to time, and when she wasn't being solemn, she flashed a 12-volt smile at Ted, who would instantly turn flame-red.

Lucky for Merv he was out of town.

All that romance was making me queasy, and I was looking forward to the crimson, green, deep yellow and electric white flash of fireworks. The papers were promising a spectacular show with new fireworks called "Five Pointed Stars" and "Yellow Ribbons".

"It's almost ten. Let's go out on the balcony, or we'll miss the show," I said.

No one paid any attention.

My father watched Mrs. Parnell through a cloud of smoke.

"So you've really had some adventures," he said.

Mrs. Parnell stuck a fresh cigarette into her holder and smiled mysteriously at him.

"But I still don't understand why this man felt so driven to kill these people," said my father.

"It was his daughter's death that sent him over the edge. A beautiful girl, she was a model in Toronto. His only child and the focus of his existence. Her death was brought on by anorexia, I believe they call it. Apparently she did a bit of drugs, too. The combination led to heart failure. She'd been a big fan of Mitzi Brochu as fashion guru. It drove Richard's wife around the bend. He was out for revenge. He wanted to kill the kind of people who create the climate where young women starve themselves to be acceptable. He wanted the image distorters to suffer. He had a thing about drug dealers too. Mitzi and her gang were perfect." Mrs. Parnell had the air of Nero Wolfe filling in the details of the nearly perfect crime.

"Yes, well," I said, intending to fill in the key details myself. But nobody gave me a glance.

"Amazing the way it all got worked out," said my father to Mrs. Parnell.

She shrugged, modestly.

"Well, I knew even Camilla would never permit a dog in the apartment with those kittens, so I had no choice but to go on over and see what the problem was."

"Very brave."

I looked at my father with irritation.

"Don't forget I provided the geraniums," Edwina said, tearing her eyes away from the saccharin spectacle of Alexa and Conn and turning her attention to Robin. "How is your sister doing, Robin? Is she getting over this?"

"Pretty much. She's getting some treatment. It shook her up when Rudy Wendtz and Sammy got killed. And when she found out her name had been on the list they found in Richard Sandes apartment, she flipped. I suppose in a way it was good for her to be shocked into looking at what she was doing to herself."

"I'm sure she'll be fine," said Edwina.

I doubted Brooke would ever be fine. Her selfishness cut too deep. But I wouldn't have mentioned it to Robin. Ted's eyes met mine when the comment was made. He felt the same way. Maybe between the two of us we could insulate Robin from whatever misery her sister would bring to her life next.

"It's a good thing Alvin was available to do all that investigating. Otherwise, how would Camilla ever have explained the situation to the police?"

This time I gave Edwina a look. I would have glared at

Alvin as well, but he was on his third round through the buffet table and he had his black leather back to me.

"Really," said Alexa, "the police would have been much better off without Camilla meddling in the investigation."

"Well," said Conn, "we were distracted by all the calls we got about Camilla's investigations. When you get complaints from Members of Parliament and television anchor people, you can't ignore them."

"But," said Alexa, tapping his nose, "you were just about to crack the case anyway. If only Camilla hadn't gotten in such hot water right then."

Well, whoop-de-doo, I thought.

"Yes," said my father to Mrs. Parnell, "we thank heaven you were there."

No one said, oh good for you, Camilla, stirring everything up like that and bringing the situation to a head. But at least *I* knew what was what.

Alexa cleared her throat.

"Actually, we have something to announce."

Everyone turned to look at her. Of course, it didn't hurt that she banged the table to get their attention.

"Conn and I," she paused to squeeze his hand, "have set a date. Valentine's Day."

What mushy drivel, I thought. But the rest of the gang seemed tickled by the news. Even I raised my glass to toast them.

"Violet," I overheard my father saying to Mrs. Parnell, "what a lovely name. I don't know how we can ever repay you. Violet."

I chug-a-lugged my champagne. And inspiration came flooding in. The perfect repayments. The perfect thank-yous. The perfect revenge.

I slipped into the bedroom. At five weeks, the kittens

looked very presentable indeed. And lively. They had already shredded my new curtains. Both Ma Calico and I were thoroughly fed up. I picked them up, basket and all, and hot-footed it back to the party.

"Congratulations to both of you," I said, fishing out a marmalade kitten and dropping it in Alexa's lap.

"Happy birthday, dear," I said to Edwina, handing over the second marmalade kitten before it ripped up my arm.

"An expression of my undying gratitude," I said to Mrs. Parnell. I popped the baby calico into the pocket of her walker.

"This will go well with your floor, Alvin," I said, attaching the inky black one to his leather jacket.

"Wicked," Alvin said, with admiration.

"Oh, Camilla," said everyone else.

"Myrtle," Robin squeaked.

The little calico cat wound herself around my leg, purring, just as the fireworks started.

Mary Jane Maffini is a lapsed librarian, now co-owner and resident schmoozer of Ottawa's tiny, perfect Prime Crime Mystery Bookstore. Her quirky characters pop up in the Canadian mystery anthologies *Cold Blood V*, *The Best of Cold Blood*, *The Ladies' Killing Circle* and *Cottage Country Killers*, and also in *Chatelaine* and *Ellery Queen's Mystery Magazine*. She is co-editor of the new mystery anthology *Menopause is Murder* and winner of the Crime Writers of Canada Arthur Ellis Award for Best Short Story in 1995. *Speak Ill of the Dead* is her first novel. She is hard at work on *The Icing on the Corpse*, the second Camilla MacPhee mystery, undeterred by her husband, birds, dogs, children and grandchildren.